BERLIN REVISITED

ALSO BY PAUL M. LEVITT

Novels

Chin Music (2001)
Dark Matters (2004)
Bogus U. (2006)
Come with Me to Babylon (2008)
The Saint-Makers (2008)
Stalin's Barber (2012)
The Denouncer (2014)
Dreams Bigger Than the Night (2015)
Provenance (2016)
Death at the Dacha: Stalin's last Movie (2020)
Yana (2020)

Plays

The Norwich Incident (1971, 1980)
The Elementary Town (1972, 1973)
In the Aviary of My Heart (1974)
The Trial of Benedict Spinoza (1974)
In the Days of My Father (1975)
A Life in the Day of Salvatore Ciascuno (1975)
In the Days of My Father (1982)
Prisoners: A Play About Elizabeth Fry (1988, 1993)
Ollie's Odyssey (1989)
*The Witch of Beacon Hill:
A Play About Harry Houdini and Margery the Medium* (1989)
The Rough Draft (1989)
Le Brouillon (1990)
The Mistress of Two Masters (1994)
Rehearsing Violetta (1995)
The Anatomy of Love or the Love of Anatomy (1997)
Hocus Pocus: Houdini's Final Act (1998)

Children's Books

The Weighty Word Book
(with Douglas Burger and Elissa S. Guralnick, 1986, 2000)
The Stolen Appaloosa and Other Indian Stories
(with Elissa S. Guralnick, 1988)
How Raven Found the Daylight
(with Elissa S. Guralnick, 2000)
Raven Finds the Daylight and Other American Indian Stories
(with Elissa S. Guralnick, 2012)

Humanities

A Structural Approach to the Analysis of Drama (1971)
J. M. Synge: A Bibliography of Published Criticism (1974)
The Cancer Reference Book: Direct and Clear Answers to Everyone's Questions (1979)
(with Elissa S. Guralnick. 1980)
The Cancer Reference Book: Direct and Clear Answers to Everyone's Questions. Rev. Ed..
(with Elissa S. Guralnick. 1983)
The Cancer Reference Book: Direct and Clear Answers to Everyone's Questions. Rev. Ed..
to Reflect British Medical Practice
(with Elissa S. Guralnick, 1984)
The ABC's of Farm Estate Planning
(with Elissa S. Guralnick, 1981)
The ABC's of Farm Estate Planning, 2md Ed.
(with Elissa S. Guralnick, 1982)
You Can Make It Back: Coping with Serious Illness.
(with Elissa S. Guralnick, 1985)
39 Forever: Living Long and Well (medical book)
(with Elissa S. Guralnick, 1986)
Joe Frisco: Comic, Jazz Dancer, and Railbird (1999)
Vaudeville Humor (2006)
My Life in Vaudeville: The Autobiography of Ed Lowry (2011)

BERLIN REVISITED

A Historical Novel

Paul M. Levitt

Cross-Cultural Communications
Merrick, New York
2021

Copyright © 2021 by Paul M. Levitt

All rights reserved under International
Copyright Conventions.
No part of this book may be reproduced in any form without permission in writing from the publisher
or the holders of the copyright,
unless by a reviewer to reprint as part of a review.

Published in the United States by
Cross-Cultural Communications
239 Wynsum Avenue, Merrick, NY 11566-4725/USA Tel: (516) 868-5635 / Fax: (516) 379-1901
E-mail: cccpoetry@aol.com

Library of Congress Control Number: 2021939342

ISBN 978-0-89304-712-2
ISBN 978-0-89304-713-9 (pbk.)

Cover & book design by Katja S. McMillan
Cover photo: *A Hanukkah menorah rests on the sill of an apartment window in Kiel.* Copyright: United States Holocaust Memorial Museum. Provenance: Shulamith Posner-Mansbach bpk-Bildagentur Copyright: Agency Agreement.
Source Record ID: NS 769
Hardcover binding by Frank Papp
Hand marbled endpapers by Lauren Rowland
Printed in the USA by The Journeyman Press

For Martin and Gloria Trotsky,
whose generous contributions to the University of Colorado made numerous initiatives possible

Acknowledgments

Three gifted women immeasurably enriched this book.

Diana Beer, a teacher of French and German, first introduced me to the Hotel Bogota and translated German documents bearing on the hotel's history.

Marion Kreith, who fled from Germany to Belgium to Cuba, before settling in America, shared her impressions about the Cuban exilic experience.

Judith Kreith, her daughter, documented her mother's exodus in a film that has been shown worldwide, *Cuba's Forgotten Jewels: A Haven in Havana* (Directed by Robin Truesdale and Judy Kreith. www.forgottenjewelsfilm.com)

A father and daughter played a major role in the production of the book.

Clayton McMillan, friend and tech maven, formatted and proofread the manuscript. In addition, he helped rewrite the revisions. My gratitude for his work is eclipsed only by my admiration for his talents.

Katja S. McMillan, his daughter, designed the cover. Taking a striking image, she made it a work of art.

PART ONE

Chapter One

While scanning German language newspapers in the reading room of the New York Public Library, I gasped to see in a Berlin newspaper, dated Thursday, 18 October 1945, an advertisement, accompanied by a photograph, requesting information bearing on the person of Ruth Rosner, my mother's married name—my last name, as in Baruch Rosner. It was she, pallid and grayer, but still exhibiting her former beauty. The ad made clear that the Allied Authorities, namely the Americans, had her in custody and wanted to prosecute her for collaborating with the Nazis. Witnesses were sought and urged to come forth to testify about her war crimes. Her trial was scheduled to begin Wednesday, 24 October, in a small courtroom three blocks from the Palace of Justice. I arrived in Berlin Monday, 22 October 1945.

The opening day of the trial, I found a seat at the back of the crowded courtroom. Listening to the appalling charges, I wept for the victims of her treachery. I knew that she had worked for the Deutsches Reich, a decision that led to my parents separating and to my mother lodging me, aged sixteen, with Walter Fertig, a kindly gentleman who kept rooms at 45 Schlüterstraße, a five-story building that housed artists and professional people, and where I first met Gemma Rosselli.

The prosecutor, Herr Wolf, who had ferreted out a large part of the story, spoke deliberately, measuring every syllable. He walked with a limp, which in no way inhibited him from pacing when he addressed the judge and jury. At certain emotional points, he would lower his head, close his eyes, and press his left thumb and index finger to the bridge of his nose, allowing him a moment of contemplation. He avoided any theatrical displays and hewed to a single line of argument, namely, that Ruth Rosner had started collaborating in 1934, and that she had chosen to work with the Nazis when others, faced with similar choices, had not.

Her defense attorney, Herr Schlagel, said that mitigating circumstances would explain her behavior. Her love of sport, he explained, was the reason she worked for the Nazis as they prepared for the 1936 Olympics. And after the Games, her help was likewise harmless. She served in the Registry Office.

Herr Wolf objected to the word help. "For six years, scouring birth and death documents," he added, "to identify Jews who were passing as Aryans."

Herr Schlagel stated that in 1942, when the authorities began deporting Berlin Jews to extermination camps, she and her parents were arrested by the Nazis. He said it was only then, to prevent their being sent to a camp, she agreed to become a Greiferin, a "catcher" for the Gestapo, identifying Jews hiding as non-Jews, referred to as "U-Boats."

The prosecutor asked Herr Schlagel to add a footnote: namely, that she received three hundred Reichsmark for each Jew she betrayed. Hence, she greedily hunted for Hebrews in every cellar and sewer, even exposing former schoolmates, while posing as a U-Boat herself. A favorite ploy of hers, he said, was to promise those in hiding food and lodging. Then once a meeting place was agreed upon and the U-Boats arrived, they were met by the Gestapo.

To rebut these damning facts, Herr Schlagel attributed her behavior to the horror of the times and contended that she saved more Jews by warning them than she identified. In a remarkable twist, he blamed the western countries and America for making a terrible situation worse by abandoning the Jews. "What," he asked rhetorically, "were people like Ruth Rosner to do upon hearing that at the Evian Conference, the thirty-two countries in attendance unanimously refused to admit any German Jews. Those countries behaved no better than Germany."

That infamy occurred in 1938. But a year later, Cuba opened its doors to Jews. For a price, the new president, Fulgencio Batista, allowed the refugees to disembark and work in the country. Those employed in the diamond industry had saved me—Baruch Rosner, twenty-four at the time—and others by paying Batista's price. My mother, like me, could have been among the saved. But upon hearing that the immigrants mostly worked in factories, she wanted no part of my plan to sail for Cuba.

******

Closing my eyes, I remembered that moment in 1942, standing on the upper deck and absorbing the vegetative smell of land, the fried empanadas sold at vending stands, the heavy, humid air, the rattling chains and rasping hawsers lowered to the pier to secure the *SS Colonial*, and the crush of passengers desperate to flee from flight and stand on welcoming soil. I smiled, vividly recalling the crowded quay: the waving, the cheering, the tears, and the women holding placards with the names of arriving loved ones. If only a placard had borne my name, and the person holding it Gemma, greeting me in her three languages, German, Italian, and Russian. On our disembarking, agents and steerers working for landlords led us, the thankful immigrants, to rental houses and apartments. As a single person, I found an inexpensive room with a family of five, ruled over by Annalie Peretz, who had married in her thirties and made up for lost time by giving birth to three sons and a daughter in six years. Childbearing, she complained, had not been kind to her hips or her bottom, both of which had doubled in size. Her heavy black hair, prematurely gray, splayed across her shoulders and held by a barrette, hinted at a lost luster. Similarly, a wrinkled forehead and tired eyes, marked by crow's feet, suggested a hard life. But for all of it, the bulges and the blemishes, her beauty lived in the kindness of her words and in the smile that haloed her lips.

Her three sons slept in one room, and her daughter, Isabella, shared her bed. Her husband had been sent packing, according to Annalie, "because he couldn't keep a job, though he had no trouble keeping girlfriends." My bedroom, formerly a pantry and narrow as a coffin, still exuded scents of fruits and vegetables. She insisted I call her "mama," and regard her children as brothers and sisters. I favored six-year-old Isabella, perhaps because her three brothers frequently teased her. But once I became her champion, she became the darling of the family, proudly helping me learn rudimentary Spanish and even absorbing enough German herself to enable the two of us to communicate in our "secret language." After dinner, when her brothers listened to the radio, I taught her how to play chess and told her about the great Cuban grandmaster José Raúl Capablanca y Graupera, world chess champion from 1921 to 1927 and considered by many as one of the greatest players of all time. I told her that Capablanca, as he was known, had been a child prodigy and she asked me to explain the word. With her usual playful wit, when she learned that he had won a championship match just shy of his thirteenth birthday, she said, "I'd better keep at it if I hope to catch him."

Over the game board, we teased each other, filling the vacuum of a fatherless home. I'd ask her, for example, whether she had behaved that day, and she would respond, "I did, but it's no fun." One evening, I asked her if she had a boyfriend, and she answered, "Yes, you." I laughed, which elicited the following reply from Isabella. "I know you already have a girlfriend. I heard you call out her name in your sleep, Gemma."

******

Mrs. Peretz worked for one of the local Catholic churches, sweeping up and polishing the reliquaries. Testifying to her devotion, she had decorated her apartment walls with pictures of Jesus, the Virgin Mary, the Last Supper, the Archangel Michael, and imagined biblical scenes. In the small sitting room, a wooden crucifix loomed large. A votary candle burned in the hallway.

With Isabella at my side, holding my hand, I applied for work in one of the gem factories. Whether owing to the child's smile or to good luck—certainly not to my fractured Spanish—I found work. Inducted into the mysteries of the diamond trade, I was taught cutting and -proved an adept cutter. For over a year, I left the crowded flat on the outskirts of Havana and made my way by bus to the factory, where I stood for most of the day using a diamond saw to cut the stone, but not before deciding on the best possible shape of the diamond to minimize waste and maximize the yield of the rough gem. With the arrival in Havana of every boat from Europe, I excused myself from my bench to stand on the wharf, where I scanned the newcomers, eyeing each woman and hoping to see Gemma. To no avail.

Sensing my despair, Mrs. Peretz asked me to join her for Sunday mass. I guardedly replied, "What for?"

"To give thanks for your deliverance," she said.

"Thanks to whom, Batista or the Jewish diamond merchants who paid my way?"

"No, to Jesus."

I grimaced. "Allow me to say, Mrs. Peretz, that your savior has a peculiar sense of salvation. He expects us to thank him for our escaping a calamity that he should have prevented in the first place."

That day, Mrs. Peretz attended church alone.

Sometimes I'd sit on the dock and, casting me eyes over the vast sea, wondering whether my absence from Germany affected anything or anyone in the inchoate universe. Feeling that I had accomplished nothing of value in life, I more than once entertained the idea of sinking under the waves. But the simple thought that Isabella would have no one to protect her, and that my drowning might frighten her, kept me from it. Tormented by loneliness, I tried to drive away the demons by attempting to understand why people make pariahs of others. Why should Jewish children have to endure the slights and slaps of Aryans who believed that making Germany Judenrein would somehow enhance their lives? The exiles faced a similar situation, with Batista having the power to determine who would disembark in Cuba and who would not. Why, I mused, do dictators love to dictate? And why, for that matter, do people enjoy lecturing others? This was just one of the many puzzles I never solved.

Disconsolately shuffling away from the dock, I would shake my head as if in communion with someone and audibly whisper, "Gemma, where are you?" So great was my loneliness that I felt that it could swallow up the world. Suffering from frequent headaches and stomach cramps, I knew their source: vacancy. One smile, one embrace from Gemma would have cured my ailing nervous system. Perhaps if I could meet another … Twice I even shouted in German, to the fright of onlookers, that if the Cuban people knew how well I spoke my own language, they wouldn't regard me as a bumbling idiot, not worth their time.

On my return to the factory, I would study the faces of the young girls and women who girdled stones, rounding them in preparation for the cutter to add the facets. I imagined that among them I would see her. Even passing conversations were subject to my parsing. Perhaps on the wind or in the breeze I would hear her melodious voice, which would, like her smile, gently excite my heart. Even later, after I arrived in the United States, her restless ghost would not let me forget her tuneful voice, with all its siren songs of Scylla and Charybdis.

******

Herr Schlagel was still speaking. His baritone register rose to make a point. "Given the circumstances," he asked, "what could she do?"

"Act honorably," Herr Wolf mumbled audibly.

Mother, sitting at the defense table, hung her head, dramatically, seeking sympathy, no doubt.

"My learned colleague," said Herr Schlagel, "speaks of honor. But does he know of the dishonorable way that Ruth Rosner's husband, Meyer, treated her for years, and the malign effect it had on her mental health and her relationship with her son?"

Although familiar to some degree with my mother's earlier collaboration, which had caused my parents to frequently quarrel, I knew nothing of her subsequent work as a Jew catcher. Nor was I privy to any mistreatment Mutter suffered. I had often seen my father exasperated, but abusive, no.

"She was victimized by an oppressive husband who asked for a divorce and custody of their son, but she refused to separate from her . . ." Here the words seemed to catch in his throat. "Only child. Such an estrangement would have been unbearable."

I wanted to yell, "Lies," but didn't wish to reveal my presence. What I clearly remembered was my father begging my mother to leave Germany for England or America. But she had refused on grounds of language and culture, saying she and her parents knew little English and disapproved of the moral laxity of the west. Who the hell was she to speak of morality? She had a lover. When she said she couldn't leave her parents, my father had offered to pay their transportation. With all her excuses exhausted, she claimed that the pain of losing old friends and having to make new ones would be too great. It was then my father had had enough and charged my mother with infidelity and cowardice.

I could still hear the accusation.

"You have been seeing Gunter Beltz for months, perhaps longer. I think he cares more for his Nazi uniform than you. He's hopelessly dim, but this is not the first time you've taken up with men beneath you, so you could appear accomplished and knowledgeable. Since I gained a position at the university you have resented playing second fiddle to a professor."

My father had received a doctorate in English history. My mother had dropped out of the Music Academy when her teacher had criticized her for not practicing enough and for not treating music seriously.

"You've always traded on your beauty," my father said, "but beauty is only skin deep. You have squandered your talents. Was it because you found thinking too taxing?"

In response, she screamed, "You've never appreciated me! Look at all the things I've done for you: the housekeeping, the child raising, the bookkeeping. Have you forgotten all the support that I've given you?"

"Material support," my father replied, "but never emotional."

Mutter ran into the bedroom and slammed the door. From behind the closed door she yelled, "You can go, but the boy stays with me!" My father stayed. With the university examination period approaching, he felt obliged to see to his students' needs. Besides, friends and family believed that conditions would improve, and that Hitler would change his tune. I can still hear my father exclaiming about himself, "Meyer Rosner has no faith that the best in German culture will prevail. Did I not witness in Opera Square, on 10 May 1933, the burning of 25,000 'un-German' books? How," my father asked incredulously, "could a civilized people ban the works of Kafka, Einstein, Heine, Proust, Thomas Mann, and other greats?" From that day on, he remained convinced that in time the fascists would burn people.

By 1935, my father was frantic to flee. He tried yet again to persuade Mutter and her parents to leave the country, but they had convinced themselves that with the forthcoming Olympic Games, minorities would no longer suffer discrimination and be accused of corrupting the master race. Moreover, she had heard on good authority that in preparation for the Olympics, antisemitic posters would be removed, and newspapers would no longer print diatribes against the Jews. My mother sincerely believed that the reformation would be permanent, but my father remained unconvinced and applied for an exit visa. Denied. Months later, a student denounced "Professor Rosner" for his antifascist classroom lectures, causing his rough removal by two policemen from the family flat. I had come upon the scene on my way home from school. Father, catching sight of me, cried out, "Write! They say letters are permitted." Bundled into the back of a truck, my father was taken to Dachau, where he disappeared behind the barbed wire. I never saw or heard from him again, but my father's plea drove me to share my feelings on paper in my lonelier moments.

My own expulsion from the family flat corresponded to my father's arrest. Now my mother had the apartment to herself and she could openly campaign to prevent antifascist groups, particularly in America, from boycotting the 1936 Olympics. Assigned by the Nazis to keep Avery Brundage, head of the IOC (the International Olympic Committee), from heeding the pleas of American Jews to spurn the Games, she entertained Mr. Brundage during his stay in Berlin with her offer of bed and board. A skirt chaser, Mr. Brundage returned her favors.

When the judge asked my mother directly whether she had ever been coerced, Herr Schlagel said that his client was too distraught to speak for herself, and that he could answer the judge's question. Conveniently ignoring his client's collaboration before becoming a Jew catcher, the defense attorney addressed her work as a Greiferin in the 1940s.

"I ask the members of the jury to imagine what it was like for Frau Rosner to appear before Adolf Eichmann's police, whom Hitler had ordered to make Berlin Judenrein. In return for helping to rid Berlin of all the Jews in hiding, the so-called U-boats, she was promised freedoms unheard of for Jews. She could keep her apartment, receive a ration card that entitled her to nutritious food, have enough money for warm clothing, and, perhaps best of all, be issued a pass indicating that she worked for the government, which was tantamount to an Aryan birth certificate and a guarantee that her family for innumerable generations was free of Jewish blood. How could any sane person, faced with the choice of internment or a privileged life, choose the former?"

"Yes, she kept her apartment," said Herr Wolf. "I'm glad you mentioned that amenity. I find it more than coincidental that when Ruth Rosner's lover, Gunter Beltz, was assigned by the Gestapo to be her minder and accomplice, he moved into her apartment." Mutter dabbed her eyes. "To work with the enemy was one thing," Herr Wolf said, "but to sleep with him as well?"

Herr Schlagel, dismissing Gunter Beltz as a mere dalliance without consequence, had one more card to play. Having blamed the Evian Conference and Meyer Rosner for Ruth's collaboration, he now tried to shift the focus of the trial from her to the unknown person who had revealed her place of hiding at war's end. Loudly, he inveighed:

"Who would denounce her? Only someone with evil intent or someone himself who had been threatened with arrest and imprisonment. Someone himself whose parents were facing the loss of their home and possessions. The evils in our midst made denouncers of us all."

The prosecutor rose and courteously objected. "The skillful counselor stirringly reminds us that the Nazis stopped at nothing to have their way. All the more reason to have resisted. Ruth Rosner, however, is not on trial for failing to resist, but for collaborating with the fascists. She was not victimized; she victimized others. The authorities had issued a warrant and reward for her arrest. But at first no one came forward. Then an anonymous letter arrived, identifying her place of hiding. The person who wrote the letter never collected the reward. He or she acted from conscience, a word foreign to the defendant. So please, counselor, do not try to put on trial a nameless citizen who acted honorably. Attend to defending the person responsible for the exposure and death of numerous innocents, Ruth Rosner."

Herr Wolf audibly sighed, as if annoyed at having to reprove his opposite, adjusted his glasses, sat, took a sip of water, and censoriously shook his head.

Mutter dramatically threw her arms in the air, cried in Yiddish, Shod mir, pity me, and struck a crucified pose, with one hand on her heart and her head thrown back.

Unable to bear witness to my mother's histrionics, which I knew all too well, I silently left the courtroom and swore to myself that I would never again set foot in Germany, unless it was to find Gemma Rosselli, who had seemingly disappeared. Her villa stood empty and, according to the office of lost persons, she was last seen in Poland.

******

Less than a year after the trial, Gemma Rosselli's letter of 15 May 1946 vanquished any thoughts I still entertained about never returning to Germany. Having last seen her in December 1942, when we had been removed from our employment at the Jewish

Berlin Revisited

Hospital in Berlin, and herded into a cattle car destined for Majdanek, I could never forget my last glimpse of her. She was holding a child by the hand. Three other men and I had forced open the door of the cattle car and, as the train entered a wooded area, prepared to jump. But Gemma feared injuring the child. So, at the last moment, she released my hand and stayed behind as I and the others leaped, amid a hail of bullets. How had she survived the camp? My numerous attempts to determine her fate had all proved futile, leading me to believe that she was dead. Her letter, which came from a Catholic refugee center devoted to reuniting families, reached me in New York, where I now worked in Midtown as a diamond cutter, earning a comfortable salary. Whenever time allowed, I haunted galleries in search of photographs by Yva Simon, the German fashion photographer for whom I had briefly apprenticed and who had helped our small resistance group forge passports. Gemma's letter, postmarked Berlin, disclosed that records recently recovered from Nazi headquarters on Friedrichstraße included information on my parents. To see them, I would have to appear in person. The authorities would not allow Gemma to make copies. She wrote that I could lodge in her Charlottenburg villa, which for a short period I had called home. By means of an old deed of purchase, she had persuaded the authorities to restore it to her. I would enjoy the company of her two children, she said.

    Had I read correctly: two children? Was she married? And to whom? Geert?

Chapter Two

Contrary to what I'd been told, deciphering the runic inscriptions of memory had not helped me overcome my longing for Gemma. Try as I had to follow medical advice, my efforts proved unavailing. Our painful odyssey seemed never to end, and my expunging the events by trying to relive them, as doctors suggested, only recalled her ghost and intensified my loss.

Berlin Revisited

I had known Gemma as a friend, a comrade, and, not least, a co-conspirator. Her name was like Holy Writ. But to keep her ghostly presence under control, as one would a chronic illness, I had, in lieu of medication, written letters to her and sent them to every conceivable address. I read whatever I could about the Majdanek concentration camp, where some of my dearest friends had died. During my worst moments, I sank into depressive moods of reflection, which doctors assured me were not unusual for such a lingering pain as mine. They gave it any number of names: survivor's guilt, shell shock, mental overload, trauma, brain fever, ocular flashback, stress disorder, and medical terms I no longer remembered. But from the start I felt the inadequacy of their diagnoses. To linger suggests a faint trace that persists, but in my case, it was a haunting, a preying on the heart, an aching void.

As much as I grieved over my missing father, and despite the many letters I had written and sent to Dachau, that pain was different from what I felt at leaving Gemma behind. Told by a psychiatrist that the most effective treatment would be to force myself to recall whatever details I could, then edit and recast them, as if making a movie, I vowed never to tell myself a different story, or to alter the ending.

******

It had begun in Berlin where, owing to Gemma's letter, I was now returning, despite my vow a year earlier never to do so again.

As much as I wanted to see her, I allowed myself a delay, to bring her a gift she would treasure. And I knew where to find it, in Czechoslovakia. A curator at the Guggenheim had told me that an original Yva Simon photograph had surfaced in Prague. Such finds were now rare. In 1943, during an Allied bombing run, what remained of her collection, after Nazi confiscations, had been destroyed in Hamburg harbor. Crated and waiting for transport, the invaluable film burned on the docks. Yva never returned from the Majdanek concentration camp, in all likelihood having died before learning of the loss of her work. I now had an opportunity to acquire one of the few original prints that survived.

Even though I had no taste for the current Czech government of Klement Gottwald, an inflexible communist ideologue who presided over a police state, I made the trip owing not only to the scarcity of Yva Simon photographs, but also to the shared memories. Even before setting out, I knew that the Ministry of Culture could, if apprised of my mission, make my task difficult with permissions and permits for removal from the country of a "national treasure." Then, too, I had to consider the problem of the exchange rate. The official one, rigged in the government's favor, could not compete with the black market; but to change money on the street ran the risk of a fine and imprisonment. My well-meaning friends suggested I take a goodly sum of Czech Korunas before leaving, not aware that the Czech government allowed visitors to bring only a small amount of the local currency into the country.

Flying from New York to Prague by way of London and Frankfurt, I remembered thanking Mr. Fleischer, the owner of my place of work, for allowing me the time off to make this trip, and his saying that there was never enough time for loved ones. At the Prague airport, I encountered all the usual indignities: my clothing inspected, my luggage and camera bag virtually disassembled, my Swiss knife examined as if it presented a threat to the state, my magazines and newspapers confiscated, and my documents scrutinized. The stone-faced custom's officer also demanded a declaration of "Purpose of Trip," and an accounting of the money I carried. Just when I thought I had cleared every obstacle, the officer, flipping the pages of my passport, paused, and then spoke to me imperfectly in German.

"Born in Berlin, 1918."

"Yes."

"You initially left Germany when?"

"In 1942.

"How did you manage to cross the border? Your name is Baruch Rosner. A Jew."

Without a pang of remorse, I lied. "Sympathetic farmers."

"And the border patrols?" Before I could answer, the officer added, "No doubt bribed," and sighed. "Scratch the surface of any Jewish undertaking and you find below money." Returning the passport, the officer asked whether I had made a hotel reservation and, if so, where? What address?

"The Stop Motel on the edge of town." I attempted to repeat the street and number, only to have my pronunciation corrected. "Beware of pickpockets," said the officer stamping the passport.

On the trolley, I sat with my legs draped over my luggage and camera bag. The young Czech women, though poorly dressed, seemed particularly attractive, unlike the stolid Russian ones I had met on a business trip to Toronto. After exiting the tram, I asked directions to the hotel and discovered to my surprise that more Czechs spoke German than English. I wondered whether some day they would speak Russian, the language of the current overseers. At the hotel, I left my passport at the desk, as required. My room, spare and functional, had a small bathroom with hot water. The towels felt like boards, and the frayed starched sheets wanted replacement, but at least they were unstained. A radio carried two stations, both in Czech, and judging from the martial music and clipped speech, I concluded that both were propaganda vehicles.

My room also included a telephone, no doubt for the authorities to monitor my calls.

To prevent the customs agents from discovering among my papers the art dealer's home address, I had memorized it; but locating it on a map proved more difficult than I had anticipated. Rather than risk alerting someone to my real intentions—not tourism—I asked a tram conductor which trolley would take me to Saint Bartholomew's Church. Told in New York City that the man I wanted to see lived in that vicinity, I was dismayed to learn that a great many street names had been changed. Near the church, I asked an old man if he spoke German. The man answered in a Deutsch flecked with Yiddish. I smiled and continued the conversation in the Jewish lingua franca. The man clasped my hands and slightly rocked from toe to heel, like a davener mimicking a flickering flame. Removing his glasses, the gentleman rubbed them on a sleeve. His rheumy eyes and parchment-like skin bespoke a life of hardship; and the large sack of rags at his feet hinted at the shmattah trade.

"Your final destination, if I may ask?" said the man. "You don't strike me as someone who plans to remain in Prague."

"Berlin."

"A word of warning. Most Germans say they knew nothing of the plight of the Jews. But for all their protestations, they were delighted to see the Jews gone."

Before I could defend the many good Germans I had known, the man inquired:

"You like music?"

"Classical," I replied.

Opening his sack, he removed a violin and to my astonishment started to play Smetana's *Moldau*. As the old Jew played, I could have sworn that the itinerant musician grew young before my very eyes. The wisps of white hair that crowned his head seemed to rise and dance. When finished, the fiddler returned the violin to the sack and once again became an aged pensioner. I offered him some money, but the man brushed away my hand, observing:

"Where you stand stands Broumarska Street."

"But the signpost says . . ."

"Named after an apparatchik. It's how the government honors 'hyenas in syrup,' Mandelstam's phrase. You do know Osip's poetry?"

"In translation."

"Buskers used to recite his verses right where we are standing now . . . in the happy days after the war . . . before the communists extinguished the pulse of the street. They said it was unseemly for people to sell from pushcarts and stalls. So the vendors all left, taking with them their golden oranges and yellow squashes, their pumpernickel breads and cheddar cheeses, their pungent sauerkraut, and fresh-cooked potato pancakes, and Hungarian soups, and roast pork with cabbage, and boiled fruit filled with dumplings. Gone in the span of a few days were the flower stands, the grinding wheels to sharpen knives and scissors, the sewing machines to mend a person's clothes, the cast iron anvils to repair a shoe, the newspaper stands, the money changers, the booths with used clothing, hats, buttons, belts, beads, briar pipes, toys, watches. All the music of the street, gone, driven away by the men with winter in their hearts."

Exhausted by his epic catalogue, the fiddler wiped some spittle from his lips and pointed me to the apartment block that housed Adam Čapek, art collector, oenophile, tennis aficionado, and scoundrel. The brass nameplate on his door said simply: Objets d'art. In response to my tapping the porpoise door knocker, a man opened a peephole, made the appropriate inquiries, and then admitted me. On entering the foyer, I sized up the collector, who resembled the American gangster Abner Zwillman, whose moniker, "Longie," captured Mr. Čapek's appearance. Everything was long: his height, face, nose, hands, fingers, and, given the size of his shoes, his feet. Čapek towered over my six feet, two inches. Fortunately, his flat, which dated from an earlier age, had high ceilings; otherwise the dealer (some might say wheeler-dealer) would have dominated the room. His taste in furniture favored fashionable Regency, when England ruled the waves and the sun never set on its empire. Mr. Čapek proudly showed me the apartment, which held pieces that could have come from a Jane Austen novel: an elegant sitting room couch with a swooping design and clawed feet, as well as double saber leg chairs with rope twist backs. In the dining room stood a tilt top table that could be folded and stored to make extra room for a party. Between rooms, in the hallway, a standing clock ticked loudly. The study was furnished with a circular library drum table, a period hat stand, desk, and bookcases. A peek into one of the bedrooms discovered a glorious mirror rising from a dressing table on a support as thin and elegant as a lily stem.

Some of the pieces, according to Mr. Čapek, came from the craftsmen Henry Holland and Thomas Hope. If Adam Čapek's intention was to recreate an earlier period, he had succeeded admirably. For antiquary reasons, this connoisseur had turned his back on the robotic world of modernism, which, he admitted, had once attracted him.

"Too mechanical," he explained.

Attired in a navy-blue velvet jacket, white ruffled shirt, pearl silk ascot, and gray trousers with thin black stripes, he looked as if he wished to imitate Oscar Wilde. Alas, he lacked Oscar's bon mots. In later years, I came to think of him as the incongruous man. Although he was stately in dress and stature and taste, his speech belied his elegance. I recalled several beautiful women who, when they opened their mouths, made exactly the wrong impression, cracking gum and dropping their g's. Čapek's command of Czech might have been perfect, but his German was ungrammatical and his English, acquired in America, a patois that made him sound like a Brooklyn tough.

"I liked da action in New York, but it ain't Prague, if yous know what I mean?"

I guessed that during Čapek's three-year U.S.A. residence learning English, he had watched too many James Cagney and George Raft movies. But who had sponsored him in America for those three years remained a mystery.

When I finally mentioned the Yva Simon photograph, Čapek replied, "Yeah, I got Scotty's letter about the pic. Word gets around fast when you got a hot item to sell. But gettin' it out of the country is another thing."

So great was his dependence on the all-purpose verb "get," I suspected that he, like most Americans, would have been rendered speechless if his English vocabulary had lacked the word, with all its varied forms and idiomatic usages.

"I can't talk too long," Čapek said. "I gotta get to another buyer."

But then he kept me from leaving, wanting to know whether the photograph would be paid for in dollars, a question I had anticipated. Before departing the States, I knew Čapek's conditions and had arranged to collect the dollars through the Swiss Embassy in Prague. When I disclosed the source of the money, the dealer visibly relaxed and suggested we enjoy a glass of Bordeaux Supérieur from the Château d'Crain collection. Pouring the wine lovingly, he seemed to have forgotten about his next appointment. Raising his delicately etched wineglass to the light, he held forth on the qualities of French wines. From the delicacy of the wine, he moved to the mechanics of tennis strokes and why the Spaniards, particularly on clay courts, looked like ballet dancers. In the middle of this encomium, he again slid into another subject: a way to take the Yva Simon picture out of the country undetected.

"I know a printer. He does jobs for me. I once gave him copies of some of her most famous pics and told him to make a calendar from them, each month a different one of Yva Simon's stylish ladies . . . you know, with fur wraps and high heels, smoking a cigarette in a holder and dripping jewelry. The calendar was a gift for a lady friend. The printer still got the plates. You can do the same. If someone asks questions, just show 'em the calendar and say, 'You pick the month. Each a Yva Simon copy. Meantime you put the real thing behind the lining of your valise. No one will ever know, especially not some bloodless border guard."

Čapek, seeing his buyer's agitation, refilled my wine glass and told me to relax. "You have my assurance." Soothing words, but once I boarded the train for Berlin, I was on my own.

"I'd like to see the photograph."

Čapek disappeared and emerged a minute later with a framed picture of a beautiful woman, gorgeously attired, holding the hand of a well-dressed child. She looked as if she were summoning a cab. A contented smile suggested she had just stepped out of the clothing store in the background from which she had purchased a camel's hair coat for her daughter.

Berlin Revisited

One look and I knew it was an Yva Simon original. Had I not worked in her studio? For a second, I found myself breathless. I had always wanted to own one of her initial prints, and now it rested in my hands. Čapek knew enough to say nothing and just let me revel in the quality and essence of the work. During my many visits to galleries, I had admired more important photo works, but none that came with the history of Yva Simon, for whom Gemma Rosselli had occasionally posed when Gemma and I lived in the Berlin apartment house, subsequently called the Bogota Hotel, where Yva's flat and studio had occupied the top two floors.

******

It took a few days for me to collect the dollars that Čapek could change, or not, on the black market for a small fortune in Korunas. I surmised that with either currency, Čapek bought favors from government officials, whom he bribed to turn a blind eye to his capitalist ventures.

On my return trip to the Stop Motel, with the framed picture in a shopping bag given me by Mr. Čapek, I took time for a beer at a neighborhood tavern. The cold Pilsen, which I gulped thirstily, was invigorating. When I looked up from my glass, people were pointing at me and laughing. In the mirror behind the bar, I could see a foam mustache on my upper lip. I chuckled. This simple event earned me an invitation to sit and chat with four men in overalls, one of whom spoke German and translated for his friends. During our small talk, I asked whether they knew a camera store in the area. They did and told me how to find it. I thanked the men, gladly paid the bill for the beers, and entered the avenue. A wind blew the falling leaves across the road. I stopped to take in the surroundings. Was it my imagination or was I being tailed? I waited a few moments, circled the block, and then continued. On a crooked lane, which undoubtedly dated from the middle ages, I found Jirí Svestka's shop. In the small front window, four framed pictures of children rested on casels. I assumed that the sign in Czech, accompanying the photographs, beckoned parents to have their children's pictures taken here.

In the shop, a woman who understood German, greeted me, identifying herself as Jirí's wife. Her husband had gone out. She had a face full of regret and, perhaps to gladden herself, wore a colorful peasant dress of red, yellow, green, and orange, with a matching head scarf. I told her that I needed a framed copy of a photograph, which I lifted from my shopping bag. She removed the photograph from the frame and told me to return in the morning to collect the developed print. With the help of a tourist bureau housed in the Stop Motel, I made train reservations to leave the next afternoon for Berlin. As I lay in bed that night, I thought of Gemma and wondered how she had become fluent in Russian. Italian and German, yes; but Russian? In the morning, I checked out of the motel, stopped at Mr. Svestka's shop, and was again waited on by the wife. As I stowed the framed original and copy in my suitcase, Mrs. Svestka said that the frame of the copy, unlike the original one, did not bear a miniscule letter Z. If I wanted, she could add the letter to the frame holding the copy. I asked her to do so and left a large bill on the counter on leaving. A few blocks from the print shop, I boarded a tram and exited at the main train station, Praha hl.n.

For a few extra korunas, I had booked a single compartment so that I could be alone with my thoughts. Train travel, disrupted by the war, had yet to return fully to normal, but thankfully the service to Berlin still operated. The train ran along the river Labe (Elbe) and cut through a picturesque gorge called the Czech Switzerland.

Periodically, canoeists and kayakers disembarked. I appreciated their enthusiasm and could hardly contain my own. The envelope with Gemma's unexpected letter lay on my lap. I had read it so often that I feared before long the paper would dissolve in my hands. Her reference to children was a nagging reminder of her infatuation with Geert. Had the Dutchman reappeared and married her? Pocketing the letter, I leaned back in my seat and reflected on the last few days in Prague, a beautiful city sadly cursed. Regimentation and grayness had descended on the people like a mist that brought not life-giving moisture but a miasma.

Why Čapek had returned to Czechoslovakia teased—and tested—my imagination. Could he be trusted? The collector's standard of living put him in the company of Czech apparatchiks. Perhaps he served the government as an agent who obtained hard currency from the West by working the art market. He certainly seemed to know art dealers, like the one in New York, who could advance his interests. What did they receive in return? If he, in fact, did work for the secret police (Státni bezpečnost), I could find myself arriving at the Czech border with Germany and have my picture confiscated. Proceeding on Shakespeare's advice to love all but trust few, I boarded the train and, on entering my compartment, used my Swiss knife to remove the screws of a recessed wooden box, which housed a coiled fire hose, and hid the original picture behind it. The framed copy and my export permit I placed in my valise, among my clothing, as if I wished to prevent any damage to either.

Shortly before the border, the train came to a halt for passport control and a search of personal belongings. A young soldier, speaking German, who looked no older than eighteen exhibited undue energy in searching my luggage. Zealously hunting for contraband, and exuding the stale odor of communist sanctimony, he exulted in finding the framed copy and exit permit, both of which he confiscated and immediately left the compartment for a few minutes. I could see from my train window the border guard talking to some official, who studied the picture and then flipped pages of a small notebook. A moment later the soldier returned, empty-handed.

"Your papers are in order, but the photograph cannot leave the country. It is state property."

"Didn't you see the paper permitting me to—"

The soldier interrupted. "All art works stamped with a Z are owned by the Ministry of Culture and export forbidden."

"Oh, if I had known . . ." I replied, feigning amazement. "Does the Ministry of Culture also reimburse me for my loss? The cost was considerable."

"You should have inquired beforehand. I'm no expert, but I fail to see the worth of a photograph of a rich woman and a spoiled brat." He shook his head. "Bourgeois trash."

Chapter Three

When the train crossed into Germany, it passed through miles of rapeseed. As far as the eye could see, the landscape shimmered with the richness of a Van Gogh canvas. Five hours later, I stood in the Berlin train station, trying to decide whether to take a tram, bus, or cab. After changing some money, Korunas for Deutsch marks, I boarded a bus traveling west on Kurfürstendamm. From my window seat, I surveyed the city's reconstruction efforts with mixed feelings. I saw neighborhoods and homes being rebuilt, suggesting a prosperity that left me feeling ambivalent. Why should Germany—any part of it—benefit from American aid? A part of me wanted to see the country suffer for eternity, while another part wanted to see the familiar streets of Wilmersdorf and Charlottenburg as they once were, undamaged.

My first stop was Charlottenburg, a section of Berlin where I had lived before my father's imprisonment in Dachau, and before my mother's decision to house me with a friend. In the old neighborhood, the trees had begun to lose their chlorophyll and take on their splendid fall colors. The day was crisp and clear, like the Friday I and other non-Aryans had been expelled from school. I walked the area looking for a familiar face; but the Jews had disappeared, and the gentile shopkeepers said they knew nothing of my parents. After several hours of futile searching for word of them, I found a place to stay.

A number of homeowners in the Wilmersdorf district, desperate to pay their heating and lighting bills, offered rooms for rent at a reasonable rate. I took one on the top floor of a three-story house, which had previously belonged, as I learned, to a Jewish family. The thin, gray-haired woman who now owned the property, Mrs. Hoffmann, had suffered the loss of her husband and son in the war. Still attractive, though clearly disoriented by the trauma of her personal losses, she aimlessly roamed from one room to the next, as if searching for her lost life. She told me the history of the house, as we sat over tea and biscuits, which I had bought at the train station.

The former owners of the house, Dr. and Mrs. Beer, had lived there with their daughter, an artist, and their son, a lawyer. The mother and children had escaped to America, but the father, an internist, insisted on remaining behind and treating the sick, among whom he counted some high Nazi officials.

"In the very room you're staying in, Dr. Beer kept his medical books. And on the windowsill stood a candelabra with eight branches."

When I told her that the candelabra was called a menorah, she guessed my religion and readily told the rest of her story.

"Dr. Beer used to treat my husband and me. When one of his patients warned him that he was to be arrested, he arranged for us to occupy his house. In return, he asked only one favor: that we should keep the candelabra safe from confiscation or vandalism. To this day it rests in my son's room, on his night table."

Later, she insisted on showing me the menorah, a handsomely crafted work from Poland. It seemed to be her way of saying, "See, I am not one of them. I am not a barbarian."

******

The next day, I walked to Charlottenburg, carrying a small grip that held the Yva Simon gift for Gemma. I had planned this day very carefully. Instead of going directly to Gemma at the villa, particularly in light of her mention of children, I would stop beforehand at my former residence, where Walter Fertig and I had lived, and capture now as much as I could of life then.

As I made my way along Kurfürstendamm, I stopped at the building that had once housed a lively cabaret. My guardian had taken me there for my birthday in 1936, the year that the Nazis, unhappy with the satire directed at them, banned all further cabaret performances. A restaurant now occupied the premises. I asked for a seat near the back, where the stage once stood, and ordered coffee and Blitzkuchen, coffee cake. The waiter noticed my bag and asked whether I wished to leave it at the front counter. I thanked him, declined, and asked for the manager, explaining that as a young boy I had once seen a cabaret show here. A few minutes later, a well-dressed portly gentleman in a black suit and vest drew up a chair beside me. As he spoke, his pencil mustache twitched, and his jelly jowls shook. A white opal, which he nervously fingered, hung from his pocket chain, which traversed his ample stomach. The stone, like one that adorned a necklace owned by Gemma Rosselli, recalled her lovely breasts, between which the opal rested, and the long-forgotten poet's words: "That stone enjoyed a double grace: both by the gem and by the place." To my question about stage props, the manager replied, "Sold, lost, or stolen." His name, Hartmut Burger, bore no resemblance to the famous conferenciers (emcees) and cabaretists, many of them Jewish, like Kurt Gerron, who had satirized Jew and gentile alike, and had made jokes of Hitler's risible absurdities, bringing audiences to tears from laughter. I could still picture the revelers, deep in their cups, slapping their thighs in delight, and deaf to the thud of boots on the cobblestones, little realizing the impending Nazi danger.

Cradling my coffee cup, I remembered sitting at a small table close enough to the stage for the performers to make eye contact with me. To this day, I could still see a pretty, young woman with a curly blonde wig and carmine lips singing:

>*My mama is a liar,*
>*My papa is a friar.*
>*My grandma's an awful thief,*
>*Stuck like glue in her belief*
>*That all mankind is rotten,*
>*And truth has been forgotten.*
>*The world, she says, is awful,*
>*And everyone's unlawful.*
>*Look at what comes of a kiss:*
>*A kid and the end of bliss.*
>*Everyone's a bloody cheat,*
>*Turn your eyes, they'll steal your seat.*

Even now, though the words of the chorus escaped me, one prescient couplet remained: "Life is short and greed's in season / We've all taken leave of reason." Such a wonderful birthday; one skit after another: singers, dancers, acrobats, a magician, comedians, and the mimics and mimes. Tipping the waiter, I took my bag, paid the cashier, and, as I walked the few blocks to my destination, repeated the words, "Look at what comes of a kiss: A kid and an end of bliss."

My thoughts flew ahead to 45 Schlüterstraße, where my guardian, Walter Fertig, and I had adjoining rooms on the second floor. We had taken our meals together, around the corner, at a favorite restaurant. Walter had come from money, and though he chose to live in a multi-family residence, with three rooms, all furnished in the Bauhaus style, he could have afforded his own flat or a country house. A uniquely kind and generous man, he fell far short of the Nazi ideal: no blonde hair, no blue eyes, no Nordic nose or mouth or bee-stung lips or ivory teeth. He resembled Everyman and could easily have passed for any dull, stolid, conventional Biedermeier. He owned a furniture store on a side street that appealed to middle-class comfort: writing desks, pianos, plump functional tables, couches, and chairs that emphasized light, native woods and geometric shapes. He also sold sentimental paintings that extolled the virtues of home, family, children, and church. Like the furniture he sold, he personified bourgeois values, except for his book collecting. In 1933, when the Nazis were confiscating books for burning, Mr. Fertig pretended to work for the Nazis and filled his small delivery truck with every book he could rescue. Returning to his shop, he stored them neatly in basement shelves. He not only loved books, but also reasoned that in time, the banned ones would fetch a handsome price. And he was right. My mother, told that he might have a copy of *The Forty Days of Musa Dagh*, by the banned writer Franz Werfel, found a copy at Mr. Fertig's shop. She paid very little. Drawn to attractive and needy women, Mr. Fertig sold them goods at reduced prices. My mother became his favorite. In all the years she frequented his shop, she never, except for that first purchase, paid him a single pfennig. Any objective observer viewing Ruth Rosner conducting business with Walter Fertig would have thought the woman bewitching and the man bewitched.

That morning in 1934 when my mother accompanied me and my possessions to Walter's apartment house, I felt orphaned, overcome by a sense of loss and early sorrow. Her explanation for moving me from the family flat rang false. She said that with the arrest of my father, she wished to live alone—to restore her mental health and to refocus her life. Perhaps for this reason I paid particular attention to the awakening city at that six a.m. hour: streets alive with trolleys umbilically tied to sparking overhead electric lines and clanking along metal rails; trains carrying their silent burghers; double-decker buses crawling from one stop to the next; taxis collecting their rich fares; private cars with their right-hand steering wheels exiting hidden garages; bicycles dangerously darting among the moving traffic that undulated like a snake; canals bustling with barges. Men in oily aprons pushed carts of grapes and lettuce and lemons and limes. Stall owners unrolled canvas covers revealing piles of clothing and shoes. Sidewalk hawkers held up pigeons for sale. Numerous store windows were whitewashed with anti-Jewish slogans and warnings, "Don't buy here, Jewish owned." Building cranes stood like giant spiders waiting to continue their construction. Poor children scavenged in trash bins, their knee socks having fallen to their ankles. A public clock chimed the quarter hour. Two sewer men descended through a hole in the road to the lower depths. A flag, promoting a Judenrein Germany, fluttered in the spring breeze. A building with rounded corners displayed women's slips on mannequins. Some shops remained shuttered. A kiosk selling newspapers attracted a pipe smoker. A woman emptied a pail of water into the cobblestone street. Several soldiers, carrying Nazi banners and flags and pictures of Hitler, passed in an open truck. An organ grinder attracted a coin from an appreciative pedestrian. A woman leaned out of a window and shook her bedding. Nurses and mothers pushed perambulators. A garbage truck lumbered to a stop. Mailmen scurried from house to house. A few children with their back satchels had already started off to school. "Cigarettin" cried a man with a leather strap around his neck supporting a wooden box. A shop selling silverware caught the morning sun, illuminating a restaurant with revolving doors. A jaunty walker sported a boater hat. Men and women in jodhpurs were riding horses in the park. A flower stand blossomed into color as the merchant arrayed his different offerings. When the train speeded up so too did the panorama of life seen through the window. There were street sweepers, women beating rugs, chauffeured cars, shoeshine boys, policemen directing traffic, charitable religious women with cans for coins, an old man picking up a cigarette butt, pedestrians dodging cars as they tried to cross a busy roadway. Advertisements rolled by in a rapid sequence: Homburg hats, fedoras, peaked workers' hats, picture hats, bonnets, roll top desks, Torpedo typewriters, rotary telephones, seal coats, Lux soap, Lufthansa flights, a circus, the Hotel Excelsior, accordions, saxophones, clarinets, violins, fireworks, hockey matches, ice skating, boxing, indoor ski jumping, tennis matches, indoor bicycle tracks, horse and boat races . . . all this bazaar of life found in the bounty that was once Berlin.

PAUL M. LEVITT

45 Schlüterstraße

Turning the corner of Kurfürstendamm, I passed a dress shop and finally arrived at the building that I had so often remembered and that had been such an important part of my life. During my mother's trial I had avoided friends, but I could no longer ignore the persistent call of 45 Schlüterstraße. Although Walter Fertig had died before my mother's trial, I felt his kindness would still inhabit the building. Entering the front door, I greeted the indolent caretaker, who introduced himself as Viktor Bobel.

"Anything you want to know about this place just ask me. I've worked here since 1941."

"In this very building I once shared an apartment with Herr Walter Fertig."

The caretaker shed his lassitude and grew animated. "I knew him. A fine gentleman. He died suddenly. When you return, we can talk."

"Yes, I'd like that."

I crossed the ornate parquet floor that led to the central staircase and small, caged elevator that had brought to Yva Simon's studio on the fifth-floor innumerable artists, authors, film stars, and models. Smiling to myself, I knew that I was returning to this address to look for yesterday, and that I had come to a place where I could hear the voices of the dead.

Relishing Yva's familiar studio, now restored, I retreated to a green parlor chair, vicariously living again our time together in this sacred space. Here Yva had used the unusual architecture to pose the youthful, ladylike photo models. By bathing the spatially opulent ambience with swirling light, she had imbued her fashion photographs with dramatic elegance and a hint of daring. My favorite picture shows a blonde-haired woman slightly lifting her skirt to examine the seam on her right stocking. The woman is standing at the bottom of a winding carpeted staircase with brass stair rods, and bending to her right, her fingertips just slightly raising the hem of her skirt, as she leans her head forward to observe the back of her leg. I still own a copy of the photograph, which captured a lost age of elegance.

And as I sat immersed in memory, the past became the present: the year 1934.

PART TWO

Chapter Four

Minutes after my mother deposited me at the apartment house in the care of Mr. Fertig, I started exploring the building. Hearing distant voices and laughter from upstairs, I tracked the sound to the top floor. As I approached, filtered lights played along the staircase. I crouched, mesmerized by the setting. A model in a long black dress, with a neck fur piece, was adjusting the pinafore and hat of a younger girl, a few years older than I. The girl was Gemma Rosselli, one of the few teenagers whom Yva Simon ever used in her photography. Both the model and the girl were strikingly beautiful and slim waisted, unlike most of the Frauen and Kinder on the street. The girl's father sat to one side, looking immensely satisfied. On seeing me peer around the door, the photographer, Yva Simon, waved at me to join the group, saying: Hallo! Bitte fühlen Sie sich wie zu Hause. (Hello! Make yourself at home.) Frightened, I bolted down the stairs to return to my room. But I kept in my mind's eye the picture of the younger girl with a ballet dancer's legs, a long neck, lovely arms, and a smile that made me feel older than my sixteen years. Before going to bed, I looked in the mirror to see how the hair on my upper lip was progressing, spun three times on one leg, and slept like a contented lover.

The next morning, I sat in the lobby hoping to catch a glimpse of the young model. According to Mr. Fertig, she lived in the building and answered to the name of Gemma Rosselli. To pass the time, I sat reading a newspaper, which featured articles about the preparations for the Olympic Games to be held in Berlin the following year, and related articles about the pros and cons of allowing German Jews to participate. In my absorption, I failed to see the person I waited for.

"Giovanotto, hey, young man," a voice near me in the lobby called. I turned. It was Signorina Gemma Rosselli, wearing a pink-striped dress. "You know," she said, "it is impolite to stare at young women you don't know. Yesterday. . ."

An excitement I'd never felt before overcame me, leaving me speechless. Her elevated eyebrows and imperious look seemed to demand a reply. Then she slightly parted her lips and laughed.

"You're staring at me again," she remarked slowly, and playfully shook a finger at me in reprimand.

Using the newspaper to cover my confusion, I stuttered that the Germans were trying to decide the fate of Jewish athletes. She looked bewildered, but before I could clarify, she tossed her head and provocatively asked:

"What did you think of me yesterday?" Then she immediately added, "What is your name?" and sat down beside me on the leather couch.

"Baruch Rosner."

My name temporarily brought the chat to a halt, as she bit her upper lip and looked over her shoulder toward the front door, as if expecting a guest. Seeing no one, she resumed the conversation. "My name is Gemma Rosselli. I live here with my father. He often takes me on business trips. We own a small villa a few blocks from here; but my father prefers to conduct his business from 45 Schlüterstraße. He says this is one of the most famous addresses in Berlin."

Incredulous, I asked, "A villa?"

"On Schloßstraße. We also have a flat here on the third floor."

The word "villa" brought to mind wealth and luxury, tennis courts and a swimming pool, none of which, in fact, the villa enjoyed.

Picking up the thread of her earlier comment, she added, "My guess is you thought badly of me yesterday."

"No, not at all."

She paused over my reply and then continued, "Listen, you don't know me. I am seventeen and know things that girls a lot older than me don't know. So, I'm a lot older than my age."

At that moment, I felt like a child. In my own defense, I blurted, "I play chess rather well."

My observation passed unnoticed as she resumed. "I know some things that would shock you. But I've learned, especially in these times, to keep secrets. If you like, though, you can tell me yours." Having little experience to draw on, I lowered my eyes and fumbled with the newspaper. "Look at me!" she commanded, and tuned her voice pleasantly to say, "I like you. I hope we can be friends. But perhaps you would rather not?" Even at sixteen, I knew that her words were meant to beguile, to teach me a lesson in craft and subtlety. But to what end? Now she was staring at the front door, as a lady with a dog entered. I took the occasion to study Gemma's face closely. She had an aquiline and handsome Roman nose, full lips, olive skin, dark curls, and, most striking of all, limpid blue shimmering eyes, with a black ring around the pupils— splendid seductive eyes.

With no little self-interest, I asked, "What business is your father in?"

She looked up and answered simply, "He sells men's footwear. He has contracts with the German government."

"Oh?"

"He supplies them with shoes. Of course, whenever he can, he sells to department stores, which love Italian leather goods. Italian styles, as you may know, are always in demand. German shoes are generally rubbish. The ersatz leather provides as much comfort and warmth as cardboard, and designs are no better than Dutch wooden clogs."

Not in the least familiar with fashions, I nodded knowingly and said, "I much prefer Italian styles to German."

She smiled. I worried: Did she see through me to the shallowness below? "Yva Simon," she observed, "is the exception. She can make any German woman or piece of clothing look elegant. That's why my father originally spoke to her about using me as a model."

Naïvely, I asked, "Do you have a mother," and then quickly added, "as beautiful as you?"

She slapped my hand playfully. "Doesn't everyone have a mother?"

Chapter Five

After we spoke, I was convinced that where Gemma stood stood the sun. That summer, I trailed her wherever and whenever I could. It was she who introduced me to Else Ernestine Neuländer-Simon, known to the photography fraternity as Yva. Born to a merchant and a milliner, Yva was the youngest of nine children. At age thirty-five, she had already published in prestigious newspapers and magazines. Her wealthy husband of one year, Alfred Simon, eleven years her senior, oversaw the business and the books. In her studio, she employed ten people. I apprenticed as the eleventh.

Although I couldn't prove it, I thought my invitation to join Yva's studio was owing to Sig. Ugo Rosselli, Gemma's father, who arranged for me to work in Yva's studio, at least for the summer. In his usual jovial manner, which I always felt hid a serious side, Ugo asked, with a chuckle, if he could "prevail" upon me for a favor. Some men, Shakespeare says, protest too much; some people, I thought, laugh too much. In both instances it invited suspicion.

"You are sixteen," he said, as he removed a gold-tipped cigarette from a silver case and tapped it on the lid.

"Soon to be seventeen," I proudly added.

"You are thoughtful for your age." He reached into his jacket and removed a Ronson lighter. He lit the cigarette, inhaled, and expelled the smoke through puckered lips, eyeing me curiously. "You are also precocious."

"I'm not sure what that means."

"Grownup."

"Thank you."

"I know about your father."

"You know something about him?" I asked excitedly, feeling my pulse quicken. "Tell me!"

Sig. Rosselli shook his head. "My German is not subtle enough. I misspoke. I know that he was taken away, but how he is faring, I have no idea. Seeing a parent arrested, I should imagine, marks the end of childhood."

Tears came to my eyes, but I said nothing. That evening, for the first time since father's arrest, I wrote a letter to him, to reconnect with the one person who knew me best. Disclosing my demons to father had always made me feel less fearful of a world in which the martial music and the jackboots on the broken glass sounded ever louder. My mother said she had no time for such adolescent "nonsense." With a framed photograph of father perched on my desk, I began writing about my personal feelings, not knowing whether my letter would ever reach him. In some ways, I hoped it didn't, because it left me so exposed.

Lieber Vater,

Mutter has lodged me with her friend Walter Fertig so that she can have the flat to herself. I held back my tears as we left the familiar for the unknown. Although I have always regarded Mr. Fertig as one of the family, my initial thoughts were of cheder and the rabbi explaining Adam's expulsion from Eden for disobedience. How could I not help but think that I too had done something wrong? For what reason I didn't know. Maybe one day Mutter will explain.

The building I am now living in at 45 Schlüterstraße has dozens of apartments. The residents seem friendly and express a genuine interest in music and literature. You would like it here. I have met a beautiful young woman I want to tell you about. Her name is Gemma Rosselli. Although only a year older than I, she seems quite sophisticated. Her looks remind me of a Botticelli painting that we once studied in class, "The Birth of Venus." I've never had a real girlfriend, and frankly I'm not sure how to act with a girl I like. If you were here, I'm sure you could advise me.

Knowing Emma, I think, will dispel some of my loneliness. Most of the boys I knew have joined one of the Hitler Youth groups. Once they put on a uniform a change comes over them. They strut and bark, ordering people this way and that. They even try to bully me, but I refuse to cower, though I admit that sometimes I begin to stutter in their presence, and I can feel my legs shaking. The one thing I can assure you, Vater, is I don't cry when they hit me, and I don't run from their taunts.

PAUL M. LEVITT

Most non-Aryans live in fear of informers, block wardens, the secret police, and of Hitler youth groups. A careless word can lead to a beating. Failure to contribute to Nazi party collections marks you as suspicious. Defending someone who is being mistreated puts you in line to be next. As a result, the streets are virtually silent, except for the occasional sound of jazz music issuing from an apartment house.

You see, many of the young people, not associated with the Nazis, want to have the freedom to listen to American music. I have not done so myself, but I understand that a great many non-Aryan boys and girls have joined gangs or groups that meet to listen to jazz and to dance. When I know more, I will write to tell you what I learn.

Alles Liebe,
Baruch

The next day, Sig. Rosselli put his arm around my shoulder and said, "If I may for a moment act as your surrogate father, I have a favor to ask, a proposal . . . Gemma can be unruly. I'd like you to join her and share her pastimes."

In return, he offered to supply me with pocket money to take her cycling, and horseback riding, and to pay for the hourly cost of a tennis court and the rental fee for a racket and balls. Naturally, I agreed. And by the end of the summer, I had learned to sit a horse and play tennis with a modicum of ease. I had also learned how to maintain the photographic equipment and the various types of lights in Yva Simon's studio.

One of Yva's assistants, Franz Stein, introduced me to the mysteries of lighting. Having thought that photographers merely pointed a camera and clicked or hit the start button of a movie camera, I discovered my mistake. Fashion photography was like portraiture. The artist sets the scene and poses the principal, all in the proper light. The requisite equipment is therefore vital. From Franz I learned about C stands that hold items in place and the different ways to alter a light source with barn doors (flaps); cutters, an opaque device that "cuts" (reduces) the light; soft boxes that modify it; snoots, black metal tubes, that change its shape; and silks that soften and reduce it. Obviously, the most important element was the light source; and to produce it indoors takes different kinds of lighting equipment, for example, flash, blackline, brownline, continuous, spyder, and gells, to say nothing of backdrops, props, posing tools, shooting tables, tripods, and monopods. These were just some of the items and lessons that occupied my apprenticeship, all of which proved indispensable when I took up forgery.

******

But equipment means nothing without the supreme eye of the beholder. Yva Simon, like no other fashion photographer of her day, could transform the common into the uncommon. Through her magic, models and objects became magnetic, drawing the viewer into the picture. Her consuming interest in making the ordinary seem extraordinary, I often thought, issued from her own appearance. Not at all beautiful—her nose was large and her teeth irregular—she did have soft features, attractive short, dark hair, and eyes like pools of love that put people at their ease and made them feel important. Her flawless milky skin gave her a childlike quality, and yet her professional habits, disciplined and steely, belied her youthful looks. Before wasting any precious film, she closely scrutinized her models: their face, eyes, legs, hands, and body. Then, of course, the garment also had to be inspected, particularly the folds and the light-absorbing qualities of the material.

Both Yva and the models worked long hours, and the pay could greatly vary. On average, magazines paid twenty-five marks for a photograph, and a title page for the *Berliner Illustrierte Zeitung*, three hundred marks. After work, weather permitting, the staff, including me, would sit on the outdoor balcony attached to her studio at a round table sipping tea or coffee, and animatedly talk about literature and the arts, trying to ignore the mounting menace. On the few occasions when the subject turned to politics, Mr. Simon always insisted that the cultured instincts of the German people would prevail and that the government's excesses wouldn't last. He cited the coming Olympics as an example of how the Nazis had already altered their behavior because Hitler wished to show the world the superiority of German youth and the wonders of Berlin. Gemma suggested that the Olympics might provide a perfect opportunity for portraiture, given the numerous athletes from different countries and the many sports. Perhaps the American decathlon champion, Glenn Morris, could be induced to sit for Yva. Little did they know that afternoon, bathed in the summer light, that Mr. Morris would become the object of Leni Riefenstahl's camera and affections.

******

Sig. Rosselli made no secret of his having asked me to entertain his daughter and satisfy what Ugo called her "restless spirit." I could imagine Gemma thinking: Poor Baruch! Becoming my plaything must make him feel like an indentured servant.

On Saturdays, we frequently rode horses in the Tiergarten Park, stopping at the zoo, buying peanuts, admiring the stately animals, and laughing at the monkeys. In serious moments, we silently admired the beauty of the woods. On one of our days out, Gemma brought up the subject of sex, nearly scaring me to death.

Asking if I thought she was pretty, she turned my face seven shades of red. Teasing me about blushing, she laughed when I attributed it to allergies. "Come now," she prodded, "answer yes or no." I replied "Very." She, presumably to put me at my ease, told me I was handsome, but instead of smiling in appreciation, I nearly choked. "Such a sweet boy!" she said.

Once, as we cantered along the trail, I felt that we were being watched, but she dismissed the idea. She said that I was becoming fearful like other Berlin Jews who saw a threat in every face and shadow. Although hundreds had already left the country—obtaining exit visas for a price—when I told her that my father's request had been denied, she minimized the danger. "The borders are not sealed," she said, "and as a last resort, one can still bribe an official." My belief that the student who betrayed my father was paid to do so moved her to reply skeptically, "But by whom?"

On Sundays, Gemma and her father attended early morning Mass, more from habit than from faith. In the afternoon, we played tennis. Our first competitive match occurred on a crisp and overcast day. She wore a sweater and sweatpants; I braved the elements in my skimpy shirt and shorts. Our opponents were blonde and quintessentially Aryan, he a low-ranking Army officer, and she a law clerk. Gemma observed that they spent their weekends on the courts, where we often saw them. Just the previous week, the nameless couple had suggested a friendly match. On the day of the mixed doubles, we finally learned the name of our opponents, Greta and Erwin.

My tennis skills had yet to improve to the point where I could keep up with the others. It took all summer until I could sustain a rally from the back court, hit aces and overheads, and poach at the net. For the moment, I was prone to rush my shots and miss easy volleys. Although Gemma kept us in the game as long as she could, my failures finally sank us. Greta and Erwin, gracious winners, praised our court sense and tenacity. Erwin even went out of his way to tell Gemma that she had elegant ground strokes and a fine feel for the game. Perhaps for this reason she was not surprised when he showed up the next day at 45 Schlüterstraße to pay her court. But Erwin wasn't the first, and always Sig. Rosselli played the role of gatekeeper, smiling and reminding the suitors that his daughter was still just a teenager.

******

To me, however, it was quite apparent that with each passing day she was becoming more lovely and shapely.

******

When Gemma told me that she and her father were planning to spend a month in Wiesbaden, for the restorative waters and spa, a sadness came over me and I felt bereft. She gave as a reason poor health, but never said whether she meant her own or her father's, and I was too polite to ask. When she saw my crestfallen look, she quickly added that they would return in late September, though not to 45 Schlüterstraße, but to their nearby villa on Schloßstraße. Knowing that she would be leaving at the end of August, I tried to make the most of the last of the summer. I accompanied Gemma to outdoor concerts, soccer matches, bicycle races, movies, and a tennis exhibition at which Baron Gottfried von Cramm displayed his balletic skills, sliding across the clay court with the ease of a skater on ice. Our activities were so frenzied that I began to suspect that it was her father who was ill. In honor of the Rossellis, Oskar Skaller, the Jewish owner of the building and a Socialist MP, who hosted literary and political salons on the first floor, organized a send-off party in his flat. To enliven the evening, he arranged to have the famous Kurt Gerron give a private vaudeville show, to which Yva and her staff were also invited. Kurt was Germany's preeminent conferencier and cabaretist. Although the satire he employed had rankled the government, this was a private performance, where he felt safe to vent his abhorrence of the Nazis in song and patter.

A heavy, loose-jawed man, though light on his feet, he gave all the guests a night to remember. With a mischievous twinkle in his eye, he began the evening with a joke:

A man from the SA, Hitler's Brownshirts, is baiting a Jew. "Tell me, who's responsible for the fact that we lost the Great War?"

The Jew replies, "The generals of course."

At first, the SA man seems pleased with this response, "Good, good," but then he reflects for a moment. "But we didn't have any Jewish generals."

The Jew answers, "Not us, the others."

Herr Gerron ended the evening with a song, accompanying himself on a portable keyboard.

If it's snowing or it's raining,
If you're investing and you're losing,
If your lady friend won't kiss you,
If you then learn she is untrue,
If the price of food seems costly,
If old friends behave most falsely,
If the flu has laid you low,
And you're snorting like a rhino,
Blame the Satanic-loving Jews,
Who are the source of all bad news.

PAUL M. LEVITT

******

Seeing Gemma and her father off at the railroad station, I returned to my room and Walter Fertig's care. With Jewish children virtually barred from the state schools since April 1933, I had been attending classes illegally. The political cloudburst subsequently occurred 15 September 1935 with the passage of two new racial laws at the Nazi party's annual NSDAP Reich Party Congress in Nürnberg. The laws took away German citizenship from Jews and outlawed both marriage and sex between Jews and non-Jews. For the first time, Jewishness was defined not by religious practice but by heredity (race). Mr. Fertig deemed it unsafe for me to continue attending a state school and engaged a tutor who lived in our building, Isaac Levy, an out-of-work teacher married to a Christian, Magda Renke, a piano teacher. The first time I met the slightly stooped and bald Mr. Levy to study math, science, history, and literature, he introduced me to his wife, who asked me which foreign language I intended to pursue. At the state school, I'd been studying English. With Gemma in mind, I replied Italian.

While the tutor and I met in a small book-lined sitting room, Magda taught me Italian and piano in an adjoining one. By midafternoon, after instructing her last student, she always appeared carrying a plate of cookies more delicious than any my mother had ever baked or bought. My mother, a terrible cook who never pretended otherwise, patronized a particular bakery in our old neighborhood. But the confections and cookies baked at that establishment couldn't hold a candle to Magda's yeast cakes, which included cinnamon, raisins, and small pieces of almond. As Mr. Levy and I nibbled on the cookies, Magda played the piano. Isaac always complemented his nosh with a cup of tea and, during the Adagio movement of a piano piece, would close his eyes, lost in the music. The first time Magda played for me, she asked if I had ever studied music. My negative reply earned me a seat next to her on the piano bench, from which she showed me fingering and taught me the notes, starting with middle C. By the end of the lesson, I was determined to add piano to my studies.

After a few weeks, I felt like the childless couple's adopted son. So comfortable were they with me, and I with them, that on one occasion, Mr. Levy felt free to say in front of me that the current state of Germany terrified him. He inveighed against the coming Olympic Games, which he argued were designed to mislead the public about Hitler's true intentions, Lebensraum and the spread of fascism. Aware of the movement in the United States to boycott the games, he said that a growing number of German intellectuals felt the same way. He confessed that he had become involved in the movement, printing fliers that others distributed calling on Germans to boycott the games.

"I have a mimeograph machine that I keep at the back of my closet, behind a false wall. If the Nazis knew about it . . ." he said, leaving the sentence incomplete.

"What would it take?" I asked, "to persuade other countries to stay away?"

"An incident."

"I don't follow you."

"That's for another time."

Although I understood his reluctance to share sensitive information, my curiosity led me to seek more details. And so, I tentatively inquired, "Who writes the fliers? And where do the paper and ink come from?"

Magda cleared her throat, as if to warn Isaac to keep his own counsel.

"We have sources," he replied, and said nothing further.

A loud knock at the door ended the silence that now shrouded the room and reinforced Magda's fear. She opened the door. In the hall stood a policeman who ordered Isaac to accompany him to headquarters for questioning. All I could think of at that moment was the mimeo machine. Isaac adjusted his binocular eyeglasses and asked for an explanation.

"According to the new laws, you are illegally married. Your wife is a Christian and you are a Jew."

Magda, taller and heavier than her husband, rose to her full height and declared, "As a good Catholic, I do not believe in divorce. He stays here with me."

Her blonde hair, blue eyes, and alabaster skin strongly argued that she was not only Nordic and Aryan, but also an idealized German Frau. The policeman seemed intimidated and backed up a few steps. She folded her arms across her chest and glared. The policeman managed to utter but one word, "Nürnberg," and in so doing precipitated a diatribe from her, the gist of which was that only God, not Hitler, could undo thousands of mixed marriages, and that German women would take to the streets if any such nonsense as the Nürnberg laws were enforced. The policeman tried to rally, saying that he would return, but clearly he was defeated and left a beaten man. Magda then turned to me and asked sweetly:

"Another cookie?"

******

I counted the days until Gemma's return, Sunday, the 29th of September. She had written me a note and asked that I share the information with Yva and her crew. The day had begun with a ground fog, which I took as an unwelcome omen. But the sun had dispelled the mist and brightened the day. I paced the lobby of the building and then slipped into an overcoat for a walk through the damp streets and golden leaves. Eventually, I found myself on the Kurfürstendamm. Although a Sunday, very few people were window shopping. In the distance, I saw a boy furtively ducking in and out of doorways, a former schoolmate, Klaus Kopf. When I looked closely, I saw that he had been distributing hand-printed postcards with the words: "Fill the unlistening streets with music. Long live swing and jazz." The card was signed "The Pirates." Both confused and cautious, I knew that the Nazi newspapers had decried the "gangs" that met secretly to listen to big band music and jazz. But these clubs, at least until now, had met in cities outside of Berlin: in Köln and Düsseldorf and Essen. Had they now formed a chapter in Berlin? I certainly hoped so. My mother used to listen on the radio to the big band music of Vincent Lopez and Paul Whiteman and Shep Fields and Fred Waring and others. Their sweet and romantic melodies, enhanced by a large string section, appealed to her dreamy personality. Vater, on the other hand, preferred the brassy jazz produced by trumpets and trombones, and the oozy sound of saxophones. Father's collection of 78 RPM records, which he played on an RCA Victor gramophone, included the music of Count Basie, Cab Calloway, Tommy Dorsey, Duke Ellington, Benny Goodman, and, of course, Louis Armstrong. If my school friend Klaus belonged to a music club, I wanted to join. Klaus's parents lived just a few blocks from my former address. I could already envision Gemma and me "cutting a rug," as the jazz cats liked to say. But first I returned to the apartment house to meet Signorina Rosselli and her father, who would be collecting their bags and other belongings before taking a taxi to the villa on Schloßstraße.

When she entered through the front glass doors of the building, I didn't recognize her at first: the ashen face, the listless gaze, the sunken cheeks. Could this be the same Gemma I'd seen a month or so before? Undoubtedly, she'd been ill. I wrapped my arms around her. She felt insubstantial, as though some vital substance had been extracted from her being. Her father, looking hale, pumped my hand and collected their possessions, which I helped move to the curb; the taxi driver loaded the bags into the vehicle. To my delight, Sig. Rosselli invited me to join them in the taxi and lend a hand when they arrived at the villa. I beamed and said it would be my pleasure to help. At the villa, I carried Gemma's valise to her room, which overlooked the garden. Although a housekeeper had opened a window to let in the fragrant air, she sat dejectedly on the bed, ignoring the fragrances and murmuring:

"You needn't say it, Baruch. I know, I look awful." She removed a handkerchief and dabbed her eyes. In a stage whisper, she said, "I was poisoned!"

"No! Tell me what happened. How could that be? Who? I mean..."

Shaking her head, she replied, "I didn't want to return to Berlin, but father insisted, for medical reasons. I would have much preferred Geneva, in fact, anywhere in Switzerland."

If Gemma had sought treatment in another country, I might never have seen her again. The very thought frightened me. To lose Gemma . . . I couldn't count the ways that her absence would diminish me. The immeasurable friendship lost. The hole in my life. Was the world so lacking in feeling that it would allow some fiend to poison the beautiful Gemma Rosselli? Now that she had returned, I wished for her to say that the one pleasure in her returning to Berlin was in seeing me. When I finally stopped stuttering and found my coherent voice, I said that once she recovered, we could go dancing.

She gazed at me vacantly and ran a hand through her hair. "I have to rest. Doctor's orders."

As I started to leave, she seemed to panic and grabbed my arm. "We must talk!" She glanced around, as if the house held hidden microphones. "But not here."

"Where?"

"In the garden," she whispered.

Ever so gently, she closed the door and, still holding my arm, let me lead her downstairs. The garden was landscaped in a way I had never seen before. Floral beds held chrysanthemums, anemones, hibiscus, lavender, red valerian, and geraniums; and ceramic planters exhibited roses, all manner of tulips, and daffodils. At the bottom of the garden stood a hillock made of logs, covered with sod, seeded in oleanders.

We pulled up lawn chairs padded with white cushions. Hers reclined, making it difficult for me to hear. An outsider would have thought she was speaking into the vacant air. And then, in moments of real importance, she would roll to her side, stare at me, and, with some urgency, aspirate the message.

Yes, they had gone to Wiesbaden, ostensibly for the salubrious thermal baths, the opera and concerts, the park and gardens, the gorgeous architecture, and not least the cozy taverns and comfortable restaurants. Suddenly, her voice became raspy and her tone fiercely sardonic.

"Do you know why we really went to Wiesbaden? To rendezvous with secret agents."

Balancing on the edge of my chair, I felt as if I might topple at any moment. "Where?" I asked incredulously.

"I thought it strange that the first stop father wanted to make was the casino, even though he disapproves of gambling." She laughed drily, and then offered a strange aside. "Unlike Dostoevsky, father played for small stakes. Or so I thought. I quickly learned that it was at the casino that he had arranged to meet two men, neither of whom I knew. One, pudgy and mild-mannered, was quiet and colorless, an erudite man who never stood out, Etienne Zabrofski. The other was the opposite: garrulous and ebullient, Stepan Poretsky. The two men spoke German fluently, though with Russian accents. Father seemed keen to conduct business with them. But it didn't take me long to discover that these men were Soviet spies."

She went on to explain that when her father and the two men promenaded along the Rhein, her father told her to remain at a polite distance. Accompanied by a mustachioed Cossack, laconic to a fault, she swore he stood seven feet tall. "My head barely rose above his belt." She presumed that he was the Soviets' bodyguard.

At this point in her story, she confessed that her father was a member of an opposition socialist group opposed to Mussolini and fascist Germany. I could barely fathom this information, not because of my political naïveté, but because Sig. Rosselli looked like a shoe salesman.

"During our promenades, I heard snatches of conversation indicating that the Russians expected father to show greater dedication to the cause. Only later did he tell me that among his shoe imports, a pair of tan oxfords always contained microfilm hidden in a heel. A mole in Mussolini's inner circle reported on Il Duce's disposition toward Hitler and the possibility of an alliance between the two fascist governments, especially in regard to impending war in

Spain. These reports were then passed on to another agent for use in Moscow."

Completely absorbed in her revelations, I whispered, "What more do they want from your father?"

Her answer left me speechless.

"We forge passports. Now they want us to print counterfeit money. But father says it's too dangerous and conveyed that opinion to the two agents. They were visibly upset. My guess is that they wanted to threaten him. At least at the time that's what I concluded."

I struggled to understand. "What are you saying?"

Again, her words confounded me.

"While we were living in the apartment building, father arranged for a printer, Mendel Brand, to move into the basement of this villa to forge passports and exit visas for political pariahs."

I knew that to counterfeit money, one needed templates and special paper. Something then occurred to me. "As far as you know, did one of the two men give your father a package?"

"Yes, Mr. Poretsky did, and insisted that father take it. Why do you ask?"

"I'll bet that package contains plates and paper. Where is it now?"

"Father probably put it in his bedroom safe."

I calculated that Sig. Rosselli had been asked before to print money, and had balked, perhaps pleading that he lacked the right ink, and templates, and paper. So, the Russians sent two agents to Germany with the prototypes for counterfeiting large bills. What could Sig. Rosselli say now?

Shaking my head, as if it were clogged, I observed, "In this context, your poisoning makes no sense. Why you?"

She replied simply, "My father."

After a moment's reflection, I sputtered, "But that makes even less sense. They need him." A pause in the conversation allowed me to consider plots and scenarios and motives. "How do you know it's the Russians?"

"I don't."

"Then who . . ."

Gemma described the last evening they all spent together. "Mr. Zabrofski suggested a restaurant. It had a winding staircase to a second-floor landing of tables. The Cassock, as always, positioned himself a short distance away. At the end of dinner, the Russians ordered tea. Father and I asked for coffee. As the waiter approached with the drinks, the Cossack stood, took the tray, and served us himself."

"That's it!" I said triumphantly.

"What is?" Gemma asked.

I couldn't answer. My insight of a moment ago dissolved almost at once. Why would the Russians behave overtly? And if the Cossack administered poison to the cup of coffee that he handed to Sig. Rosselli, how did Gemma end up with it? They had not exchanged cups. And if the Russians intended the poison for Gemma, was it to serve as a warning to Sig. Rosselli to do the Kremlin's work—or else? Neither Zabrofski nor Poretsky had access to the coffee cups, only the Cossack. Was he the explanation?

I wanted to know more, but Gemma was tiring and asked me to help her back into the house. As she leaned on my arm, I asked, "What about the other Russian, the quiet one?" At that moment, I saw a face at the window, her father's.

"I think you're wanted inside."

Not yet willing to abandon the field, she inhaled deeply and said, "As we sipped our tea and coffee, Etienne Zabrofski asked my father whether he approved of the arrests in Moscow, but before father could reply, Mr. Zabrofski remarked that it was a shame that Trotsky had slipped through the net, and that dissidents were dangerous. He then lectured father on the virtue of orthodoxy, saying that believers always know the rules and what to expect, whereas in the Western countries indecision was rife. He declared that obedience was the source of all other virtues, and that when we follow orders, we are relieved of the responsibility of choice and of error. Father chuckled and said that Etienne sounded like St. Ignatius of Loyola, but I heard something more ominous in the words: a threat. At that moment, I feared we would not escape the evening unharmed. Then I felt a dreadful pain in my stomach and fell to the floor with convulsions. The restaurant called the police, who accompanied father and me to the hospital. Etienne, Stepan, and the Cossack disappeared. At the hospital they pumped my stomach and said without further tests they supposed it was food poisoning."

Reaching her room, Gemma fell into bed exhausted, as her father watched from the door. I then accompanied Sig. Rosselli downstairs and into the kitchen, where Ugo opened the ice box looking for a snack.

I remarked, "The poisoning must have terrified you." Ugo nodded. "What do they want?" I asked, unsure of the actors in this drama.

A pensive Sig. Rosselli, in no mood to accommodate my desire to know more, advised that some things do not stand much looking into.

Chapter Six

My initial shock on hearing about the poisoning gave way to a sense of oppressive loneliness, no doubt because of my having depended unduly on Walter Fertig and Gemma's friendship. With her bedridden, I felt deprived. My world had begun to shrink with the arrest of my father, my exile from the family flat, the prohibition of my attending state schools, and the absence of neighborhood friends and familiar Jewish faces. Only Mr. Fertig and Gemma had stood between me and despair. It now seemed apparent that the person I held dearest needed my help. But how could I protect Gemma? If everything she said about her father was true, then he had to be wary of the Nazis on one side, and the Stalinists on the other. What I failed to comprehend from her disclosures was how the forgery and counterfeiting could be conducted from the villa cellar. But her current mental state, unfortunately, did not invite further questions.

After Sig. Rosselli and I had parted in the kitchen, the latter took to his library. Minutes later, I knocked and entered a small paneled room lined with glass bookcases of Italian classics: Dante and Petrarch and Boccaccio and Ariosto. The shelves also held books by famous Germans: Hegel, Goethe, Schiller, Nietzsche, and Schopenhauer. Although I looked for books by, on, or about Hitler, I saw none, not even *Mein Kampf*. Its absence could present a danger; and yet its absence heartened me, mitigating my fear, at least for the moment, that Sig. Rosselli could be a double agent.

Invited to make myself comfortable, I settled into a wide-armed leather chair. Ugo sat at his desk, with his head to one side resting on his hand. For several seconds, we silently stared at one another, as if each were taking the measure of the other. Then I blurted, "I'd like to join you . . . I mean your anti-Nazi activities." To my surprise, Sig. Rosselli showed no alarm that I was privy to the Rosselli activities and wished to enlist.

"Let me suggest, young man," he said, "you leave your current rooms and lodge here at the villa. That way you can keep an eye on us, and we on you. On the third floor, you will find a comfortable space, which I will arrange to have dusted and fitted with a bed and bureau." Immediately, my thoughts turned to Mr. Fertig and what he would say. Certainly, the kindly gentleman would approve of the arrangement. So I eagerly accepted, and we shook hands. "Before you go," said Ugo, "give me a minute more. For one thing, never speak of any of our work while you are in the house. Silence is golden. For a second thing, I can see you have a yen for Gemma. It's only fair, then, that I tell you she can be very stubborn. She had to be. That's how she survived her childhood."

From my confused expression, Sig. Rosselli could see that Gemma had not told me about her roots.

Berlin Revisited

"She was born in 1917 . . . in Russia . . . in Voronezh. In 1925, when I adopted her, she had lived in an orphanage for three years. To this day, she still has dreams of childhood desertion and disorder."

******

That evening, as usual, I met Mr. Fertig for dinner at the Il Forno restaurant. While I sipped my pastina in brodo, my guardian enjoyed the spaghetti vongole, which I think he could have eaten every meal. Since Mr. Fertig paid the bill, I didn't complain about how often we ate at this restaurant. It was my impression that Walter and Sig. Fellini, the owner of the Forno, had some arrangement whereby we received meals for free. In return, Sig. Fellini had the pick of Walter's store. Ugo had praised the food and, coming from Italy, he would have known if the fare were lacking. It was at this meal that I guardedly expressed my wish to join the anti-Nazi underground.

Mr. Fertig asked simply, "Why?"

"People say the more serious the crime, the greater the wish to avenge it. Just look around at what's happening to Jews and others."

"Do you plan to shoot all the members of the National Socialist Party?"

"Assassinating one or two prominent Nazis would have symbolic importance across the world."

Mr. Fertig smiled. "A philosopher you ought to be. No, I take that back," and, after looking around, whispered, "too many university professors, like doctors, become Nazis."

"Why is that?"

"Self-interest, I guess, sprinkled with a large dose of cowardice. They don't want to be on some forbidden list. But once you eat the Nazi's food, you become beholden to them."

I studied my soup, as if I could divine some truth in it. The only thought that came to me was a saying that my father often used: Whose bread I eat, his man I am. "Mr. Simon thinks that all this," and I waved a hand toward the boulevard, "will blow over. He says it's just a passing fancy. Yva disagrees." I intended to say more, but an *SS* man entered the restaurant and arrogantly looked over the customers. Then without any provocation, he ordered everyone to stand and salute, "Heil Hitler!" His sudden appearance and equally abrupt departure moved me to remark, "Mr. Simon insists the clown will soon disappear, but I don't think so."

Mopping up his spaghetti sauce with a piece of bread, Walter sadly mumbled, "I'm afraid I agree with you."

Although his reply made me want to ask him more about the madness that had beset our country, I had Gemma on the mind, leading me to introduce the subject of Sig. Rosselli, a subject that I knew interested him, as it did others at 45 Schlüterstraße, because of the gentleman's comings and goings.

"You do realize," Walter replied, "that he's not her real father, but a stepfather? He has a great deal of money, though you wouldn't know it from their modest flat. I understand that in Italy he owns an estate and for some reason has earned Mussolini's favor." As if to mock the very thought of it, Mr. Fertig added, "Perhaps he's a spy."

"What does that make Gemma?" I asked, fueling Walter's favorite pastime, conspiracy theories, which under the Nazis ran rampant. Most of them concerned the fate of Jews, but others treated war and waste and want. Would Hitler eventually order troops into the Sudetenland; would the expense of armaments be curtailed; would there be food enough to feed the nation?

Walter, whose mind characteristically flitted from one idea to another, asked me if I'd ever read Joseph Conrad's *The Secret Agent*. "It's his best book in my estimation." Walter, who read voraciously, brought books from his shop to his flat. Like the basement of his store, his room had tomes stacked from floor to ceiling. The other residents in the building treated his room as a lending library.

"May I borrow it?"

"Borrow! Just take it."

I wondered how best to introduce the subject of my moving to the villa. Not wishing to hurt the kindly man, I eased into the matter. "I helped the Rossellis unpack at their villa. It's quite spacious inside. Larger than it looks from the outside."

"I'm sure it's lovely, but what does their villa have to do with Joseph Conrad?"

Mr. Fertig had just provided me the occasion to tell him that Sig. Rosselli had invited me to live at the villa. With a rush of words, I did, leaving the older man confused.

"You mean leave 45 Schlüterstraße? I promised your mother. I thought you liked . . ."

Once I explained that Gemma was unwell and that Sig. Rosselli had asked me to look after her, the old man softened.

"Of course. It makes sense. But once she's recovered, you'll return?" Before I could answer, Mr. Fertig added, "I trust we'll still have dinner together every night. I so look forward to it."

I equivocated. "Just give me a week or two . . . enough time for Gemma to recover. For now, I'll move a few things over to the villa."

At the apartment building, I packed a suitcase with changes of clothes and toiletries. Mr. Fertig, looking forlorn, stood and watched. Before I lugged the valise downstairs, Walter handed me a copy of *The Secret Agent*.

"Conrad's own father," he said, "was involved in the nasty business of spying."

"My own father," I replied, "got in trouble just for speaking up."

"The first rule of spy craft, I gather, is to cultivate silence. Silence never betrays. Which reminds me: What should I tell your mother?"

"Nothing. After all, my change of address is only temporary.

"As you wish."

What I wished was to gain the affection of Gemma Rosselli, but that satisfaction would have to wait.

******

Mr. Fertig's comment about Conrad's father lodged uneasily among my thoughts. As I unpacked at the villa, I wondered about Sig. Rosselli's loyalties. Were they to Italy, Germany, the worldwide socialist movement, or to himself and family? My ruminations, however, were interrupted by Ugo, who entered my room and gently closed the door.

"I have two favors to ask," he said.

"Whatever I can do to help, tell me."

For a second time the Ronson lighter appeared, as Sig. Rosselli lit a French cigarette. The scent reminded me of railway stations. Ugo walked to the one window in the room and looked down at the road. He ran a finger over a glass pane and observed, "Newly cleaned." What did he see outside: spies, shadows, sunlight? I decided that Sig. Rosselli held in his head information enough to fill a library.

"Nothing is ever what it seems," he said gnomically. "If you look across the way, you will see a perfectly innocent-looking house. But if you look harder, you will see the kitchen curtains imprinted with small swastikas. And the man who lives in that house is a Lutheran pastor."

"Maybe he hangs the curtains to disguise his real intentions."

"A man is what he hides."

"Oh?"

"My first favor concerns our villa basement. For now, I think it best you pretend not to hear anything."

"Granted! And the second favor?"

He pulled on his cigarette and seemed to swallow the smoke. "I fear that I am being followed. By whom I do not know. I would like you to follow me at a safe distance and, if I am correct, follow my stalker to determine who he or she is and for whom the person works. Tomorrow morning, I shall leave the house at eight for an appointment with the German police, where I have contacts. The forecast is for rain. If you lack an umbrella, I have a large one you can use."

With this request from Sig. Rosselli, I realized I knew even less than I imagined. The only thing I could say for sure was that Gemma's father would be dressed and groomed impeccably. At 45 Schlüterstraße, he never left his flat without looking like one of the manikins in a high-class men's shop. Perhaps because he trafficked in shoes, his attitude toward them bordered on the obsessive. From what I could observe, he fetishized them, frequently removing from his jacket a carefully folded flannel cloth with which he buffed his oxfords. Once, when I saw him stumble on the front steps of the apartment house and scuff his shoes, Ugo made directly for his rooms and returned moments later with a different pair: same color but slightly different style. At least once a month, a box stamped "Firenze" and addressed to Sig. Ugo Rosselli had brought shoes to the apartment for him and his daughter. My mother used to say that clothes made the man, but I thought that in Sig. Rosselli's case, it was shoes.

The next day, as Sig. Rosselli predicted, it rained. The large umbrella that I unfolded made it all the easier to hide my face. Sig. Rosselli wore rubbers and opened a large black brolly with a carved handle. I had seen him with it before. Looking for all the world like a man who had nothing to hide, he never glanced back and made no attempt at evasiveness. He behaved like a well-assured and well-positioned gentleman. I trailed him down the street and on and off two trains. I watched him stride down Friedrichstraße to an imposing structure with two guards in front of the high iron fence. The building reputedly housed the Gestapo. He took out his wallet and showed identification that admitted him. I couldn't imagine that the secret police were interested in Italian shoes, given their preference for drab ones, like their Marschstiefel, the marching boot of German soldiers. Perhaps he was selling dress shoes for after-hour wear or special occasions, though the German high command seemed never to appear out of uniform. At the end of the street, I sat in a café, sipping hot chocolate, waiting and watching.

Several people exited from the building before Sig. Rosselli. One of them, a woman with dark hair pulled back into a bun, seated herself at the same café serving me. She ordered black coffee and a sweet roll but had little time to enjoy either because Sig. Rosselli passed through the gates and started in the opposite direction. The woman pocketed the roll, left money on the table, and took up a position not far behind. I paid my bill and trailed the woman. Sig. Rosselli never looked back. Striding confidently, like a man on a mission, he went to the S-Bahn station, where I stood behind a trestle and watched. When Sig. Rosselli and the woman entered the train, I waited until the last moment and then boarded.

At the Tiergarten station Sig. Rosselli and the woman left the train, with me following cautiously. Entering the park, the three of us, discreetly spaced, started down one of the lanes. At the juncture of two wooded paths, a gazebo provided shade and shelter. Sig. Rosselli lowered his umbrella and stepped inside. I ducked into the trees and watched. The woman strode past the structure and seemed to disappear down the path to the right. Not more than a minute or two passed and an ashen-faced man in a rumpled raincoat came from the other direction. He joined Sig. Rosselli. At first, they behaved as if they were strangers. The other man then tipped his hat. Sig. Rosselli did the same. A nurse pushing a pram approached. The other man stepped out from the gazebo, exchanged a few words with the nurse, and bending over the pram ostensibly admired the child. Even from a distance, I could see the man remove an envelope from the carriage, slip it inside his raincoat, and return to the shelter. Only then did the two men speak. In less than a minute, each man gave the other an envelope.

Sig. Rosselli departed first. He raised his umbrella and retraced his steps toward the station. From a clump of trees, a man in a common gray suit fell in a few yards behind Sig. Rosselli. Was he part of the cloak-and-dagger game? I continued to remain out of sight, undecided how to proceed. Chance made the choice when the mystery woman appeared again; this time, however, she shadowed the man who had exchanged envelopes with Ugo. The man opened his umbrella and walked off in the opposite direction from

Sig. Rosselli. Leaving my hiding place, I followed the woman following the man. I reasoned that their destinations might explain their identities. But if they split off, whom should I follow? I chided myself. The woman, of course. She was the one, after all, who had been tailing Sig. Rosselli.

Crossing the park, I saw embassy row in the distance. It appeared as if both people were headed there. From a lane on my right, a German youth group and their leader approached. I dallied and fell in behind them. Their chattering attracted the attention of the woman, who paused to look over her shoulder, while the man continued on his way. It soon became apparent that the youth group and the two strangers were all headed for embassy row. The youth group stopped outside the American Embassy, where the leader explained that the ambassador, William Dodd, was a historian and therefore familiar with the glorious history of Germany. A second later, music issued from an open window in the embassy: jazz.

Ambassador Dodd's daughter was reputed to be a fan. The youth leader turned to his group and said with contempt "decadent"; then they moved down the pavement to the next embassy. The man from the gazebo stopped at the sound of the music. We exchanged smiles. The man approached. In a strangely accented German, he said, "Decadence is in the ear of the listener." A minute or two later, he entered the Soviet embassy. The woman had crossed to the other side of the road and waited until the man was out of sight before continuing to the Italian embassy, where she politely greeted the guard and passed through the front door.

******

During my absence from 45 Schlüterstraße, Yva Simon had received a visit from a government official who had given her a list of women to pose and photograph, shady ladies who were all associated with the German high command; in other words, prostitutes and Nazi girlfriends. Yva sweetly purred, "I'm always glad to promote the purity of the race and German morality," and, being no one's fool, agreed to the request—and a price. She wanted to keep her studio and wanted the high command to pay for film and equipment. For a while, the Nazis kept their promise, until it no longer suited their purpose. Fewer than two years later, Yva would have to turn over the management of the studio to an "Aryan" friend and subsequently leave the premises entirely. But for now, she had her staff, including me, prepare the studio for the arrival of the Nazi beauties.

Scheduled every hour, these "ladies" behaved like spoiled royalty. With raised noses, as if the hoi polloi offended them, they waddled into the studio on high heels. Most of them smoked, either with or without cigarette holders. Fluffy boas trailed from their necks. Their skimpy dresses, practically diaphanous, covered less than they revealed. Although Nazi propaganda inveighed against the morals of the 1920s, these women looked like American flappers, shebas on the prowl for sheiks. Yva immediately directed them to the lavatory to remove the layers of rouge, lipstick, and mascara. Underneath the varnish, many of them were actually pretty, others not at all.

That first day, the staff posed and photographed five women; the second, six; the third, four. I remembered the last day best, as well I should have, because the first person to arrive was Heidi Jugend, a girl whom I had known, in the state school, as Myra Huberman. But that was before the wholesale expulsion of Jews from the school. Two or three years older than me, she was clearly trying to pass as a gentile with her blonde Aryan good looks. Adding a Nazi boyfriend to the mix made it all the easier to pass. Myra and I recognized each other at once. She put a finger to her lips, and I nodded. For her sake, I said nothing. After all, the most popular saying in Germany was: The walls have ears.

After Yva took pictures of her, sitting on a chair with her legs crossed, pointing a finger into the distance, and standing on the bottom step of the staircase leading to the balcony, Myra retired to the lavatory to repaint her face. When she returned, she gestured to me to follow. Discreetly trailing after her, I met her on the sidewalk.

"You're taller," she said.

"Yes."

"The moment I saw you I recognized you."

"May I call you Myra? Heidi doesn't suit you."

"Yes, but not in front of others." She stared at her glossy fingernails. "I don't know whether I should tell you."

"Tell me what?"

She lit a cigarette, inhaled, and let the smoke trail listlessly through her carmine-painted lips. "If you promise to keep my life a secret, I'll tell you one."

"You have my word."

"Your mother is working for the Nazi high command."

I had thought she did clerical work. Myra's revelation left me speechless. I finally summoned enough courage to ask, "Doing what? And how do you know?"

"I have a position at the Adlon Hotel with the chief detective. We spy on the guests."

Defensively, I said, "She's just trying to defeat the movement to boycott the Olympics. It's nothing worse than that."

For the moment she ignored my explanation. Then, without any apologies, she explained, "I'm now a kept woman. My family and I receive the protection of Generalleutnant Schmitz. He found me the job. I have a room in the basement equipped with all kinds of electronic listening devices."

Her eyes darted around, as if she were wary of spies. I could feel her unease, and cautiously asked the fraught question, "Is my mother helping the Nazis in more ways than just the Olympics?"

"She acts as a hostess, entertaining foreign dignitaries, in order to obtain important information. We keep transcripts of all her calls and conversations from inside the hotel."

Upset by Myra's disclosure, I asked, "Is my mother safe; am I? And what about you?"

"Every Jew in Germany is unsafe, but with the Olympics coming on, we'll be all right until they end. At this minute, the only danger I face is from the Nazi pornographers." I blinked. Did I hear right? "They take the prettiest girls and put them in bondage films that portray the Jews as lascivious ravishers." With that comment, she departed.

As I watched her sway down the pavement on her elevated shoes, I wondered whether her comment about pornography also pertained to my mother, or to younger women only, like Gemma.

Chapter Seven

Three boys, with swept-back long hair glowing from brilliantine, passed down the avenue singing in English, "It don't mean a thing if it ain't got that swing." The Duke Ellington song reminded me immediately of Klaus Kopf, my former classmate distributing postcards. I had always liked Klaus and admired his outspokenness, as well as his piano playing, when he performed with the school orchestra. Having no male friends my own age and feeling the lack, I decided to call on Klaus. That evening I set out. Returning to the old neighborhood imbued me with a frisson of expectation. I scanned the lobby mailboxes and saw the name Kopf. But what if Klaus no longer lived with his parents?

Berlin Revisited

Climbing the steps to the second floor, I chased the chords of a Bach Fugue to number 212 at the end of the shabby hallway. For a moment, I listened outside the door. Klaus's father, a piano refinisher, might be the source of the music. Or Klaus himself. I gently rapped on the door. A woman about my mother's age, but not nearly as attractive, answered the door. Her graying hair had been fashioned into lyrical loops around her ears, but rouge and powder could not mask her wrinkles. I introduced myself, and the woman graciously said that she remembered meeting me once in the neighborhood. Over her shoulder, I could see Klaus at the piano.

"Come in and enjoy the music. Klaus says that playing Bach keeps his fingers tuned." She laughed. "You can make of that statement whatever you wish. I've never been sure myself what he means."

Klaus came from the piano and warmly said, "Baruch, such a pleasure. What brings you here?"

"Swing and jazz."

At once, Klaus grew serious. "The postcards. I saw you in the distance."

"Yes."

"But as you see," he said defensively, "I play Bach not Count Basie."

I could understand Klaus's caution. After all, one never knew who worked for the secret police to help ferret out "decadent" music.

Mrs. Kopf invited me to stay for tea and pointed to one of the black leather lounge chairs. A polished mahogany Bechstein grand piano held pride of place. Behind it, stood a ten-foot pink velour tufted couch, flanked at one end by an Art Deco lemon tree brass cabinet and at the other end by a gramophone. The Kopfs appeared to have money. Over tea, I would learn that the furnishings had come from Klaus's maternal grandparents. Even the handsome piano had been passed down from one generation to the next, refinished and reconditioned by Klaus's father, currently out of town.

Unchanged since I knew him at school, Klaus resembled a puppet on strings. He dangled. His skinny arms hung limp at his sides. His tousled hair and rumpled clothes bespoke his preference for the demi-monde. One look at his large calloused hands made people think he worked as a mason or some similar occupation. But the fingers were really quite delicate, especially when they caressed the keys of a piano. Having long admired Klaus, I praised him exceedingly.

After bringing a small porcelain pot of English tea and crackers, Mrs. Kopf retreated to the kitchen, leaving us to pour for ourselves.

"Let it steep a minute," said Klaus, who fell silent, leaving the next words of the conversation to me.

Imbued by my parents with the social graces, I felt more at home among adults than with people of my own age. A middling athlete and a competent chess player, I had never exhibited the kind of skills that attract numerous friends. Preferring to watch the world go by rather than to take part in the action, I thought of myself as a goer rather than a doer. I particularly liked attending artistic events: concerts, readings, exhibitions, movies. Although I had never excelled in any of the arts, by temperament I loved music most. In response to Klaus's silent stare, I inanely confessed that as a child, I used to run after the organ grinder, who periodically passed through the neighborhood. When Klaus frowned, I knew that what I'd just said made me sound like a dolt. Still Klaus said nothing. Upbraiding myself for coming to see Klaus and not explaining my mission, I blurted:

"I like jazz and want to join a like-minded group."

There! I had just made myself vulnerable.

"Most of these groups," Klaus said, "are on the Nazi blacklist. If you're found with them, it could land you in jail—or worse."

"I know the official line. Patriotic young people join Nazi youth groups. If you don't join, you are an enemy of the people."

Klaus opened the brass cabinet and removed a package of cigarettes. "Smoke?" he asked. "No thanks." Tipping one out, he lit it with a stick match, dragged deeply, and then let the smoke slowly dissipate as he spoke. "Do you remember Alf Tropp? He belonged to the Boy Scouts. Several Hitler Youth members cornered him and said he should leave the Scouts and join them. He refused. A boy pulled a knife. He and Alf fought. By the end of the scuffle, Alf had a cut hand and the other boy a slashed cheek. The result? Alf had to steal out of the country to avoid arrest. If you join a jazz group and you're found out, you could end up thrashed and thrown in jail. Are you still interested?"

"That's why I'm here."

"Drink up and we'll listen to some great swing. But you'll have to sit close to the gramophone. I keep the sound turned down, so our neighbors don't hear."

Having heard through the grapevine that my father had been arrested, Klaus trusted that I was not an informer and shared his record collection. As we swayed to the music, I knew what my next letter would say.

Lieber Vater,

I have made a good friend. Yes, I know what you're thinking. How can I say "a good friend" until he has proved himself honest and trustworthy? Like a number of jazz lovers, he has no time for the Nazis and refuses to serve in the Hitler Youth. I spent an evening with him listening to your favorite jazz musicians. His gramophone lacks the resonant sound of Mr. Skaller's, but just hearing Count Basie, Cab Calloway, Jimmy and Tommy Dorsey, Benny Goodman, Fletcher Henderson, Earl Hines, and Artie Shaw made me wish you were there for the ride, as you used to say. And quite a ride it was. I went home lightheaded.

So many of the jazz artists are American Negroes, and Jewish audiences love them. Both groups are pariahs, and just as you can hear the plaintive cry of the old rabbis in their prayers, you can hear the bleeding souls of the blacks in their music. For reasons that are unclear to me, the Nazis let some Negroes live and perform in Germany, though they are not allowed to play swing or jazz. I wonder how long the government will allow them to stay. But what do they have to go back to?

In a few days, I will accompany Klaus to a jazz session, which is being held in the cellar of a beer tavern. Klaus said that the singing and general disorder of the tavern above covers the sound of the music below. I hope to make friends at the session and hear not only records on a gramophone but also some live music. Klaus, for example, will be playing the saxophone (he also knows how to play the trombone and, of course, the piano), and another boy I knew in school will be playing the clarinet. God, how I wish I knew a musical instrument. You used to beg me to practice the piano. Now that I'm trying to get back to it (Isaac Levy's wife is tutoring me), I could kick myself for quitting my childhood lessons and thinking that riding my bicycle was more fun.

Mutter was the real musical talent in the family. When she played the piano, I imagined myself in a concert hall. To give it up just because of a disagreement with the piano teacher seems wasteful to me. Such talent! If only she had passed it along to me. I remember once sitting at the keyboard, trying to figure out a Mozart étude, and mother entered the room. "Baruch," she said, "you have a tin ear." Maybe that was the reason I quit. But I shouldn't blame her. I quit because I didn't have the self-discipline, as you used to call it. I see now that self-discipline eclipses even genius, because if you don't perfect and polish your skills, the genius in you will atrophy and die.

But who am I, a teenager, lecturing you, a professor and Doctor of History.

Alles Liebe,
Baruch

The jam session took place on a Saturday night. Upstairs in the tavern, workingmen guzzled beer and loudly caroused. From the sound of shuffling feet, I concluded that some of the men were dancing. Downstairs in the dank cellar, young men and women, dressed in the most unconventional styles, waited for Klaus and his friends to connect the gramophone to an outlet among the spider web of electrical wires hanging overhead. Once they made the connection and all the lights came on, I could see that most of the swing and jazz set came from middle-class homes. Their clothes bespoke money. Although the styles varied, the majority mimicked the dress of Hollywood movie stars. The girls wore heavy make-up in different colors, and in imitation of men's styles dressed in pinched-waist outfits and trouser suits. I felt surrounded by Katharine Hepburn look-alikes puffing on long, slim cigarette holders.

Both sexes wore their hair long, not short like the fascist youth groups, as a way of thumbing their noses at the latter. Boys favored zoot suits and knee-length loose-fitting double-breasted jackets that sported wide lapels in imitation of American jazz musicians. A great many of the boys had arrived in trench coats, à la American gangsters. James Cagney would have felt sartorially at home in this company.

Most of the people seemed to know one another. I was clearly the outsider; I therefore stayed close to Klaus. When the music began, so too did the dancing. But though I had seen this kind of dancing in movies, I had no idea how to move my feet to the beat. I watched for a long time, thrilled to be free of the regimentation of the city and the polkas of the government-approved dance halls. Klaus urged me to dance, but I declined saying I knew nobody and would just make a fool of myself.

"Cut in and let the girl lead you," said Klaus.

"I couldn't."

A minute or two later, a drunken, red-faced, reveler appeared from upstairs, glared, belched loudly, separated a couple dancing cheek to cheek, and roughly embraced the girl. Her partner, too intimated to engage the sot in a fight, retreated to a corner. Whirling her round and round, and lifting her off her feet, the lout caused her to grow visibly dizzy and ill. As they swung past me, she reached out a hand to me and said:

"Get me away from him!"

Never one for a fight, I stepped back, like her boyfriend, distancing myself from the fray. The girl looked on the point of collapse, until Klaus came up behind the brute and crowned him with a metal bar. The drunk fell like a bag of cement and immediately passed out. That misadventure led to the group dispersing, but not before agreeing to meet somewhere else in the following weeks. Standing by myself, I felt ashamed for my cowardice. I could have at least tried to extricate the girl from the man's grip. But I had always run from altercations. Such was my nature. I recalled a time when a neighbor boy was bullying me, and my father, who witnessed the scene from a window, yelled, "Don't let him push you around. Punch him!" I had replied, "He's older than me." My exasperated father rejoined, "What the hell does that have to do with it. Slug him!" In response, I had slunk away, and for months afterward could hardly face my father, so great was my humiliation.

To assuage my guilty feelings for not trying to help the girl, I approached Klaus and proposed that the group meet next time at 45 Schlüterstraße, where I would arrange with the owner of the building, Oskar Skaller, to host a musical evening, free of interruptions. Klaus liked the idea and agreed to bring his records. He even suggested that I help him select the ones they wanted to play on Oskar's Excelsior floor cabinet gramophone. Of all nights, on the night of the party, my mother showed up at the apartment house and wanted me to join her for dinner. I declined. She appealed to Walter Fertig, who, unable to say no to her, inadvertently mentioned the evening plans for a jazz session, which included Klaus's friends and the few whom I felt close to, particularly Gemma, the Simons, Yva's assistants, and the Levys. My mother, whom I'd barely seen since the start of summer, left in a huff. So estranged had we become that I ignored her annoyance.

Gemma had recovered sufficiently to declare that a party was just what the doctor ordered and that she was ready to dance. The flat had already begun to fill with Mr. Fertig, the Simons, and Yva's crew. Gemma arrived in a white sheath dress that only an Italian could have designed: sleek, elegant, and free of ornamentation except for a black belt and thin green thread that circled the low neckline. She immediately became the cynosure of all the young men, especially me. Mr. Skaller had brought in dishes of cold meat, cheese, biscuits, wines, and sparkling water. Later in the evening, a chef from a nearby restaurant arrived with loaves of bread, mashed potatoes and gravy, and a large leg of lamb. Even before the music had begun, Klaus and friends were already dancing. In a space created by Mr. Skaller having rearranged the furniture, they started to jitterbug.

"Teach me!" Gemma cried excitedly.

Her request was directed at Klaus.

"Me, too," I added.

Klaus put on the gramophone Cab Calloway's "Happy Feet." At once, Gemma realized that she was wearing the wrong dress for the freewheeling dance. She whispered to Yva, darted from the room, and returned two minutes later dressed in a flowing pink skirt. She removed her patent leather black pumps and danced bare-footed. Standing in front of Klaus, she held out her arms as if to say: "I'm ready; take my hand; lead me; and show me the steps." He moved the stylus to the beginning and started the record again. Everyone watched as he instructed Gemma in the fine art of jitterbugging. As they went through the motions, Magda and Isaac arrived not wishing to miss any of the fun, so painfully absent under the Nazis. The party goers formed a circle to watch Klaus instruct Gemma. In no time, most of the guests were standing in place and imitating the steps. Then Magda took Isaac's hand and they started dancing, exhibiting surprising agility and quickness. The Simons did likewise. Yva was graceful, Alfred a klutz. Before long, Gemma swung out of Klaus's orbit and took my hand. A moment later we were shimmying and swinging, quickly moving from the basics to the cuddle and triple step to jitterbug turns and even an occasional flea hop.

Berlin Revisited

A succession of jazz records kept us all trying to keep up. As exhaustion set in and the dancers began to collapse on the couch and chairs, Klaus played a slower jazz tune, Benny Goodman's "Stompin' at the Savoy." At the end of the dancing, all the guests were ready for food and drink. By midnight, my head was swimming and my eyes failed to focus. That night, Gemma and I, light-headed, waltzed back to the villa. She weaved to her room. When I reached mine, I fell into bed fully dressed and immediately succumbed to a grotesque dream that included caricatures from the Nazis' cinematic hate campaign.

A naked Myra Huberman, tied to a tree in the woods, stood with her head bowed in shame. Two stereotyped Jews, unshaven and hook-nosed, lasciviously drooled over her. I recognized the men. They were the ones who appeared in Nazi propaganda posters, depicting on the left side of the poster a healthy young Aryan couple resting on a hillside, enjoying nature, and on the right, two leering Jewish men sitting next to a buxom woman, as the three of them watch a pornographic movie. Presumably the Jewish men intend to ravish the pure maiden. Then my mother appeared on the wooded path. She wiggled her finger and hips to entice the two Jewish men to follow her into the forest. They did, but before they could catch up with her, a uniformed Nazi, who resembled a stormtrooper, stepped out from behind a tree with a pistol in hand. The two Jews stopped in their tracks, turned, and started to run in the other direction. But after a few steps, their pants came undone and their trousers fell to their ankles, a scene reminiscent of one that I had recently seen in an anti-Jewish movie cartoon; and like the cartoon, the officer removed his belt and thrashed their backsides. In my dream I could hear the howls of the delighted audience. Then I awakened.

In the morning I had a headache from the wine and wild imaginings of my nightmare. To clear my head, I took a walk and found myself sitting on a bench in the park-like area in front of the Trinitatiskirche. Occasionally, an elderly woman passed through the heavy wooden doors of the church to attend morning services. A cold breeze felt good on my face. Pedestrians passed. I wondered what their lives were like. Would I want to change places with them? Certainly not with the old man in a wheelchair, pushed by a young woman in a nurse's uniform. Who was the man? One of the millions of elderly men walking the planet. My father used to say that before criticizing, I should try to live in someone else's skin for a day. What would that be like? As a young boy, I had been to the Jewish Hospital in Berlin to have my tonsils removed. Afterwards, the doctor had brought me a dish of ice cream. It might be nice to live in his bones. Dr. Baruch Rosner. Specialty: surgery. "Calling Dr. Rosner, calling Dr. Rosner! You're wanted in the emergency room. Calling Dr. Rosner!" And Dr. Rosner finds lying there on a bed, covered with blood, an *SS* officer, who has shot himself cleaning his pistol; or has he tried to kill himself? I enter the soldier's life.

Name, Otto Gluten. Recently married and commissioned. First posting, Dachau. From the innumerable rumors, I imagined the grisly scenes: torture, shootings, forced labor, dysentery, people from every walk of life. All deemed anti-state, all judged anti-Nazi. Otto recognized one of the prisoners, Meyer Rosner, a former teacher of his at the university. They had frequently spoken. Otto feels humiliated that Prof. Rosner is at Dachau, sent there by the government to which he has pledged his loyalty. With each passing day, the prison conditions undermine Otto's certainty, until one evening, on leave, he shoots himself. He is brought to the Jewish Hospital.

Does Dr. Rosner save his life? Or does he render Otto Gluten a favor by letting him bleed to death? If he lets him die, the Nazis will say that a Jew doctor killed him. If he stanches the bleeding and patches him up, will Otto participate in some future war on the eastern front and die there in the cold of winter? Perhaps Dr. Rosner can persuade him to help his father escape. Perhaps . . .

******

Seeing Gemma come into view surprised me. She had been looking for me and guessed that I might be in the park, a favorite retreat. Glad to have found me, she said that one of Klaus's friends, in attendance at the party the night before, had telephoned the villa to report that Klaus had been arrested for disseminating degenerate art, namely, playing some of his jazz records in Oskar Skaller's flat.

"Who in the building would denounce him?" I asked rhetorically. "Who else knew about the party?"

"Perhaps Klaus told others," Gemma hazarded.

"Outside of the tenants, the only person who knew about the gathering was my mother. A bitter woman, yes, but treachery of this sort would gain her nothing. Money and possessions drove her, not spite. She'd have no reason to turn Klaus in; it had to be someone in the building."

My suspicions fell on the manager, a lover of order and rules. With one call he could ingratiate himself with the Gestapo. The manager and Yva and Mr. Skaller owned the only private phones. But until I could be sure, I resolved to trust as few people as possible.

Chapter Eight

Alarmed by Myra Huberman's revelations concerning my mother, I waited for Myra outside the hotel to ask if I could listen to the taped conversations. She bundled me in through a back door, reserved for the staff. Her room was, as she had said, cluttered with electronic equipment, which I quickly discovered she knew how to use. In school she'd been studying to become an engineer. Trading on her knowledge of machinery, as well as her blonde hair and blue eyes, she volunteered to work for the secret police; in return, her parents received two exit visas. For my protection, she had picked a time when the house detective, Rolf Kimmelman, would be spending the day with his widowed mother in Wannsee. Myra said he was also part of a special unit charged with finding wooded spots in the Wannsee area suitable for German Fraülein to have sex with Olympic athletes. The plan was to select men and women for their Aryan qualities. And to protect the women from the stigma of being unwed mothers, the government would have them give birth in the countryside or in another city and place the offspring with acceptable Nazi families. The birth mother, in return, would receive welfare and special favors for her contribution to the Master Race.

I had heard rumors of the government pairing "racially valuable" unwed women with *SS* officers to produce racially pure children, who were subsequently placed in German homes, and all in the service of eugenics. When I shared with Myra my loathing of this Nazi practice, she said that Herr Kimmelman had told her all about Lebensborn, and had remarked, only partly in jest, that if she acquired the right papers, she could easily pass for an Aryan.

"Eugenics!" I exclaimed. "Only Germans could fall for it."

"It started in America."

"Probably with the Bundists."

A troubled Myra shook her head despondently. "I hate to tell you, Baruch, but in some impoverished Polish towns, like Gdynia and Bydgoszcz, mothers will sell you a child for forty Reichsmarks."

Feeling dirtied by Myra's disclosures, I wondered whether now was the time to listen to my mother's misdeeds. After a moment's reflection, I decided not to gamble on another day. With Rolf Kimmelman out of the office, I needn't fear discovery. Adjusting the headphones, I listened to several tapes, enough to persuade me that my mother used her charms in the service of the current government. She tried to inveigle information from diplomats and even slept with them. Her pillow talk was clearly designed to compromise her prey. One of the men she entertained was Avery Brundage, president of the United States Olympic Committee and the Amateur Athletic Union. I strained to hear as Brundage told her that if not for the pressure of American Jews, the threat of a boycott of the Games would disappear. He saw the coming Olympics as an opportunity to advance democracy and Capitalism and to provide a bulwark against Communism. He inveighed against the American ambassador, William Dodd, for his antifascist views, and praised the National Socialists' passion for order and for putting slackers and parasites, like gypsies and Jews, in work camps. My mother opined that all the antisemitic posters and slogans and newspaper articles in Berlin would hurt his cause.

He replied, "I have it on good authority that prior to the games, they'll be removed." He then said something unintelligible, succeeded by: "What the Nazis do later is another matter."

On one of the tapes, I could hear the click of glasses and surmised that my mother and Mr. Brundage were drinking cocktails. What were they cheering? At that moment, although not apposite, I remembered being told that anti-Nazi elements were planning some incident before the start of the February winter games—officially designated "IV Olympische Winterspiele 1936 Garmisch-Partenkirchen"—to provoke Hitler to initiate a mad act that would persuade the rest of the world to boycott the summer games.

On another tape, Avery Brundage made clear that he had the Adlon's permission, for the greater good, to avail himself of anything in the hotel—like a suite of rooms for an afternoon tryst—paid for by the German government. Most enlightening was Brundage talking to the German Minister of Finance. The American was assuring the Count that he would deliver on his promise to see that American Jewish organizations would not prevent the summer Olympic Games from taking place.

"But," said Brundage, "I expect you to hold up your end of the bargain. My construction company receives the contract to build the new German embassy in Washington."

From the newspapers, I knew that Brundage owned a large and successful architectural and building company run out of its Chicago office. What Myra's tape made apparent was that Brundage's public pieties about the purity of sport and the importance of keeping politics out of the Games served his own interests. He was using his influence to keep the Games on track in return for German business. Brundage's morality was clearly moored to money. How, though, could I make this information public? And if I could, would it even matter?

My thoughts wandered to Isaac Levy. Surely, he could devise a plan to expose Brundage and the Count. But to my chagrin, I learned on approaching the Levys that they had another plan in the works and thought the "exposure plan" would be less effective than the one they and their friends in the underground had in mind, one that I would hear about shortly. When I tried to learn more from Isaac, he said:

"Ask the Signorina."

I had suspected that the Rossellis coordinated their work with the underground. When I approached Gemma, she indicated a wish to see Rossini's opera "L'Italiana in Algeri," playing at a small nearby theatre. "Take me and we'll talk along the way."

Sig. Rosselli kindly bought me a new suit, double-breasted and black. Gemma wore an incomparable red velvet dress with matching shoes. Even before we arrived at the opera house, I knew that every head would turn when she made her entrance. Surprisingly, a great many Italians were in attendance. Where did they come from? Unlike stiff Germans, they gushed over Gemma's elegant dress and praised her good looks. "Che bella!" I heard repeated throughout the lobby. Near the Will-Call window I saw a disconcerting figure: a short, pudgy man who seemed to be following us.

The opera, which neither of us knew, turned out to be an ironic choice: the story of a captive Italian woman, Isabella, who has landed in Algiers owing to a shipwreck. She bewails having to make her way in a strange country, separated from her fiancé, Lindoro. As the opera progressed, Gemma whispered a running commentary, seeing herself in the person of Isabella.

"If Algeria is strange," she said, "what is one to make of Germany today?"

Isabella, told that she will be a handsome addition to the bey Mustafà's harem, reconciles herself to her fate with the knowledge that she has the ability to tame unruly men.

"Had she known the Nazis," Gemma murmured, "she would know that some men are insatiable."

The bey, known as "the scourge of women," elicited a knowing laugh from Gemma. Through assertiveness and guile, Isabella manages to have her way with Mustafà, and to escape with Lindoro for Italy. At the end of the opera, Gemma commented:

"If only it were so."

I was left wondering who in her life played the role of Lindoro? With whom would she retreat to Firenze? Might it be some admirer of hers whom I had failed to note? Or by some lucky chance, might I be the chosen one? From my lips to God's ears, as the Yiddish proverb translated.

On the sidewalk in front of the theatre, a number of Italian men ostentatiously bowed and scraped before the lovely Gemma, but she merely answered their adulation with simple replies: "Thank you" and "How kind of you to say." As we returned to the villa in a cab, I heard Gemma murmur, "Yes, a disguise. Perhaps that's the ticket."

In a trailing taxi, I could see Mr. Pudgy, whom I mentally labeled Herr Fettsack, Mr. Fatso.

"Now tell me what's afoot," I whispered.

A few days later, I heard raised voices coming from the basement. Although virtually every night muted sounds had issued from the cellar, I assumed they had to do with the clandestine press, which I had promised to ignore. This evening, however, I heard discordant voices, among them Sig. Rosselli's. At almost the same moment, Gemma appeared at my room and indicated that I should follow her. She unlocked the door to the basement and slowly made her way down the steps, with me at her back. We came to a landing from which one could see a printing press, a brightly lit workbench, shelves of paper and ink, rows of type, photographic equipment, and a steel safe, which I later learned held blank passports stolen from embassies and town halls. The punishment for such thefts was summary execution.

A tall, skinny asthmatic man, Mendel Brand, removed a hand-rolled cigarette from the corner of his mouth, looked up at the landing and said, "You must be Baruch Rosner, the young man Sig. Rosselli has been talking about. Right, Ugo?"

Sig. Rosselli nodded and waved us down the remaining steps. In an unlit corner sat two people I had seen before, the man from the gazebo and the woman who followed him. On the other side of the room sat a smiling Isaac Levy.

Noting my surprise, Ugo said, "I see you're wondering who these people are and why they're here. Let me explain. Isaac you know. Our other friends here belong to the Democratic Socialist Party. Comrade Vasily Kozlov works in the Soviet embassy's cryptography office and, through various means, shares important information. Comrade Leda Noncentini is a member of the Italian secret service, ostensibly on the side of the fascists but actually on ours. To protect against Nazi surveillance, I asked Leda to shadow me, and you to follow. That way I could be sure that the Nazis were not sniffing around. We have found that some of our people are being stopped at the Swiss border and turned over to the German authorities. I am certain that the source of our trouble is Wilhelm Gustloff. It's time to cut off the head of the snake."

Until sued for libel, Gustloff had put a great deal of effort into distributing the Tsarist forgery, *The Protocols of the Elders of Zion*. He kept an office in Davos, not far from Bern. He worked for the Swiss government as a meteorologist but devoted most of his energy to the Nazi Party organization for German citizens abroad, which he founded.

"We have no doubt," declared Isaac Levy, "that his antisemitic activities are funded from Berlin, and that he hopes one day to lead the Swiss Nazi Party. He protests that the German refugees entering Switzerland will destroy the Swiss national character, and that most refugees are Jews, rapists, murderers, and thieves, all bearing forged passports."

Mendel Brand interrupted. "As I said before, we are in the business of forgery, not killing."

"Allow me, Mendel, to disagree," said Sig. Rosselli. "We are in the business of killing fascism and replacing it with democratic socialism. As Isaac said earlier, we have it on good authority that Wilhelm Gustloff and his fellow Nazi sympathizers present a danger to us. They have already detected some forgeries, not ours, but others."

"The Swiss," Leda said, "nurture neutrality. To murder one of their nationals is to invite attention."

"Neutral!" Ugo scoffed. "The Swiss function as the international banking capital of the world. All sides, east and west, park their money there. Like Sweden, they sell everything from bread to ball bearings to whoever will pay. The denomination of the currency doesn't matter. If a war comes, and we all pray it doesn't, the French and Italian speaking areas of the country, I think, might reject National Socialism. Bern is a different matter. The German population in that city is proud of the gains being made in what they call the 'New Germany.' These people are willing, for the moment, to give Hitler the benefit of the doubt. The Swiss fascists are well aware of this fact and have been working quietly behind the scenes to increase membership in the Bern Nazi party."

Perhaps owing to the hours I had spent in Yva Simon's studio, I panned the room with a photographic eye, noticing for the first time the dress of the people. Isaac in a jacket and tie resembled a commonplace clerk. Vasily in a drab gray suit looked the part of every Soviet apparatchik, a perfect spy because no one could pick him out of a crowd, except perhaps for his thick-lensed wire glasses. Leda, who had literally let her hair down from a bun to shoulder-length waves, had soft features and Mediterranean coloring. If not for her Roman nose, she would have passed for an inconspicuous forty-year-old wife. Her long blue dress, the sort found on pushcarts in every commercial square, was one piece and buttoned at the front. Mendel Brand wore a butcher's apron, long-sleeved denim shirt, and a worker's cap, like Lenin's, with a leather peak. His hands, stained with ink, were delicate, marked by long, slender fingers.

For a moment, all talk of assassination ended. Actually, no one spoke at all. I wondered: Was it the prospect of a Nazi Switzerland that scared them? Murder? Or were they aghast at the thought of the haven next door disappearing, even given the difficulties of crossing the border?

Then Sig. Rosselli became the focus of everyone in the room with the declaration, "I know the man." For a moment, all breathing seemed to stop. "I met him once. His wife, Hedwig, did secretarial work for Hitler. Herr Gustloff knows the pulse of the Nazis and has the ear of Berlin."

"Which ought to make us all the more cautious," warned Mendel, sighing audibly.

"I fear," said Vasily, "kill Gustloff and he'll become a martyr. The Nazis will use his death to justify untold atrocities."

Leda replied, "Unless it can be made to look like a fellow Nazi killed him."

"Unlikely," added Mendel.

Ugo Rosselli, clearly the author of the assassination plot, argued, "There are armed men, Swiss patriots, who would, to preserve their freedom, assassinate Herr Gustloff. But I'd prefer a lone killer."

Leda asked, "At the risk of inviting Hitler's displeasure?"

"Corporal Adolf," he said disparagingly, "won't do anything this year lest he endanger the winter and summer Olympics. An assassination on this scale could very well persuade the IOC to cancel the Olympics lest the Games put athletes at risk."

So this was the "plan" that had caused Isaac to tell me to ignore the financial deal between Brundage and the Count. Murder made the headlines; graft, the back pages.

"And who do you have in mind for this assignment, Ugo?" asked Vasily.

"Dr. David Frankfurter, a Jewish dentist from Croatia, who studied in Germany and now lives in Switzerland."

"Never heard of him," scoffed Vasily.

"He is partially crippled and moves sideways, like a crab. Except for his disability, he doesn't look unusual. His parents were German. He speaks the language like a native Berliner. His dark hair, wide forehead and neck, turned-up nose, small mouth and full lips make him appear non-Aryan. He's actually rather good looking. Some women would undoubtedly find him appealing, despite his impediment."

Mendel, who had been weighing the comments about assassination, remarked, "When I first started forging documents and photographing stolen papers, I was approached by a moviemaker, a minor one, who asked me whether I had any interest in filming a crime thriller. The more I thought about it, the more I realized that a good script—and ours was not—required an extraordinary amount of detail, everything from motivation to the execution of the crime to capture or escape. Most people underestimate the many questions the killer has to ask himself."

"Unless," interrupted Ugo, "the killer has no wish to escape."

"But then you have no crime thriller," remarked Leda.

"Thriller, no, but a possible psychological study, yes."

Admitting to voraciously reading detective novels, Vasily jumped into the conversation. "The first thing the killer has to consider is the instrument or means of death: weapon, poison, drowning, suffocating, car accident, et cetera."

"And what is the second thing?" asked Sig. Rosselli.

Vasily, relishing the moment, enthusiastically replied, "Any good killer has to have a well-planned escape or getaway. The killer doesn't want to leave any tracks. He—or she—must therefore decide how to avoid witnesses."

"And," said Leda, "how to reach the victim: by car, foot, public transport, bicycle, motorcycle, horse, for example, disguised as a mounted policeman, or some other imaginative means."

Perhaps thinking of fashion photography, Gemma, who until now had been mute, observed that a male killer might want to dress as a woman.

"A favorite Muslim trick," said Isaac.

By this time, completely absorbed in the complexity of crime, I commented, "If the killer wishes to dispose of the body that could present a real problem."

Gemma eagerly volunteered, "What about alibis and aliases?"

"Good point!" Leda said. "But the trouble with alibis is they depend on others. And the more people involved in a secret, the less secret it is."

"What about diplomatic immunity?" Gemma added.

Ugo demurred. "That has nothing to do with David Frankfurter. Who would take him in?"

Gemma stood and turned a full circle as if to enlist the attention of everyone present. "What," she speculated, "if the victim could be lured to a remote place?"

"With what inducements?" asked Sig. Rosselli.

"Feminine charms, money, lies, nationalism. You name it."

"I suppose it's possible."

Vasily digressed and pointed out that in 18th-century England, most misdemeanors were treated as capital crimes. Germany, he hazarded, was moving in that direction.

Adding to that idea, I observed that if my guardian, Mr. Fertig, were present, he would add book burning to the list of criminal acts. "But he often says that a worse crime than burning a book is not reading one."

Leda commented, "No non-sequiturs, please. Dr. Frankfurter isn't going to kill Gustloff for his not reading books."

Feeling the sting of the reproof, I reacted like most inexperienced arguers and thought that a more detailed explanation would make my point. "In light of the book bonfires, Mr. Fertig was determined to save as many as he could. He drove his small delivery truck through local neighborhoods, decrying degenerate literature and offering to transport such smut to the fire. By the end of the day, his wagon was full. Those books now line the shelves of his cellar."

"I suggest we get back to the subject," said Ugo. "We've strayed."

"Yes," said Mendel emphatically, enough silly talk about murder and methods. Our work is forgery."

On that note, the meeting broke up, and the participants agreed to meet several days later. Embracing me, Isaac whispered that I should forget that he had attended this meeting and that even Magda mustn't know. Then I watched as the guests ascended the stairs. Only Mendel and I remained. Gemma called. I replied that I wished to learn more about Mendel's work, and that I would be along presently. Turning to Mendel, I said, "My father tried but failed to find a forger. They sent him to Dachau. Teach me how to do it." Mendel reached for a camera. "I already know a lot about photography."

"Good, I can use an experienced hand."

Mendel explained that although the market for forgeries was insatiable, good ones were rare. Innumerable people were looking for passports, from Jews to army deserters; and with the Gestapo growing ever-more determined to round up pariahs, the forgeries had to be letter perfect.

Passports of deceased foreigners, he said, were collected by the Gestapo and could sometimes be bought from a corrupt officer who "forgot" to burn them as ordered. The going price: four hundred marks apiece. A touch-up of an existing document was relatively easy but having to create an official paper from scratch or from stolen blank forms was daunting. The ideal situation occurred when a perfectly good passport reported lost, say, from a devout Nazi, bore a description that could be assigned to someone roughly similar in appearance. Then all that the forger needed was to change the photograph.

"The three-step process," he said, "makes it difficult. One, you must reproduce that part of the official rubber stamp that partially covers the photo. Two, you transfer that reproduction onto the new photo. And three, you must generate worn-looking lettering so that the forged part will match the rest of the stamp. It's excruciating work, especially fashioning the rubber stamp. In fact, any stamp accepted as the ultimate evidence of legitimacy and authorization by German officialdom is always scrutinized with care. The stamp is, as forgers know, a German's supreme swastika."

Mendel related the story of how a master forger taught him to take a small blank patch of newsprint margins from a newspaper, moisten it, and press the passport's stamp against it. "The forger, at one time an artist, used overlay paper and a tiny paintbrush to transfer the copied piece of rubber stamp onto the altered passport. It worked!"

"How," I asked, "do you remove the 'Jew' stamp from a real passport?"

"Not with solvents. Escharotics don't work, so I began producing identification papers from materials I produced myself, especially the cardboard and paper. I even fabricate the watermark, stamp, ink, and photographs that I attach with a hole-punch to the fake passports. To make the forgeries look old, I use a special dust. Once I start work on a passport, I lock the doors and pull the shades. Any distraction can be fatal. The work is exacting. Every ID card can mean the difference between life and death. The old man who taught me the art of forgery never tired of repeating that we work in a fate factory."

Never before having been in the cellar, I started exploring some of the shelves, finding not only passports, but also food ration cards, identity papers with the imprimatur of the police, ID's validated by the post office, and other official documents.

"By the time I went to work for Ugo," said a justly proud Mendel, "I had learned how to forge army identification papers, which required thirty-six different rubber stamps." He rolled a cigarette and inhaled; as the smoke exited his mouth, he coughed and wheezed, "I am resolved to save as many people as I can."

That night I began a new apprenticeship.

******

Not until after midnight did I return to my room bearing in mind Mendel's lessons in the art of forgery. Slipping under the covers, I wondered what else I could do to help the cause. At some point in the discussion, it had occurred to me that someone had to deliver the forged documents to the waiting party. No Jew or runaway soldier was going to show up at the Rosselli villa to collect forged papers, not with neighbors whose curtains displayed swastikas. It was then I decided that Gemma and I, acting like a young married couple, could serve as Mendel's couriers. The next step was to inform Mendel of my idea—and wait to be called.

Before drifting off to sleep, I imagined myself invited to participate in the Olympic Winter Games in Garmisch-Partenkirchen. But in which sport? Ski jumping? Too scary. Figure skating. That was for Sonia Henie. Toboggan? Too dangerous. Slalom or downhill racing. A possibility. Cross country? Yes, because one could ski off the course and keep on going until he crossed the Swiss border.

Berlin Revisited

In the morning, Sig. Rosselli was sitting at a card table hunched over a map of Bavaria. After I greeted him and asked after his health, Ugo presciently pointed to Garmisch-Partenkirchen, as if he had read my nighttime thoughts. "Here," he said, "from February six to sixteen, the Nazis will show off their Übermensch winter athletes. Fans will come from all parts of the globe to ooh and ahh and will unknowingly endorse this repugnant regime. But behind the government's fanfare and patriotic slogans will remain the same truth: the Nazis are thugs and murderers; they are intent on destroying the very ideals the Olympics proclaim. I tell you, something must be done to capture the attention of the world."

"Is there anything I can do?" I timidly inquired.

Ugo paused and studied me. "As a matter of fact, yes. I can't leave at the moment, and we need to get a forged passport and visa to David Frankfurter in Bern. We also need someone to make a drop in Firenze; our contact is waiting. Are you game?"

Chapter Nine

After several months of apprenticing with Mendel, acting as a go-between, and continuing my school lessons with Isaac Levy, I found myself at the train station, being seen off by Gemma Rosselli. Given a new name—Carlo Martini—I carried Swiss francs, Italian lire, and forged documents. I also carried a train ticket for Bern, dated Saturday, 1 February 1936, as well as a rail ticket to Firenze. I had been given several of Mendel's masterpieces for distribution not only to David Frankfurter, but also to the Italian underground, which used as a collection point the church of Santa Croce. Sig. Rosselli had emphasized the importance of this courier work, and warned me that I'd be frequently tested, particularly at the borders. Ugo explained that I would be given a service passport, issued to government employees for work-related travel. "When your train stops at the border and the police ask to see your papers, try to look bored." All the false documents will be disguised as pages sewn into the binding of a book."

At the border, an indifferent guard, on seeing my service passport, merely thumbed through the pages and noticed nothing amiss. I was then asked about my work.

"Photography," I said, "a lighting technician."

"Where's your equipment?"

"You don't expect me to carry around shooting tables, tripods, and monopods. The supplies I need are waiting for me in Bern. When I return, I'll give you a copy of one of the pictures. A mountain scene, perhaps. Would you like that?"

The border guard seemed pleased and let me pass without any further questions. To enable Dr. Frankfurter to identify me when I arrived at the train station, I had been told to wear a red scarf and blue beret. I was also told not to be surprised to see a man in his twenties crab walking toward me.

"Carlo!" shouted David, who had been given my code name. Across the platform, I saw a crippled young fellow coming toward me. "It's been far too long," David said, embracing me.

We took a cab to David's apartment, where the doctor explained that he was the victim of periostitis, a disease that inflames the band of tissue that surrounds bones. He had endured seven operations, but none had freed him from acute pain, swelling and weakness in his legs, fevers, chills, and inflammation-induced pus.

An icy rain had made the streets slippery. I helped David out of the cab, through the front door, and into the elevator. The apartment, haphazardly furnished, was cluttered with medical books, paper pads, and city maps. Pictures covered the walls. In a corner, next to a floor lamp, a metal stand supported a Hermes typewriter. On a plain coffee table in front of a worn beige couch lay a pile of books, among them a copy of *The Protocols of the Elders of Zion*. Strips of paper indicated the various pages he had referenced. Remarking on all the misery and pain occasioned by *The Protocols*, even in Bern, David sat on the couch, opened the book, and read aloud a passage, ostensibly written by Jews:

"It is indispensable for us to undermine all faith, to tear out of the mind of the 'goyim' the very principle of god-head and the spirit, and to put in its place arithmetical calculations and material needs."

He closed the book and opined unemotionally that those who traded in this filth deserved to die. Wishing to change the subject, I walked around the room, admiring the wall pictures and photographs of colorful Croatian land and seascapes. Noting my interest, David drily observed:

"A beautiful country with a surfeit of religious zealots and fascist sympathizers. My father was chief rabbi in Vinkovci, the oldest inhabited town in Europe. The Ustaše forced him to step down. Those bloody fascists will be the death of the country."

Removing a book on dentistry from the pile in front of him, David remarked, "I grew up in a German-speaking house and went to dental school in Leipzig and then in Frankfurt, the home of my ancestors. So Bern in some ways feels familiar, in other ways not. I don't always understand Bernese German, for example. But I've just about completed my work here."

A pause ensued. Outside, rain pelted the windows. The radiators knocked, and the air inside the flat became heavy. I asked how Hitler's election had been received in Bern.

David's reply led me to think that my query had gone unheard.

"It's probably snowing in Davos."

I made no reply.

"The skiers and skaters will be happy." He stood and stretched. Then he went to a window and, looking out, spoke with his back to me. "Any resistance on the part of the Swiss would cost them their independence, so too would collaboration. The Swiss love nothing more than tranquility and their chocolate, eaten to the muffled sound of a ticking clock."

David turned and grimaced. I asked was he in pain, not knowing whether the source of his facial expression was the dispassionate Swiss or his medical condition.

"Pain," he replied simply, and crab walked across the room, putting a hand on my shoulder. "This weather makes my condition all the worse." Then, with a steely look, he told me, "I need someone to accompany me to Davos—to carry a pistol in a canvas bag. Of late, I have the feeling I'm being watched. We'll take the bus but not sit together. Davos isn't far." As gravely as a mortician, he added, "The day of the event is this Tuesday, February 4th. The winter Olympics begin two days later."

Confused, I stammered, "Sig. Rosselli told me to give you these papers," and carefully removed several pages from the book. "He didn't mention any other assignment."

"I plan to shoot Wilhelm Gustloff," David said casually and coldly. He then opened a cupboard drawer and removed a gun. "With this!" He held up a J. P. Sauer and Sohn semi-automatic pistol.

Seated on the couch with an open dental book on my lap, I looked down and read the chapter heading, "Extraction," which I took as an omen.

David eased into a rocking chair and rubbed his legs. "In Germany, at this time, nothing can be done. Perhaps a major incident in another country can remind the western democracies that the Olympic Games are meant merely to showcase fascism." He shook his head and said vacantly, "Who knows?"

Out of fright, I pleaded, "Sig. Rosselli never spoke of my participating." He forced a laugh, but did not try to counter my objection. "It's not my line of work."

"You won't be involved. Dress in your few belongings, even if it means layering your clothing and being uncomfortable. Just follow me to the house. Once I'm sure we haven't been followed and that the house is unguarded, I'll determine if Gustloff is at home. Only then will I signal you. Casually approach, as if we were strangers. Hand me the canvas satchel, then take the bus directly to Bern and the train to Firenze. I'll do the rest."

On 4 February 1936, David Frankfurter went to Wilhelm Gustloff's home in Davos, knocked at the door, determined his victim was at home alone with his wife, Hedwig Gustloff, received the pistol, and followed her into the house. She showed him to the study and asked him to wait because Wilhelm was on the telephone. Frankfurter sat in a chair facing a picture of Hitler. Herr Gustloff entered and asked the reason for Frankfurter's visit. His reply, which he later related, caused a moment of consternation. "I am a Jew." Before Herr Gustloff could order Frankfurter from the house, David removed the pistol that he had purchased in Bern and shot Wilhelm five times, in the head, neck, and chest.

According to a witness, Frankfurter left the house with the cries of Hedwig Gustloff at his back, walked next door, asked to use the telephone, called the police, and confessed to the murder. Taken to the police station, he calmly signed a written confession that detailed exactly what happened, omitting the person of Baruch Rosner.

Sentenced to life imprisonment, he was released at the end of World War II and allowed to immigrate to Palestine.

As Ugo had hoped, the news of the assassination commanded screaming newspaper headlines throughout Europe. But Hitler did not take the bait. As much as the Führer wanted to launch an immediate purge of German Jews, he feared that he would jeopardize the winter and summer Olympics. Instead, he declared Wilhelm Gustloff a Blutzeuge, a martyr of the Nazi cause, toured his coffin on a special train through half a dozen German cities, personally condoled with the widow, who thereafter received a monthly "honorary payment" of 400 Reichsmark, and cited the murder as part of the propaganda used to justify Kristallnacht, two years later.

I left Bern unnoticed on a train for Firenze, where I took a cab to an address given me by Sig. Rosselli on Via del Pratolino, an apartment house. I admired the huge front doors and rang a buzzer to the Baldini flat. A moment later, someone rang me into the building. As I started up the steps to apartment number seven, I saw standing at the top of the staircase a young woman, about my age, blonde, beaming, and beautifully dressed.

"You found us," she said in Italian," and then added in German, "Willkommen." Her name was Gabriella Baldini.

As I discovered, she spoke three languages, the third, English. Her parents worked long hours, her mother as a seamstress and her father as a museum guide. She had a sister and brother, neither of whom lived at home. A language student, she planned to attend the university in Bologna. After introducing me to her mother, who worked at home, she showed me to a back bedroom that overlooked a small garden. The bed was narrow; and affixed to the wall above the headboard was a reproduction of a 12th-century painting of a Madonna and child. She asked if I had eaten, and before I could reply, invited me into the kitchen for some homemade pasta. After tasting her fettuccine, I knew I would never find its equal at Il Forno. How Mr. Fertig would have loved this meal. Gabriella also served me a cup of coffee that made me think that every previous brew tasted like dishwater. Via del Pratolino was beginning to resemble Paradiso.

Sitting at the dining room table, Gabriella and I chatted until late in the night. She told me what to expect the next day when I set out for Santa Croce. She described the Blackshirts, who enforced fascist order in the country.

"They are mostly former soldiers, trained to impose Mussolini's authority. There are also youth groups, like the Balilla and the Avanguardista. The first enrolls children ages eight to fourteen; the second, fourteen to eighteen. Like the secret police, in their black uniforms with white braids across their chests, they parade around like peacocks, accosting peaceful citizens by demanding to see their papers."

She also warned me not to be surprised if I saw a person bound to a lamppost and forced to drink castor oil until he vomited; or beaten around the kidneys until he pissed blood, staining his pants.

"What do the priests say?" I asked.

"Nothing. The Church and Fasci have made common cause, particularly when it comes to women. Mussolini wants to double the population and has advised husbands to tell their wives: 'Either children or beatings.' The Church regards women as hand maidens to men. They're to cook, clean, sew, and procreate."

"If I'm stopped, what do I say?"

She thought a moment and then a thin smile crossed her lips. "Bark at them what they bark at everyone else: 'Me ne frego.' I don't give a damn. That will give them pause."

"But will it work?"

"Probably. The Fasci are none too bright."

A train rumbled past the building, and I walked to the window to watch. I hadn't realized that tracks ran just across the roadway. Gabriella said, "Freight trains, but who knows what the freight is?"

Then out of the blue she asked, "Do you like opera? There's a good one at the Teatro della Pergola, which is on the way to Santa Croce. Verdi's *Il Trovatore*."

The next morning, I rose early, breakfasted on bread and cheese, as well as a cup of the incomparable coffee. I then left for Santa Croce, with my briefcase of forged papers.

******

On my way to the bus, I passed a chocolate shop and made a mental note to buy a cake for the family. I would do so on my return. The bus was crowded, and silent, perhaps because of the presence of two Fasci di Combattimenti, with undercut hair, and dressed in black shirts, wide black belts, black pants, and black boots. I stood at the rear and looked out the window at the passing streets. Associating Italians with spirit and warmth and gregariousness, I saw neither outside nor inside any expression of those qualities. Fascism had brought fear and fatalism. At the Piazza San Marco, I quickly left the bus and slipped into a bookstore, where I bought a German-Italian grammar, and a book entitled *Famous Operas: Plot Outlines*. After paying for my purchases and asking directions, I started for the Teatro della Pergola.

Expecting to find the theatre on a grand square, I was surprised to locate it on a narrow lane, tucked away from the confusion of the main avenues. At the box office, I bought two tickets for "Trovatore." In the distance I could see Il Duomo and knew that the church of Santa Croce was to the southeast of that magnificent structure sporting Brunelleschi's dome. As I walked toward the Piazza del Duomo, I passed a shop with a picture of Benito Mussolini in the front window, and wondered: What's worse, the known or the unknown? Living under fascism or communism, one knows the rules and the regimen. If one violates them, he knows what to expect. But not everyone lives on the straight and narrow. I could imagine turning the corner and unexpectedly facing a roadblock, with secret police checking papers. My briefcase held a dozen forged passports and exit visas. How would I explain having them? I decided that the unknown held more dangers than the known.

In the Piazza del Duomo I stopped to admire the Baptistery doors fashioned by Lorenzo Ghiberti and raised my eyes to scan Giotto's Campanile. What a magnificent city, I thought, and remembered Magda calling it il centro del universo. The Piazza Santa Croce, with its famous surrounding palazzi, its fountain, and its statue of Dante, seemed to kneel before the Basilica of Santa Croce, the largest Franciscan church in the world and the burial place of such giants as Michelangelo, Machiavelli, Marconi, Cherubini, Galileo, and Rossini. According to the pamphlet I collected at the front door, the sixteen chapels were decorated by Giotto and his students. In one of those chapels, I planned to meet Father Virgilio Gallo, sympathetic to the partisans. I had been told that the good friar had a club foot, which made it all the easier to identify him. Seeing a friar dressed in a brown Franciscan robe, which symbolized for St. Francis the destitution of the peasants, I handed him a card with the name "Virgilio Gallo." The friar, rotund and red-cheeked, replied in simple Italian that Brother Gallo was ill and could not be seen for several days.

Wary of entrusting my briefcase to anyone but Father Gallo, I scribbled my name and address, presuming that the information would be given to the ailing man. Seemingly dumb to the fact that I had not uttered a word, the plump friar stifled a burp and started talking effusively, as if his mouth had been stoppered and was now free to speak. And speak he did. Fortunately, Magda had taught me enough Italian to enable me to understand that the good friar wished to enlighten me about the ideal of poverty in St. Francis, about the Church canonizing Francis when it could have condemned him for apostasy, about the Wolf of Gubbio, and about a dozen other things. To stop the flood, I handed the friar a donation and bolted from the church.

Hastening across the square, and still in possession of the false documents, I decided to avoid public transportation and take a cab back to Via del Pratolino, where I would ask Signora Baldini to sew the documents into my clothing. In return, she could keep the handsome leather briefcase. As I exited the square, I saw two men approaching with white braids that ran from the top of their right shoulders to their left breast pocket and guessed at once that they were OVRA, secret police. I could feel a trickle of pee wetting my underwear and realized I was involuntarily pissing myself. I had read that fear could have this effect, but I never thought it could happen to me. When the two men were nearly upon me, I shot up my right arm in a fascist salute and cried, "Me ne frego!" The men stopped, did the same, and continued past me. Gabriella had told me that all the churches in the city were spied upon by the secret police, whose work was made easier by their identifying homosexual priests and blackmailing them to work for the OVRA. She said the same was true of the Vatican.

A stoic cab driver drove me home, but so scared was I that I forgot to stop at the chocolate shop, an errand that would have to wait for another day. I had been given a key to the building and let myself in, going straight to my room to change my underwear.

At dinner that night, which I took with the Baldinis at their dining room table, I showed Gabriella the theatre tickets and said I hoped she was free, apologizing for not asking her first. She glowed.

"Kindness," she observed, "never needs an apology."

"May I ask a favor?"

"Of course," replied Gabriella.

"I need someone to sew some important documents into my clothing."

Expecting Mrs. Baldini to volunteer, I was surprised when Gabriella said, "Just bring them to me after dinner."

The next day I slept late and remained in my room studying my German-Italian grammar book. In the evening, I took Gabriella to the opera. I had asked her to call a cab, and she had puckishly answered, "if you promise to go to dinner afterward."

I was silently thankful for all the money that Sig. Rosselli had given me, though it was dwindling fast.

Gabriella, like Gemma, knew how to dress and turn heads. She wore a black long-sleeve V neck sequined mermaid gown featuring paisley sleeve details. The contrast of her blonde hair and floor-length black dress did not escape the beau-monde. Even women stopped to look. Bemused, I wondered how I, unschooled in the ways of love and courtship, had come to enjoy the company of two stunning Italian women. Unlike the German girls I had known, Italian women of the same age seemed like adults, not adolescents. I started to hyperventilate from excitement and didn't calm down until I had reached my seat in the balcony. When the men on the main floor began to glance upward to admire Gabriella, I suddenly wished I had taken her to a movie.

Before the start of the opera, Gabriella outlined the story. During the performance, the searing music held me fast as the preposterous plot unfolded.

After the opera, a dinner of veal and fresh fish delighted us in the Piazza della Signoria. With floodlights playing on the Palazzo Vecchio, and the arcade of Benvenuto Cellini visible in the shadows, the night was ripe for romance. But I had no idea where to go or how to begin, so after dinner we walked along the Arno, paused on the Ponte Vecchio to admire the shops, took a chocolate drink across the road from the Pitti Palace, and snuggled into a cab for the ride home. It was an evening I often remembered, and though I swore to repeat it with whomever I married, I never did.

The next day, Gabriella and I returned to the same area and visited the Uffizi Gallery. As we admired the stunning collection, Gabriella told me that Mussolini had agreed to sell William Randolph Hearst some masterpieces for huge sums of money, which Il Duce needed to finance his wars of conquest in Africa. Paintings disappeared every day, though not the popular treasures. I especially liked the 13th-century religious paintings. Gabriella pointed to the stick-like fingers of the figures and remarked that the Madonna's hands were as large as her head, and that the child's face resembled a man's. "The painters of that period," she explained, "hadn't yet learned how to draw hands, which may be the most difficult of all objects to capture accurately. They knew little about perspective and depth, which is why the paintings all look one dimensional and flat. And since they regarded children as adults, they painted them as grownups."

"I suppose," I said, imagining what an art history class might teach, "that a historian could look at these paintings and come away with some idea of how the people dressed and lived."

"The wealthy people. And the background architecture often provides a snapshot of the city or town."

Several hours later, we left the gallery and enjoyed a gelato at a small stand on a narrow side street. Gemma recommended the light chocolate. One taste and I knew that no ice cream in Germany could compete.

"Tomorrow," I said glumly, "I have to return to Santa Croce."

She nodded. "In your jacket lined with passports?"

"The same."

"Are you worried about being stopped?"

"Honestly, yes."

"What if I accompanied you?"

"I'd be a lot less frightened. You speak the language. The best I can do is ask for directions to the gabinetto."

"You're too hard on yourself. Your Italian isn't so bad."

"But not good."

She merely squeezed my hand.

******

The bus was crowded as it made its way to the Piazza San Marco, where we exited and walked arm in arm down Via Cavour to Il Duomo and then through the market area to Santa Croce. Although we passed several men in uniform, no one asked to see our papers. But on entering the church, we were stopped, in this instance, by a brown-robed friar. Gabriella spoke for us both, though I gleaned enough to feel panicky.

"My cousin from Germany," she said, "wishes to speak to Brother Gallo."

I smiled broadly as if to say, "Me!"

"He has been ill."

The friar studied my face skeptically.

"Father Gallo treated my cousin's tumor with prayer at this time last year. Before my cousin returns to Berlin, he would like the father to pray over him once again."

Sympathy suffused the friar's face, saying he understood.

Gabriella took my arm and moved me toward the friar. "Pardon my manners. I neglected to introduce you to Carlo Martini."

The hand that I shook felt like a dead fish. But the weak handshake was the least of my frights. Gabriella had taken a false step. By introducing me as Carlo Martini, she had led the man to believe that I could speak Italian.

And sure enough, the friar asked, "Parlate Italiano?" using the formal voi form that Mussolini was promulgating.

Gabriella quickly recovered her wits and replied that Carlo had a throat tumor that limited his speech. She pointed to my neck, and I dutifully croaked.

The friar apologized, "Mi dispiace," introduced himself as Brother Sandino, said how glad he was to make our acquaintance, "Sono molto lieto di far la sua conoscenza," and said he'd return in a moment.

Gabriella's upper lip had broken out in a sweat, which I dabbed with my handkerchief.

"How stupid of me," she said. "I wasn't thinking. He may well be a spy working for the government. I could kick myself."

We stood in front of the tomb of Galileo Galilei. A German-speaking guide, leading a small group of frowsy-looking women tourists, explained that the tomb was erected in 1737, designed by Giulio Foggini, and contained a bust of Galileo Galilei, by Giovanni Battista Foggini, and figures representing Astronomy and Geometry. Staring at the bust, I murmured, "I wish I had some of his genius. I could use it about now."

When the friar returned, he directed Gabriella and me to follow him. He passed through the ancient cloister, one of three in the basilica, and entered a small room, sparsely furnished with a wooden table, a bench, and three chairs. On the table stood a pitcher of milk and a plate with bread and cheese. The three of us sat facing the table and waited silently until a door opened and Friar Virgilio Gallo hobbled in and seated himself on the bench. A frail, pale-faced man, the friar breathed laboriously, like a consumptive in the final stages of his illness. A wry smile seemed to say yes, the end is nigh. He leaned forward on the table, revealing the small wooden cross hanging from his neck, folded his hands, and asked how he could be of help.

Terrified, I worried that with Friar Sandino sitting next to me, I'd have no occasion to hand Friar Gallo the forged papers.

Gabriella said she trusted that Friar Gallo remembered her cousin, who had come from Berlin, to once again receive his blessing for the tumor in his neck. I sat hoping that she had supplied him with enough information to signal that I was the "courier from Berlin."

Father Gallo shook his head and asked Brother Sandino if he would be so kind as to bring him a small footstool for his deformità. As soon as Sandino left the room, Friar Gallo reached beneath his robe and removed a satchel, which he slid across the table to me, saying "Ti aspettavo. Dobbiamo agire tempestivamente," which Gabriella translated: "I was waiting for you. We must act quickly."

As fast as I could, I divested myself of the passports and visas, stuffing them into the satchel, which Friar Gallo slipped back under his robe.

"Mangia," said the friar, pointing to the food. "Eat!" He then poured himself a glass of milk and broke off a piece of bread to go with his cheese. To calm my nerves, I did the same. Gabriella, whose composure had returned, said that she preferred wine with her pane e formaggio, bread and cheese.

On those words, Friar Sandino returned with a footrest and watched as Friar Gallo stroked my neck and murmured a prayer for healing, while I knelt.

******

Passing down the nave of the basilica, I stopped and slipped into one of the rows. Gabriella could guess why. With my head resting on the wooden rail of the row in front of me, I recited a Jewish prayer, "Shema Yisrael Adonai Elohenu Adonai Ehad."

In the piazza, I suggested we stop for a glass of vino, in honor of Gabriella's good work. At a small taverna overlooking the river, we watched as two young men rowed their racing scull down river and back. "Like Sisyphus," I said, "no matter how well we live, we lose." I rubbed my nose and added, "A teacher told me that once."

"Do you know of the Masaccio at the Santa Maria del Carmine? No? Then let me show it to you."

We made our way to the south bank and to the Brancacci Chapel, with its famous fresco, "Expulsion from the Garden of Eden." Captivated, I stood wordlessly for a long time. Finally, I said, "From the little history I've read and from what I've seen in Germany, people are always trying to expel others. It's the original sin, first introduced by God."

On the side streets branching from the church stood artists' studios. Several of them were offering copies of "Expulsion from the Garden of Eden," some even framed. Pensively, I shared my thoughts, feeling touched by an epiphany. "Isn't a large part of our beings spent copying others? I mean copying in its largest sense: manners, morals, religious and political beliefs, habits, customs, even food and dress, and of course language."

"You seem to be suggesting that all of life is a forgery."

"Isn't it?"

"How do you mean?"

"We imitate our parents, in most everything we do and become, unless they alienate us."

"So, then, how does change occur?"

"As far as I can tell, slowly."

Why I had introduced the subject of imitation was a mystery. But the moment I did, I felt as if someone else had taken possession of my body. The painting had tapped a vein in me, a philosophical one, which I'd never given voice to. I suddenly felt a changed person, an adult with independent ideas. In making a case for imitation and forgery, I was expressing my own thoughtful opinion. How long this independence would last, I didn't know, but hoped for its permanence.

"Sometimes," I added in response to her question, "I think change enters us involuntarily, brought on by one's imagination."

We entered a small craftsman's shop, permeated by the smell of wood shavings, and were met by the carver, with chisel in hand. He had been fashioning a Madonna and Child from a pungent block of cedar. But the figures were distorted, and certainly not traditional. I stared, and the carver bravely remarked:

"You're wondering why the acute angles and the misshapen postures. Simple. Just look around, and you will see that under this regime women have become breeders and the children warriors. The world is out of kilter."

Berlin Revisited

Our arrival at Via del Pratolino corresponded with a train stopping across the road. Rail inspectors were opening the car doors to expel stowaways, Romani. An animal-like cry came from one of the cars, as a gypsy family was discovered hiding inside. Gabriella and I squeezed through an aperture in the fence. Two policemen were removing the family and their sparse belongings. A little girl, no more than two and tied to her mother's back, peered out from her ragged clothes and smiled, oblivious to the danger. As the police led away the family of three, the mother disengaged the child and threw her towards me. I caught her before she could hit the ground. Then the gypsies ran, with the police in frantic pursuit. The child, although looking bewildered, never cried. Gabriella immediately took control of the little girl and made for her building across the avenue. When we arrived, Mrs. Baldini wanted to know what we were planning to do with the child. Gabriella replied candidly, "Keep her safe." Mrs. Baldini opened her mouth, as if to object; then she closed it and walked into the kitchen, leaving Gabriella and me in the sitting room with the child.

Making a place for the child on the couch, Gabriella put me in charge while she warmed some milk and buttered a few pieces of toasted bread. Unaccustomed to caring for young children, I patted her head, as one would a dog. When Gabriella returned, the child, without a word, devoured the food. A bath ensued, with Gabriella shampooing the child's long, black hair. Gabriella asked her if the bath felt good, but the child showed no comprehension.

"She doesn't speak Italian," said Gabriella, "and I don't know Romany."

"Then you'd better start teaching her the basics, unless you want me to take her to Germany."

"She stays here with me until I can find her parents."

"And your mother: what will she say?"

"She'll complain, but a month from now she'll be hugging the girl and treating her like a daughter. Which leads me to ask: 'What name shall we give her?'"

"I've always liked the name Adriana."

"Then Adriana it shall be."

The day that I left from the train station, Gabriella and Adriana, clutching her hand, accompanied me. I hugged them both; then I thanked Gabriella for all her help, and whispered in her ear, "Ti amo."

She replied, "And I love you, too."

Standing in the open door of the train, I said, "You can still change your mind and let me take her to Berlin."

Pulling the child close to her, she said, "Adriana stays with me. Where I go, she goes."

Those were the last words I ever heard Gabriella speak. As the train pulled out of the station, Firenze was left behind. I never saw it again.

PART THREE

Chapter Ten

A whistle blew, and the train began to slow for its approach to the central station. As a precaution, no one met me. I took a cab not to the villa but to 45 Schlüterstraße, where the Jewish residents, still stunned by the recent news of David Frankfurter's assassination of Wilhelm Gustloff, were in a state of fear and shock, and also elation. Before returning to the villa, I remained with Walter Fertig for the next few days, listening to Walter's excited reporting of the winter Olympics, and how the Scandinavians had won a majority of the medals. The foreign press praised the victors, and also reported that hoteliers and property owners had conspicuously displayed signs warning Jews to find lodging elsewhere. As that proved impossible, Jews boycotted the winter games.

******

Berlin Revisited

Only years later did I ever say a word about the murder. I quickly came to realize that forging passports and exit visas was one thing, being party to an assassination quite another.

Now that the winter games had come and gone, with the Norwegian team excelling, the Nazi officials rationalized the results and seemed more intent on preparing for the summer games, when German athletes were likely to win the most golds, than in Jew baiting. Their preparations included sanitizing Berlin, building first-rate facilities, and quarrying stone from the Alps for the construction of a world-class stadium to hold 100,000. The crowning architectural feature, the Bell Tower (1,247 feet high), held the Olympic Bell, inscribed with the Olympic Rings and an eagle. It also bore between two swastikas the motto: "I call the youth of the world." All antisemitic posters were ordered removed, and graffiti whitewashed; all flags, banners, and propaganda were removed from Berlin and stored in a warehouse. Innkeepers and landlords were told to admit people of every religion and race. Since 1933, most every shop and public building, including libraries, had displayed signs that read "Juden unerwünscht": Jews not welcome. Before the Olympics, Nazi newspapers, in every German city, contained hideous caricatures of Jews with huge bellies, hooked noses, glinting animalistic eyes and warnings not to associate with these "beasts." All the antisemitic banners and signs removed from German buildings and lampposts on Hitler's orders would be reinstated as soon as the foreigners left.

For now, Hitler basked in the warm glow of a Germany, clean and orderly, that showcased the virtues of fascism. The world's finest winter athletes had returned to their home countries praising the "New Germany" for its well-organized games and society. Even antifascist countries complimented the Reich on the equality and fairness their skiers and jumpers and bobsledders and skaters and hockey players had experienced. Germany had become a model for the rest of the world. So taken were some of the athletes with the culture of the country, they chose to stay behind. What the athletes never saw were the dilapidated training facilities for German-Jewish athletes, who were subsequently kept from the games, and the Nazi minions who kept the Jewish athletes of other countries out of sight.

To explain the victories of the Scandinavian countries, the German press was told to emphasize the Aryan characteristics of the Norwegians, as well as those of the Swedes and Finns, who also did well. With a few choice quotations from fellow travelers, the word went out that based on the Winter Olympics at Garmisch-Partenkirchen, fascism had much to recommend it.

******

Lieber Vater,

Although the Nazis have whitewashed over the graffiti with calcimine on thousands of Berlin walls, one can still make out under the chalk the old slogans. Mutter used to say that when the goyim cleaned a stove, on the outside it shone, and inside, filth. The same can be said about the Nazis. They parade in shiny uniforms and polished boots, talking about a master race, but underneath, you find smallness and bigotry. They have clean faces and dirty hands.

Mr. Fertig says they have made a deal with the devil. In return for order and discipline, the country has sold its aesthetic soul. Theatre has lost its vitality; art and artists are condemned as degenerate; composers and musicians and writers flee to other countries. Where, Mr. Fertig frequently asks, will it end?

Berlin Revisited

To show my disgust for the current government—and because I love the music—I have joined a swing and jazz club. Twelve of us make up the core of the group. On weekends, when the weather allows, we hike in the woods and build a campfire to cook our food. I asked Gemma to join us, but she said that her father needed her at the villa. To be truthful, I don't think she likes clubs and group activities, even though she likes jazz. If I had to choose between the swing club and Gemma, I would of course take Gemma. But in her absence, it's nice to have other friends, even though none of them means as much to me as Gemma.

I sometimes ask myself what I would do without her, a question that comes from one of your favorite operas, Gluck's "Orfeo," and the aria "Que fará senza Euridice?" The way I feel now, I would like to marry her when I am older and have the means to support us. But whether I survive—or the Rossellis—is another story. Every day, I think of you and pray that we will soon be reunited.

Alles Liebe,
Baruch

With the approach of summer, Yva Simon suggested posing a model in clothing reminiscent of tennis and track. With business sadly declining because of Nazi bans and prohibitions, she was seeking ways to capitalize on the coming Wimbledon Championships (22 June–3 July) and the hoopla of the coming games in Berlin (1 August–16 August). She invited the staff, including Gemma and me, to view five slides she had taken of prospective models. For each woman in the slide, she provided a fictitious back story to complement the particular scene she had in mind.

"This one has just come from the grass courts; this one has a secret lover among the athletes, hence the sly look; this one, with the come-hither smile, longs to be a track star; this one could pass for a swimmer; and the final one should bring to mind a Nordic femme fatale, imperious and peerless."

I found the last slide unsettling. The woman eerily resembled my mother. Tormented by painful memories of disparaging comments that passed between my parents, I remembered that before my father's arrest, he said that Mutti had everything in life except the privilege of giving herself unselfishly to another human being. Peering at the last slide, I volunteered, "She cares only for herself."

"Which," asked Yva, "should we feature: the woman wearing either a swimsuit, without a cap so we can see her curly hair, or the clothing of an Olympic participant? I also have in mind a javelin thrower or a sprinter, wearing shorts and a polo shirt. "What's your choice?"

Statuesque Gemma, of all people, remarked that a swimsuit photo was just another pose. But a woman in the act of throwing a javelin or crouching at the start of a race brought energy to the picture. The other staff members concurred; they also agreed that the last woman, the imperious one, would make the best model. They liked the turned-up nose, the small mouth, the sculpted cheekbones, and the dark eyes. Her svelte figure and ample bosom also won her votes. As one of the staffers said, "She's a knockout, but what do her legs look like?"

Yva projected another slide on the screen, in which the same model was wearing shorts. "I anticipated your question, Horst."

"What a peach!" he exclaimed.

"Well, then," said Yva, "let's give her a history, to provide context for the shot."

Again, thinking of my mother, as well as our old flat on Wilmersdorfer Straße, I unhelpfully confused fact and fiction. "Like the enclosed garden outside her window, she blooms with the season. In winter, she hibernates, rarely venturing outdoors; in spring, she flowers, frequenting dance halls and jazz concerts."

Horst, a whiz at building props, dismissed my comment with a laugh and a wave of his hand. "We are talking about an athlete, a young woman who has grown up with sports. Indoor sports facilities in winter, outdoor tracks in good weather. Her polo shirts and skirts will show her off to good advantage."

Yva smiled indulgently and added, "Let's say she's Jewish, but wishes otherwise, and therefore tries to pass as Nordic. Her blonde hair and facial features make her pretense all the easier. She wants to compete in the Olympics or, at least, be part of the practice team. The men fancy her, but she has eyes only for the German decathlon champion, Erwin Huber. In part, but only in part, I am thinking of Helene Mayer, the Mischling whose father was Jewish and her mother Lutheran. The mix contributes to her furtive look."

Yva went on to explain that the woman is edgy, as if concerned that at any moment she will be exposed or exiled or exploited. Haunted by her past and hopeful for the present, she wants to impress with both her face and her feats. But success, as modern women know, comes at a cost. To the Nazis it means home and motherhood, certainly not a professorship in a university or a political role. Athletics straddle the line.

"Would she prefer to marry a decathlon champion or win a medal herself?" asked Yva. "That ambiguity is what I want the photograph to show."

Horst, a sallow-cheeked chain smoker, with a chipped front tooth, inhaled and suggested, "What about two shots, side by side? One featuring the athlete, the other the feminine."

"Or transparently superimposed," added Yva. "That might be just the winning combination."

The staff smiled approvingly.

Melchior Kramer, a lighting expert who used to race cars and now limped from a spinal injury, asked a question that excited the group. "Do you think we could induce Leni Riefenstahl to pose for us? I understand she'll be filming the Olympics. It would be quite a coup."

They all knew the name because of her acting career and her immensely successful film the year before, "The Triumph of the Will." Rumors abounded that she was a faithful Nazi, though others disagreed. It took many years before the truth emerged; a secret recording captured her fervently espousing fascism. But at the moment, whether she'd be willing to help Yva and the team was unknown. Once again, I thought of my mother, this time in the context of her Nazi contacts, including the sympathetic Avery Brundage. Perhaps my mother could ask Leni or have someone in the party approach her. I therefore volunteered to contact my mother, if Yva approved. It was a dicey proposition. Leni in some ways was competing with Yva, even though the former was a world-famous filmmaker and the latter had not yet attained an international reputation as a fashion photographer.

Yva wanted time to mull over the idea. A few days later, she discreetly inquired if I wouldn't mind talking to my mother about trying to reach Leni. Of course I agreed.

Although mother had a telephone, not once since the day she dropped me off to live with Walter Fertig had she called. When I rang her, she seemed annoyed. After I told Mutti that I needed her help and mentioned Mr. Brundage, a name that undoubtedly made her wonder how I knew about her connection to him, she suggested, "Why don't we meet for lunch at the Adlon Hotel?"

Even though I wore my Sabbath best, I looked out of place among the high Nazi functionaries, diplomats, and wealthy businessmen who frequented the Adlon, the finest hotel in Berlin and perhaps even in all of Europe. Having always entered the hotel through a rear door to reach my friend Myra, I now used the front door, which led into an enormous lobby with imposing marble columns. Decorated in a mix of neo-Baroque and Louis XVI styles, the ground floor housed a restaurant, a café, a palm court, a ladies' lounge, a library, a music room, a barber shop, a cigar shop, an interior garden with a Japanese styled elephant fountain, and numerous grand ballrooms. My mother was already seated in the restaurant. She extended a hand to me, but not a hug. Her first words were:

"Couldn't you find something better to wear?"

A group of Nazis, seated at the next table, occasionally stole glances at my beautiful mother. Their starched black uniforms and highly polished boots reminded me of ravens, birds of death. Their proximity meant that mother and I would have to converse in whispers.

"The woman I work for—"

"Yva Simon," mother interjected. "A known Jewess."

"And you," I replied bitterly, "what are you?"

"I plan to be baptized in the Lutheran Church. You are welcome to join me. In fact, I recommend it."

Thinking of what father would say, I responded, "Then they win, and we lose."

"Have it your way."

Mother stared at the tablecloth and with a well-manicured fingernail traced some lines in the linen. Only she knew what those pictographs meant, if anything. A secret code? A wish to see me leave? A sign? But to whom? It occurred to me that living in Germany made diviners of us all. Every person I passed on the sidewalk, every car, bus, cab, store window, street sign, advertisement, flag, banner, gesture, grimace, smile or sneeze made me ask what they meant. Were they intended for me? A Jew? No wonder so many people stayed indoors and hardly ventured outside. The omens were everywhere.

"The Olympics," I hazarded, "could provide a wonderful opportunity for Yva Simon if you—"

My mother, looking put upon, was saved by the waitress who took our order. One glance at the menu and the prices led me to ask for a hot roll and butter and a cup of tea. Mutti paid no heed to cost and ordered a full lunch: soup, salad, lamb chops, potatoes, and a glass of Chardonnay. Who's paying, I wondered? It was certainly not Mutti. In fact, at the end of the lunch she merely signed the bill and slid it back to the waitress. But for now, I wanted to determine if she would help the studio. I tried a new opening, a direct one.

"Mr. Brundage, I understand, is a friend of yours. He—"

"Gossip," she replied sharply, "nothing more."

"Do you happen to know Leni Riefenstahl?" There, I had said it, with no further circumlocutions.

"I've met her once or twice."

"Do you know her well enough to ask her a favor?"

"Not in the least."

"Do you know someone who does?"

"Baruch, what is this all about?"

I told my mother what a boon it would be to the studio to have Leni pose in a fashion photograph, advertising the Olympics, with Yva's imprimatur.

"Not a chance," Mutti bluntly replied, bit into a lamb chop, and daintily dabbed her mouth with the linen napkin.

I tried one last desperate gambit. "Mr. Brundage might be willing to help."

"I hardly know the man."

"Really?" I said as incredulously as I could.

My tone succeeded, because mother asked, "What are you suggesting?"

Taking my time to answer, I buttered my roll, now cold, reached across the table for some marmalade, and slathered a spoonful on the bread. As I munched the bread, I started to speak, but she stopped me and scolded:

"How many times have I told you not to talk with food in your mouth?"

A moment later, I continued in an insinuating manner. "I must say, your English sounds quite good."

"I have no idea what you're referring to."

Sipping my tea slowly, I stared at her. At first, she failed to flinch, and then diverted her eyes. Not wishing to expose Myra Huberman, I stalled. "You know very well what I mean."

Pause.

She frowned, planted her elbows on the table, and leaned toward me in a menacing manner. "It's that floozy maid, Hannah, isn't it? She's always nosing around."

Fearing I'd cause the dismissal of some innocent person, I quickly tried to disabuse my mother of her suspicions by pointing her in another direction. "One of Brundage's staff members was overheard in a bar."

With this untruth, apparently uttered too loudly, one of the Nazis at the next table stood and introduced himself. "And you," he said to my mother, "are Fräulein Logenheit. I have seen you here before and have taken the liberty to inquire—" He failed to complete the sentence. "I trust that you will not take offense." He slightly bowed. "Your work for the . . ." He looked at me. "For the government is widely appreciated. Perhaps one day you will agree to be my guest for dinner."

My mother, now compromised, smiled insincerely and said, "Danke." Her admirer bowed again and with a click of the heels returned to his table.

"Logenheit!" I repeated.

"It's my professional name."

For a moment we sat in silence. I pondered the meaning of the word "professional," and she stared into space, thinking what, I had no idea, except possibly the easiest and fastest way to escape.

"I think," she said, "we have exhausted this topic of conversation. I must be off."

"Then there is nothing you can do for our studio?"

"Nothing."

She stood. I remained seated.

"Aren't you going to see me to the door?"

"Before you go, "I replied, "answer one question. Why are you working for the enemy?"

Rather indecorously she plopped back into the chair. Clutching her handbag, as if she feared someone might steal it, she reached across the table and took my arm, but not affectionately. "Are you blind? Do you not see where the country is heading? If you wish to remain in Germany, as I do, then you must accommodate, seem what you're not, look the other way. The future will be better. You understand? The important thing is to survive! Nothing else matters. Now is not the time for moral posturing. Besides, you're unsuited for politics. Were it not for me, you would have been arrested for belonging to that jazz group. I am trying to keep you alive. And do you care? If you do, show it!"

She sat stiffly, with chin thrust upward, proudly, as if to declare, "I am the master of all fights now."

Looking at her face, I saw clearly how beauty deceives, and angrily answered, "You turned in Klaus Kopf."

Unrepentant, she said coldly, "I did it for your own good, for your own safety. You should be glad that I did. The Nazis have forbidden that kind of music."

"Perhaps," I replied, with a catch in my throat, "you read the morning papers. A bargeman hauled Klaus's tortured body from the Landwehr canal last night."

******

We left separately. I watched her signal a cab and depart. Destination unknown. When the cab was out of sight, I circled behind the Adlon and entered the staff door, passing some hotel employees who paid me no heed. I went to Myra'a apartment and knocked: once, twice. Then she opened the door. She was not alone. The man sitting with headphones and cavesdropping on some poor soul was presumably the house detective, Rolf Kimmelman. She introduced me. Instead of a lean and hungry aspect, which I had assumed, Rolf was round-faced, fat, and quite jolly. I supposed his warmth disarmed people, a useful asset for a detective. Rolf excused himself and left. Once Myra and I were alone, I told her about my lunch with "Fräulein Langenheit."

"I should have told you about her name change, but I didn't want to upset you."

Although my next comment sounded like a non-sequitur, it was really not. "Throughout the city, the government is removing the antisemitic banners and flags. Packing them up and hauling them away. They did the same for the winter Olympics. Do you have any idea where they're being stored?"

She chuckled mischievously. "The same warehouse where they're filming their pornography. I've been there. It's just outside of town near Tempelhof Airport."

"Can you get me a pass?"

"What for?"

"Souvenirs."

"Liar."

"Arson."

"Don't be a fool. They'll shoot you."

"Not if I'm cautious."

I knew that Myra wished to protect me, but she shrugged and said that she'd ask Rolf for a pass. As I exited her room, she told me to keep my pants buttoned. A few days later, I dropped by the Adlon and collected a letter of entrée. I waited until Saturday to make my way to the warehouse, a non-descript, square, flat-topped structure. Reasoning that Jews were supposed to be in synagogue on the Sabbath, I figured I was less likely to be thought one. My plan, concocted in light of David Frankfurter's rash deed, was to set fire to the building. I carried a knapsack packed with accelerants. But before I could enter, I had to pass inspection by a guard.

The sentinel wanted to know what I intended to do with the flammable liquids. I laughed and said they were for special effects on the studio stage. Why else would I have been issued a pass?

"You know," I joked, "to burn Jewish asses." The man waved me through, commenting he'd like to see the scene for himself. Myra had outlined the layout of the warehouse. To reach the large storage area to the rear, I had to pass through the film studio, where they were producing the antisemitic pornography. I entered a door marked for staff only and slipped into an inconspicuous corner where I could observe through a slit in the black felt curtains the action on stage.

The lights came up on a setting for a grocery store. Jazz music played in the background, as a large man seated at a small counter fingered an enormous cash register. Every time he hit one of the keys, instead of a number appearing in the register window, the word Betrüger popped up. Cheat! A pretty, young blonde woman entered from the wings and asked for credit. She said that her family was starving and could not afford the price of food or clothes. He replied that he could accommodate her for the right price. "Which is?" she asked. He pointed to one side of the stage where a curtain slowly opened to reveal a bed with restraints. Before she could speak, two men dragged her from the counter to the bed, rudely undressed her, and fastened her hands and legs to the bedposts.

It was now that the man, whom I had seen only from the back turned to face the camera. He was sporting a false nose, made to look unnaturally hooked and long, a padded stomach, and a dangling watch chain with a pendant of the Star of David. But these effects were the least of the caricature. He was also wearing an enormous phallus that jutted out from his pants. The fair-haired woman was clearly intended to represent an Aryan beauty about to be ravished by a Jewish satyr. She cried out in defense of her purity and innocence. He reached into his pocket and removed a handful of bills that he spilled over her nakedness. But his attempt to buy her cooperation and silence elicited even louder cries, to which the putative Jew responded with satanic laughter. As he moved in for the seduction, the lights dimmed and the next scene, one that took only a moment to reconfigure, opened with a sign on an easel that said "Jewess," and depicted a naked woman on the bed in the same position; but when the man showered her with money, she smiled and invited him to seduce her.

This crude pornography, I mused, was meant for whom? Surely not for public cinemas. For private consumption? My bewilderment was compounded when I felt a hand on my shoulder and turned to see the smiling face of Sig. Rosselli.

"What are you doing here?" I asked.

"Myra."

"Myra?"

"The resistance coordinates its efforts."

"Then you are here to prevent me—"

"Yes."

I said nothing.

"You are no doubt wondering," said Sig. Rosselli, "what becomes of this trash."

"It did occur to me."

The older man ran a hand through his dark, thick hair. "Just between us," he whispered, "whatever I tell you must remain secret. I buy this Dreck from the Nazis and sell it to Arab countries. The Saudi sheikhs love it. They pay handsomely. The money helps support our cause. If the Grand Mufti of Jerusalem, Haj Amin al-Husseini, knew that the money goes to the resistance, he would die of shame and shock."

"Who's he?"

Ugo patted my head. "He opposes the British in Palestine and is a friend of Hitler's."

"Can anyone just walk in and buy this stuff?"

"Not exactly. Fritz Moeller is in charge. We work with him. He keeps us informed about the detention camps. Come, I'll introduce you."

Mr. Moeller's office, a comfortable retreat of overstuffed furniture, with cluttered bookshelves and pictures of movie stars, constituted a library of ancient Greek and Latin writers. To one side: Homer, Thucydides, Plato, Aristotle, Aesop, Sophocles, Aeschylus, and Euripides. To the other side: Horace, Ovid, Cicero, Vergil, Plautus, Terence, Pliny, Seneca, Diogenes, and Zeno. Those names I recognized; others were unfamiliar. Had the books been printed in Greek and Latin, instead of German, I would have been at a loss.

"Do you read all these writers?" I asked Mr. Moeller on being introduced to him.

Fritz, clean shaven, with a head of curly, unruly hair, wore a blue artist's frock, as if preparing to sculpt a block of stone. Fat pink cheeks and puffy eyes made him look like a fish, the resemblance enhanced by his round mouth gulping air, owing to an asthmatic condition.

"When time allows. I try to read every night. It keeps me from thinking about what takes place in the streets."

"And you, young man, what is your place in the scheme of things?"

"I work for a fashion photographer and for Sig. Rosselli," I said, and quickly added, "I have a tutor who is introducing me to some of the authors on your bookshelves."

Mr. Moeller looked at Sig. Rosselli, who nodded, and then checked to make sure the office door was locked.

"You are no doubt asking yourself," Mr. Moeller hazarded, "how I can read such wonderful literature and produce such terrible films. The answer is simple. The pornography pays, and the film studio camouflages my important filmic work." He removed an inhaler from his pocket and breathed deeply. After wiping his nose, he slid aside some books, revealing a wall safe. "This is where I store evidence of the camps. The Germans, as you know, are a fastidious people. They keep immaculate records, even of concentration camps and detention centers. They film the prisoners, in life and death. The films are then collected in a film archive. You might say that the archivist and I have an arrangement. He receives free copies of my films, and I receive free copies of his. Someday there will be a reckoning and I want to have the evidence to back up the claims of brutality and bestiality."

I felt a lump in my throat and could only burble an answer. "I . . . see."

Sig. Rosselli added, "Mr. Moeller is our archivist."

Fritz smiled and asked me if I would like one of the pornographic films as a souvenir.

Finding my voice, I said, "Yes, please. It might prove useful." Handed a blue movie, packaged in cardboard and stamped "Pornographie," I tucked it into a side pocket of my knapsack.

Fritz chuckled and wagged a finger at me. "You know the Russian Politburo often watches such films, also the Nazi high command. They are all sexual predators."

Berlin Revisited

I returned to the city with Sig. Rosselli, well aware of the irony that I now owned a blue film when I had intended to torch the building, with its pornographic film studio and stored Nazi paraphernalia.

Chapter Eleven

On August 9, Sunday, I sat in the Olympiastadion with the Rossellis and the Simons. The featured race was the 4X4 100 meters sprint relay. Ugo, immensely excited because the Italian team was reputed to be the equal of the Americans, wondered about Team USA's tactics. Did they have something up their sleeve? A few hours before the start of the race, the U.S. track coach, Dean Cromwell, made a change. He replaced Marty Glickman and Sam Stoller, two Jewish sprinters unrivalled for their flawless baton pass, with Jesse Owens and Ralph Metcalf. I was secretly crushed. Yes, Owens and Metcalf had come in first and second in the 100-meter dash, but Glickman and Stoller were faster than the other two members of the relay team. The gun sounded, and the race began. From the start, the American team led. The Yanks clocked 39.8 seconds, a world record, the second-place Italian team, 41.1 seconds, and the Germans came in third with a time of 41.2. Ugo sensed my disappointment.

"At least feel good for Gemma and me. The Italian team's second place finish pushed the Germans to third. Not a bad day's work."

"What we have just seen is Brundage's doing. You can bet on it."

Gemma, sitting next to me, was strangely quiet, but the Simons were jubilant that Jesse Owens, a Negro, had won a fourth gold medal.

"So much for the master race," said Mr. Simon.

When I asked Gemma, "Why so pensive?" she whispered, "Yva should have used a Negro model for her Olympic photograph."

"Jesse Owens?" I innocently asked.

"A Negress," she replied.

I sat tongue-tied. The thought of it had never crossed my mind. But I could see Gemma's point.

"Actually," she continued sotto voce, "I suggested it. An Ethiopian model, I know. Really quite a beauty. She could have used the work."

"No market for such a photo," I replied, "unless you're thinking of other places, other continents."

She stared at me regretfully. "You're wrong," she objected, "dead wrong." The force of her annoyance surprised me, but I didn't contradict her; instead, I admired her peevish beauty, including the look she beamed at me when she wanted me to feel, without her saying so, that I was still too young and inexperienced.

As we left the stadium, Ugo exclaimed, "Gli italiani, bravi!"

In light of Gemma's comments, Yva's Olympic photograph, lost to Allied bombing, now felt like a reproach. But why? Its artistry was indisputable; its timeliness perfect; but Gemma's words lingered. Was she suggesting that I had participated in glorifying the so-called Aryan race by agreeing to Yva's project? Who, though, would have published a black model? Which magazine? None that I knew. Even in the United States, the Negro had no public face. They were lepers, like America's Jews.

******

Germany basked in the glow of the XIth Olympiad. In subsequent press reports, visitors and correspondents praised the hospitality and organization of the games. The German press could not help but crow over the fact that German athletes had won the most medals. When *The New York Times* wrote that the Games put Germans "back in the fold of nations," and even made them "more human again," most other papers agreed. Some even found reason to believe that this amiable interlude would endure. A few reporters, however, were more skeptical. Taking the time to look into the dark recesses of Berlin and other German towns, they found not a glittering brave new world, but a racist and militaristic one. Ironically, while reporters were filing their post-game panegyrics and writing about Germany as a peaceful country, Hitler continued to talk about bringing German-speaking areas of other countries into the Fatherland's orbit. He also spoke of taking over the Olympics forever.

Two weeks after the Olympics ended, the antisemitic banners, flags, and posters returned. Conditions in the country worsened for the Jews, and the demand for forged exit visas and passports increased. Mendel asked me to bring, by means of a circuitous route, Herman Ehrmann, a professor of political science, and his wife, to the villa. His was a sad story, though not an unusual one. Having escaped the torment of teaching in the provinces, where he had been threatened and bullied for being a Jew, he had received from the chancellor of Humboldt University in Berlin a good position in political philosophy. Then the Nazis ordered German universities to make themselves Judenrein. The chancellor summoned Ehrmann and recommended that he disavow his Judaism and convert to Protestantism. Ehrmann refused, and the chancellor said he "would have to take steps." The Ehrmanns, driven from jobs and home, were now on the Nazis blacklist and living in the attic of a sympathetic neighbor. With a chance to teach in America, the Ehrmanns had, through Jewish friends, contacted Mendel Brand to provide the necessary documents that would allow them to flee the country. Mendel needed photos of the two and some background information that would give them new identities. Mendel had put me in charge of passport pictures, with the understanding that I would handle the cameras and Mendel the rest.

Shutting the gate of the villa, I carried in my briefcase the pornographic film, as I often did, lest Gemma find it in my room. Gemma, from her bedroom window, could see a black Mercedes slowly following me. She threw a pink boa around her neck and left the house. Catching up to me, she put her arm through mine and related the danger. "Don't look around. Remember, we've used this ruse before. We are a young married couple." I patted her hand and said:

"Perhaps someday."

"Now's not the time for feathers and flippancy!" she chided.

Glumly, I suggested we walk together for a block or two and then separate. "They won't know which one to follow."

"And if they follow you?" she asked. "Shouldn't you tell me the assignment?"

"What you don't know can't hurt you. A cliché, but true."

"Stop and hug me. Perhaps the car will pass." We stopped and embraced. She whispered. Was it my imagination or had I heard correctly? She had leaned into me, put her head on my shoulder, and said, "Don't let go." Or did she say, "Let's go"? She had not yet fully recovered from the poisoning; she might have unguardedly said the second because she actually felt that way. My spinning head, besotted with young love, suddenly could not distinguish fact from fancy.

The car slowed and stopped. Gemma, at my insistence, went one way and I another. I knew what to do next. Following Mendel's advice, I walked into a Nazi recruiting office. The car slowed and then sped away.

"Ah, so you wish to join the glorious National Socialist Party?" asked the uniformed man behind the desk.

"Pardon me for intruding, but may I use your lavatory?"

The official's upper lip, sporting a mustache like Hitler's, twitched several times. Indignantly, the man declared, "This is a government office, not a public urinal."

Hearing a tram coming, I wheeled and quickly left just in time to board the back of the trolley. I studied the passengers and the street. All clear! A minute or two later, the conductor approached to see my ticket. In no mood to pay, I jumped from the trolley before it could come to a full stop, darted into a café, and ordered a coffee. When I finished, I exited through a back door.

The building and attic in which the Ehrmanns had taken refuge were not hard to find. Before entering the building, I made it a point to circle the block. No one followed. I entered, climbed the steps to the top floor, and gently knocked.

"Yes?"

"Teatime," I said, repeating the password that Mendel told me to use.

Professor Ehrmann opened the door and invited me in. "If it's teatime," said the professor kindly, "I'll put the kettle on." And he did.

Between sips of tea, he told me how he and his wife had come to this sorry pass, where they had to steal out of their country.

"The Gestapo came to campus. First, they spoke to the Chancellor, who gave them a list of the faculty. Then they sought out the Jews. I objected to their interrogation. They merely scoffed. So, I wrote a letter to the Chancellor. I kept a copy. You can read it for yourself."

He went to a cardboard box filled with papers, rummaged through it, and proudly handed me the following letter:

Dear Chancellor Dorfner,

Permit me to bring to your attention a forced visit I had with two Nazis. These men said they were known to you, an admission that I took to mean that you did not object to their questioning me. They wanted to know whether I was an Aryan or a non-Aryan. For reasons of principle I declined to answer. I indicated that the question was relevant neither to my work in political philosophy nor to the tradition of humanistic research nor to the long history of freedom at Humboldt University. I further pointed out that their question was inconsistent with the necessity of the academic community to maintain an atmosphere of free inquiry and the free association of scholars in their unhampered pursuit of truth. Finally, I stated that their question was not in keeping with the spirit and intent of the explicitly formulated principles of the university.

When the two men said that my refusal to answer their question was tantamount to a declaration of my Jewish race, I told them that what they had learned in Nazi police classes was incompatible with what I had learned at Oxford and the Sorbonne. The men said that foreign universities were shit and there was now a new order in Germany.

I scoffed, and one of the men struck me across the face with his glove. Because of my concern, and in the interest of clarity, I am writing to determine where you stand in this matter. If you would be so kind as to tell me, I will make myself available at your convenience.

******

When I looked up, after reading the letter, I saw Mrs. Ehrmann crying. Her husband put an arm around her and assured her that with Mendel Brand's help, they would escape the country. He had even had Eleanor Roosevelt's assurance of safe passage to the United States.

I led the Ehrmanns through back streets and alleys to the villa. But a block from the house, I saw the black Mercedes parked outside the front gate. For a moment I debated whether to turn back or brazenly face the enemy.

"Start coughing," I told the Ehrmanns. "And double over while walking, as though you're in pain. If the men in that black car down the way stop us, I intend to tell them you have tuberculosis. That ought to make them leave immediately."

The Ehrmanns removed handkerchiefs and covered their mouths. I walked ahead. When I drew adjacent to the villa, with the Ehrmanns coughing behind me, two uniformed men exited the car. One of them was Herr Fettsack, Mr. Fatso. They flashed Nazi badges, and the thinner one asked:

"Are you Baruch Rosner?"

"Yes."

"Your mother suggested we have a long talk with you at Nazi headquarters on Friedrichstraße. Your friends, too."

"They are seeking medical attention in the villa. They have TB."

The two Nazis remained unmoved.

"Tuberculosis," I repeated.

"There are worse things," said Herr Fettsack and commanded that they all get in the car. The Ehrmanns stood terrified on the sidewalk, unable to move.

The other policeman took my knapsack. "Was ist das?" he asked and removed the pornographic film that I had tucked away in a side pocket.

Seeing my opportunity, I said in a muffled voice, "It's a racy porn film. I'll give it to you in return for my silence. No one need ever know that defenders of home and hearth, of maidenhood and marriage, watch such smut."

The two Nazis looked at each other. One nodded. Without a further word, they took the film, entered the car, and drove off.

After the Ehrmanns and I entered the villa, Herman asked, "What did they say about your mother?"

For the first time, I realized that I had become the keeper of my mother's reputation.

"My mother," I said ruefully, "is hostage to the Nazis. They use her to get at people like us."

"Us?" said a bewildered Mrs. Ehrmann. "You mean Jews? But aren't you one yourself . . . and your mother?"

Before one of the Ehrmanns could ask me what I meant by "hostage," I said that time was running short and they had better talk to Mendel. Leading them into the basement, I introduced everyone and set up my photographic equipment.

Later, in my room, I sat on the bed and reflected on my mother's behavior. Should I once again be asked, I needed to construct some plausible explanation. I knew the dictionary definition of hostage: a person held or seized until some condition is met. But what other services could my mother possibly render? She had no access to jewels or money. Conversion? The Nazis scorned former Jews. Voluntarily migrate to another country? Then why was the government making it so difficult to leave and expropriating Jewish property? Yes, my mother was a beautiful woman; but a great many Aryan women were equally attractive. My father, if returned to the classroom—an unlikely event—would certainly not recant. What good then was my mother to the Nazis? An escort for Avery Brundage? The authorities could find any number of women to sleep with important men to gain their favor. My grandparents were aged and feckless, so they couldn't figure into the equation.

I, Baruch, had to be the key to the puzzle. But I was just a teenager, temporarily staying in the Rosselli villa. I paused in my ruminations. Information! That had to be it. I had been living at 45 Schlüterstraße, home to numerous artistic and cultured people. The Nazis hated intellectuals; they didn't trust them. My mother had caused the arrest of Klaus Kopf and regarded me as knowledgeable about many of the other tenants. And currently I was living at the Rosselli villa, from which I had left for Switzerland to aid Dr. David Frankfurter. If the villa had been wiretapped . . . No wonder Mendel regularly checked the cellar and Sig. Rosselli's library for bugs. Now I knew why I had been warned never to say anything compromising in the house. The Nazis, I concluded, wanted my mother to induce me to work for the government as an informer. I would poison myself first.

Berlin Revisited

Many hours later, I heard my name being called. I went downstairs, where Mendel instructed me to photograph the Ehrmanns again. He didn't like the first set. Once he studied the new pictures and determined that they had the look of authenticity, he affixed the pictures to the passports, stamped the exit visas, and told me to take the Ehrmanns to a certain location. They now had what they needed to make their way to America: new identities and papers. On the Nazi blacklist for being intellectuals, the Ehrmanns were instructed by Mendel to speak low German and to use colloquialisms.

With Sig. Rosselli's help, they hoped to reach Lisbon. After a hasty goodbye, we left the house by way of the garden, took the footpath to the end of the wall, through a metal gate, which the gardeners entered to maintain the flowers and tend the lawn, and into a small roadway. By way of twists and turns, we arrived at the elevated railway that took us to the U-Bahn Station, Tiergarten, rendezvousing with a garrulous, though not unintelligent, Milanese truck driver, Giovanni Cielo, who had occasionally delivered boxes of shoes for Sig. Rosselli. Often stopping in Switzerland to visit his estranged wife and son in Lugano, he knew the border area and the Italian Lake District as well as a mapmaker. He also knew that the Italian polizia diffidently patrolled this part of the country, with its winding road to Milano.

Years later, when I saw the couple in Colorado, they vividly described their escape. Never having ridden in a truck, they peered through the large front window, leaned back on the elevated bench seat, and elbowed each other contentedly. Cielo, an art lover, began immediately to talk about Masaccio and the infamous order of the Church Fathers directing him to paint over the genitals and breasts in his canvases. He expounded on how little art historians knew about the life of the painter, a man whose work taught others linear perspective and moved the art world from the Gothic to the use of perspective and chiaroscuro to achieve greater realism, a subject that by association led Giovanni Cielo to observe that in the interests of realism the Ehrmanns had better close their eyes and nap, a respite that should have put an end to Giovanni's verbosity, but did not, since he merely inhaled deeply and on a long exhale predicted that before the Ehrmanns reached Milano and the bustle of passengers and vendors and carabinieri to board a Paris-bound train that would, as Mussolini had promised, arrive on time, they would have to take care to purchase tickets immediately and not be late for the train, destined for Bordeaux, known for its Gothic Cathédrale Saint-André and its wine-growing region in southwestern France, a pleasure they would miss as they continued on to Toulouse, famous for Catharism, a Christian heresy that thrived between the 12th and 14th centuries before being ruthlessly suppressed by the Catholic Church, and continue on to Marseille, teeming with immigrants trying to obtain transit visas to cross the border into Spain or to board a boat for a neutral country, like Portugal, precisely the Ehrmanns' plan, where they would take passage in Lisbon to America, docking in New York City, where they would be met by a representative of the Emergency Rescue Committee.

******

Out of breath and panting, I left the telegraph office, where I had heard news of the Ehrmann's safe arrival and ran to the villa. Calling everyone into the garden, now drooping from the chill of November, I announced that the "package had arrived safely."

"Excellent!" said Sig. Rosselli, looking older than his forty-eight years, having acquired deep furrows that ran from the bridge of his nose to the corners of his lips. The tension of manipulating

Nazis and dodging Stalin's agents had not only weathered his face but also slowed his step. He occasionally complained of angina pains and would take a pill to ease the discomfort.

"The bad news," Ugo said, "is that all Jewish passports are now invalid for foreign travel."

It was then that Mendel requested that I deliver a newly forged exit visa to a prominent person. Knowing that I was on the Nazi watch list, Gemma, over the objections of her father, volunteered to act in my stead as the courier. Ugo grumbled but eventually agreed. The visa was for the movie actor and singer Manasse Herbst, who had made a name for himself between 1930 and 1932, participating in 416 sold-out performances in Berlin of the operetta "White Horse Inn." Reputed to be the lover of the famous tennis player Gottfried Alexander Maximilian Walter Kurt Freiherr von Cramm, the German amateur tennis champion who won the French Open twice and was currently ranked number two in the world, Herbst, a Jew, was accused of sexual deviance and interrogated by the Gestapo. Fearing imprisonment, he wanted to flee the country but could not secure the papers to do so. The visa that Mendel forged was in Manasse's name, to be delivered to the von Cramm apartment. Gemma joined Mendel in his basement printing shop and took possession of the envelope with the visa. When Mendel suggested she not carry it in her handbag, he helped her pin it to the inside of her coat jacket.

Von Cramm's apartment was under surveillance because the Gestapo suspected him of being a homosexual. Having lost badly to Fred Perry in the 1936 Wimbledon Championships (6-1, 6-1, 6-0), von Cramm had fallen from the Führer's favor. This information had come from Myra in the Adlon Hotel. I had shared it with Sig. Rosselli, who had then concluded it was too dangerous for Gemma to make "the drop."

Gemma's argument was simple but irrefutable: If I went to von Cramm's apartment, the Nazis would treat it as a sexual rendezvous; but if a woman showed up, they would be less likely to look closely. Myra had told me that the Gestapo had assigned a minder or two to watch von Cramm. With that fact in mind, Gemma dressed alluringly in blue satin, with a cape coat and a pillbox hat, not for von Cramm's sake but for the minders'. Uneasy about her decision, I decided to follow her from a distance—just in case, a decision Sig. Rosselli hardly approved. Lest she see me, I left before her.

Arriving at Dernburgstraße in Charlottenburg, she was not surprised when she found two members of the Gestapo policing the hallway. They lasciviously eyed her.

"I wish to visit Herr von Cramm in apartment number thirty-five," she said, recounting the event to me.

"Empty your purse!"

She opened the snap and instead of turning the bag upside down, she slowly removed each item, with a smile and sway of the hips, reasoning that by the time she arrived at the end, the minders would have lost focus and waved her through. And indeed she was right. Taking the elevator to the third floor, she walked a short distance down a carpeted hallway to von Cramm's apartment. A handsome man, with Aryan features, answered the door, Gottfried. Gemma looked down the hall and saw one of the minders, who had scurried up the stairs. She waved to him.

After she loudly told von Cramm that she had come to interview him for an English newspaper about the upcoming Davis Cup match between Germany and the United States, she said the password for Herbst, "Uffizi."

"I love the paintings on your walls. They remind me of the Uffizi."

Von Cramm scribbled on a pad. "Be wary of what you say. They may be listening." She assumed, not incorrectly, that the apartment was bugged, and that the minder down the hall would position himself so he could hear. In High von Cramm German he remarked:

"My taste runs to the Italian Renaissance."

These words indicated that he understood the point of her visit. Slowly circumnavigating the room, she walked to a corner, away from the windows, and unpinned the envelope, which she handed to von Cramm. He wordlessly moved a painting aside and put the visa in a wall safe. She was afraid that anything she said might be misconstrued, so she decided to engage in inanities. Seating herself in an antique yellow parlor chair, framed in mahogany, she disingenuously said:

"Let's begin with your childhood. I understand you had an English governess."

That statement, she suddenly realized, exhausted all she knew about the man's personal life. Thankfully, he offered her a cup of coffee and filled in the details.

"As a kid, I was always up to mischief. I shot birds with my BB gun and fed the horses pepper."

"You have a reputation for playing beautiful tennis—having seen you I can attest to the accuracy of that point—and never humiliating your opponent."

"Why make an enemy of a fellow tennis player by beating him love and love?"

"That's what Budge did to you at Wimbledon. Do you hold it against him?"

"I like Don, but I couldn't understand his pouring it on. I would have given my opponent a few easy points, just to make the score more respectable."

"I understand you've lost a few matches doing just that."

"True, but better to be a gracious loser than a fierce winner."

She had brought along her own note paper for this moment. She wrote: "Talk some more about your childhood. I've run out of questions to ask."

He nodded and spoke candidly for thirty minutes. Gemma, again loudly, thanked him for his time and his hospitality. Von Cramm opened the door for her and, she noted, watched her hip-swaying exit down the hallway. The same minder as before was standing next to the elevator. "Going down," he said ironically, and to his embarrassment, she replied, "Not with you."

Chapter Twelve

Mr. Fertig no longer asked me if I'd be returning to 45 Schlüterstraße. After two years of splitting time between the apartment house and the villa, the others and I agreed that lodging with the Rosellis was the best idea, particularly since the government had ordered Yva to relinquish her studio to an Aryan. Alfred Simon stepped down as the business manager, and the studio was turned over to Yva's friend, Dr. Charlotte Weidler, an art historian, who allowed Yva and the staff to continue their work on the premises. With Jews banned from many professional occupations, including teaching, accounting, and dentistry, I felt Germany evermore stifling. Even so, I continued my private studies with Mr. Levy and took pleasure in playing chess with Gemma, who intuitively knew when I felt depressed. We often sat and talked in the library and ate at a nearby café. We grew closer, perhaps because I was quickly maturing. She tried to keep up my spirits by assuring me that the constant surveillance I experienced would eventually melt away, like winter snows in spring. I reminded her what the poet Shelley said, "Lift not the painted veil which those who live call life." The closer one looked at the Nazis, the grimmer the picture. Trying to dismiss my sadness, she urged me to continue my work with Yva and the studio and promised me that one sunny day we would travel together to Italy.

PAUL M. LEVITT

Lieber Vater,

Commissions and sales of Yva Simon's fashion photos have diminished, and foreign sales have almost disappeared. Yva thinks the government is selling reproductions of her pictures in other countries. At least a few German magazines still use her work, a consoling thought but not one that will pay the butcher and baker.

I have noticed of late that few of the gentiles in our apartment building seem to notice or care about the military buildup and vile antisemitism in the country. When I asked Mr. and Mrs. Esterhazy, who live across the hall, how they felt about current conditions in Germany, they praised Hitler for restoring order and putting people to work. Mr. Esterhazy even patted his stomach and said, "Full, just the way I like it." His wife added that for them nothing much had changed. They could still go to the movies and bicycle races; they could still attend concerts and cafés; and best of all, they agreed, was that the world once again respected Germany. No more living down the humiliation of Versailles.

If the Esterhazys, who are kind and good-hearted, feel this way, what must the discontented think? I sometimes have the impression I am living in two worlds, one sane, and the other utterly mad. How could we have arrived at such a pass? Perhaps it is for this reason that Mutter tries to keep a foot in both worlds. But always at my back, I hear Isaac Levy quoting the Talmud: "Who can protest, and does not, is an accomplice." I shall never lend myself to the hellfire and hatred.

Alles Liebe,
Baruch

Berlin Revisited

On 12 March 1938, German troops marched into Austria and annexed the country as part of the Third Reich. Between March and November, the Simons moved twice, first to Düsseldorf Strasse 22, then into a house with Yva's sister, Gertrud Gotthelf. On 9-10 November, the Night of Broken Glass (Kristallnacht), the Nazis looted thousands of Jewish shops and businesses in Germany and Austria. Over a thousand synagogues were set on fire. More than thirty thousand Jews were arrested, ninety-one killed. Among the arrested was yours truly, Baruch Rosner.

Sig. Rosselli was out of contact on a business trip to Amsterdam. Gemma, not knowing how to reach my mother, went to the Adlon Hotel and found Myra Huberman. Through her undercover work, she had the means to get a message to Mutter that her son was in jail. A few days later, without any explanation, I was released. I had little time to celebrate with Gemma because someone in Amsterdam had tried to kill Ugo, and he was currently being treated at the city hospital for a stab wound.

******

As Sig. Rosselli later explained, in painful detail, from the moment he had arrived in Amsterdam, he feared that Stalin's agents would make an attempt on his life. He had never told Gemma or others at the villa that he was a member of the International Left Opposition. Formed in 1923, the Left Opposition opposed the growing influence of Stalinism and the Vozhd's belief that socialism could work in Russia without the support of a worldwide revolution. Labeled as Trotskyists, because Trotsky was the de facto leader, the members of the movement were expelled from the Soviet Communist party (CSPU) in 1927 and forced to leave the Soviet Union. Shortly thereafter, the International Left Opposition was created.

Always paranoid, Stalin sent agents around the globe to assassinate members of the International. Sig. Rosselli said that he had used his business connections to travel throughout Europe to distribute Left Opposition propaganda. In the Netherlands, his first stop was an art gallery, "The Palette," that had nothing to do with politics. Ugo made it a point of promoting Yva Simon's work wherever he traveled. Amsterdam was no different. At the gallery, he talked to the proprietor about Yva Simon and showed him examples of her photographs.

"How do I know they come from the original negatives?"

Ugo looked around the gallery. Every inch of wall space seemed to be taken, but most of the contemporary collection was in the neo-Nazi classical, superman genre.

Ugo removed from his black leather attaché case a thin portfolio that held five of Yva's most striking works. He spread them out on a viewing table, stepped back, and invited the owner to admire them.

"But I have to know whether they're photographic copies or prints from the original negatives."

"Just look," he said, as he held up a picture. "No liquid looking surfaces. Nothing bent. The background objects are straight, not in the least warped. No distortions anywhere. And note the light and shadows, perfect!"

"You're an admirable salesman. Let me see everything you brought."

Fifteen minutes later, Ugo left the shop with a check made out to Yva Simon. He chuckled as he thought of the proprietor saying he would be selling reproductions to newspaper stands and gift shops, the type of transaction the gallery itself wished to prevent. Ugo's next stop was a houseboat on the Prinsengracht Canal, not to sell photographs, but to engage in politics. A cold wind rudely barreled down the boulevard, and he pulled up the collar of his overcoat.

As he strode the cobblestone streets, he periodically paused and listened. Although he felt certain that his footsteps were being tracked by another, he could see nothing out of the ordinary, only berthed houseboats and, at the end of the canal, an idling motorboat. His destination, the houseboat bearing the name October, was chained to the canal wall and kept from chafing by some fenders of old car tires. It wanted paint. The original red and gold colors had either faded or flaked. On reaching the ramp that led from the road to the October, he gripped the rope handrail and descended to the deck, where he was met by Comrade Visser, the owner, who warmly embraced him and said:

"The others have arrived."

Ducking his head to enter the cabin, Sig. Rosselli saw three men in workers' caps seated at a table. They introduced themselves as Comrades Jansen, Bakker, and Smit. In their thirties, the men's weather-beaten faces made them look years older. Their leather jackets, patched at the elbow, their ragged sweaters and calloused hands testified to their manual labors.

Taking his seat among the men, Sig. Rosselli said, "It's best to pull the shades. Anyone on the street can see into this room."

Once the shades were drawn, Sig. Rosselli opened his black attaché case and removed pamphlets, fliers, and letters, which he distributed among the men. "The recruiting material," he explained, "was printed in Paris."

Comrade Bakker snickered. "The wealthy émigrés who pay to have this stuff printed are the very ones a revolution would eliminate."

"Stalin's word, 'eliminate,'" said Comrade Smit, who had been sucking on a pipe stem. "People aren't murdered or assassinated; they are eliminated."

Comrade Visser, standing at the door of the cabin, remarked that the immediate danger was not the bourgeoisie but the fascists. "We have them right here in Amsterdam, men who would use any means to ingratiate themselves with the Nazis and capitalize on antisemitism."

"All the more reason," said Ugo, "to press our socialist cause."

Comrade Smit, who had not spoken, cleared his throat, which sounded to Ugo like a sputtering boat propeller, and remarked, "The Dutch authorities think they're immune to Hitler. Fools!" The word "fools" undoubtedly whistled on his breath.

"They say Stalin is worse," said the man sucking the pipe stem.

Comrade Visser slapped his forehead and exclaimed, "Ugo, I haven't even mentioned our new member, Comrade Aal, who will be along shortly. His wife's been ill. At that moment a single shot tore through one of the houseboat windows, on the canal side. Comrade Bakker slumped, and a red spot sprouted like a bloom on the back of his head. "Get down!" cried Comrade Visser, and the men scrambled underneath the table. But no further shots came from the water. Looking out the back window of his houseboat, Comrade Visser could see a motorboat speeding away down the canal. "They must have pulled alongside and shot at point-blank range."

"The bullet was meant for me," said Ugo. "Had the shades been up, I'd probably be dead."

"How do you know?" asked Comrade Smit, trying to stanch the blood issuing from Comrade Bakker's head.

"It's not the first time," replied Ugo.

Berlin Revisited

"I'll call the hospital at once," said Comrade Visser.

Ugo took that statement as his exit line, leaving behind his written material, heading out the door, and striding up the ramp. On the cobblestone street, he was immediately greeted by a man who asked for directions.

"Scusi, signore, conoscere il distretto a luci rosse?"

The fact that the man addressed him in Italian should have made Ugo immediately wary. How did the man know Ugo was Italian? But without thinking, Ugo started to respond and pointed toward the red-light district. At that moment the man plunged a knife into Ugo's chest and fled. Ugo could vaguely remember hearing sirens and being wheeled into the emergency room, where a bright light floated overhead. Lying next to him on a hospital gurney was Comrade Bakker, whose wife arrived just in time to hear the doctor pronounce her husband dead. Then everything went dark.

Recovering in the intensive care unit, Ugo said his mind wandered. He remembered, though not clearly, October 1922 and the Marcia su Roma, Mussolini's march on Rome. It had begun as a planned mass demonstration and insurrection to take place on 28 October 1922. Ugo Rosselli was then thirty-one years old, from a working-class family. His father, a tanner, warned him to stay clear of the Mussolini demonstrations, particularly since Ugo was a Democratic Socialist. "So was Mussolini once," replied Ugo. "Yes, but not anymore," said his father. "He's now a fierce nationalist." When the fascist Blackshirts entered Rome, even the revisionist Zionists joined them, thinking of the paradise to come. Prime Minister Luigi Facta's wish to declare a state of siege was overruled by the king. The next day, 29 October 1922, King Victor Emmanuel III appointed Mussolini as Prime Minister, thereby averting armed conflict and transferring political power to the fascists in the Kingdom of Italy.

To escape deportation to Sicily and internment, Ugo fled Rome in late 1922 and found his way to the Soviet Union, where he joined the party of Lenin. While working to radicalize those in the Russian-Italian community, he met Laura Brancati. She had attended one of Ugo's propaganda sessions, introducing herself afterwards as the daughter of Roman émigrés fleeing Italian fascism. A marvelous cook, she could seemingly conjure a meal out of scraps. During a time of famine, Ugo had brought her and her family, spices and condiments cadged from the local Soviet. Whether it was owing to his wiliness or winsomeness, Laura took a liking to him, and shortly afterwards they became lovers. As he lay in bed remembering, he could smell the cooking. His recall of scents was greater than his visual memories, and he thought of the stinging taste of oregano, basil mixed with oil, garlic, and tomatoes; the flavoring of parsley, tonic rosemary, sacred thyme, and the queen of spices, sage. How could anyone forget? Nor could he forget their first real date, at a tributary of the River Don. They bailed a rowboat for an outing on the water, and then paddled to an island in the middle, by which time the boat was again taking on water. Stopping, they bailed some more, laughed, and spent an hour lying in the grass and exchanging real and made-up stories about their lives. For are we not, after all, a creation of our own making? She wished to be known as a stalwart defender of women's rights, and he, an indefatigable voice for the right of workers to share in the profits of their labors. And so, like us all, they mythologized themselves into the persons they wished to be, and perhaps, in fact, were.

In the months and weeks ahead, they conducted dangerous missions together and, as much from necessity as love, became as close as the fingers in a fist. Each depended on the other, not only for safety, but also for emotional sustenance. They married. After Lenin's death in 1924, Ugo fell in with those loyal to Trotsky; she joined with Stalin and the Right Opposition. But her impatience for revolution now, and his willingness to wait for Europe to erupt and carry Russia with it, became more than an ideological difference; it grew into a factional fight. They thought that by adopting a child, parenting would assuage their differences. Good Bolsheviks were expected to adopt homeless children. The orphanage in Voronezh to which they were directed had already placed the youngest children. Older children were harder to place. The director recommended a seven-year-old girl, Gemma Bronshtein, who from the first seemed to prefer her father, although father and daughter often had to communicate with looks and gestures until she quickly learned Italian. Giving her the family name Rosselli, her parents wished to erase her former life and begin anew. Her mother wanted her to be steely; her father preferred to see her evolve, slowly becoming the flower rooted in her genes. Her mother, less patient, gladly let a sympathetic Ugo teach her Italian verbs and listen to her bedtime fears. Laura soon realized that she lacked the patience to be a good mother and much preferred the more exciting life of a revolutionary. Ugo, on the other hand, relished the role of a father.

They hoped to bridge their differences by consulting a priest, Father Lorenzo, who was sympathetic to Italian emigres, and who advised, in defiance of church doctrine, that it was better for the couple to part than to feud. A priest trained to speak Russian and understand Greek Orthodoxy, Father Lorenzo had graduated from the Russicum in Rome, a school devoted to training young men to travel abroad and convert Catholics of the Greek or Russian belief to the Roman persuasion, and to bring Bolsheviks into the western fold. Father Lorenzo genuinely believed in his mission: to save the Italian-Russian community from eastern Catholicism and atheistic Bolshevism. When he had first counseled prayer to heal the couple's divisions, Laura had ruffled his feathers by asking him how long it took for orisons to reach the Divine Presence. Father Lorenzo had replied that the Lord was ever-present. "Even," she asked, "when he is 180 million light years away?" Perhaps for this reason, Father Lorenzo had concluded that divorce was no sin.

The decision to part found the couple in agreement about child custody, particularly since Laura had been diagnosed with consumption. Taking Gemma aside, Ugo explained that for precautionary reasons he and Laura had to separate. Unless she objected, she would go with him. Not surprisingly she happily agreed. Ugo remembered the parting well. Laura had accompanied him and Gemma to the station. He and the child boarded the train. Just as it started to move, Laura reached up to give Gemma a final hug. Ugo held one arm of the child, and Laura the other. For a moment it looked as if neither would release her; but at the last second, Laura relinquished her grip and Gemma now belonged to Ugo, who could see tears running down Laura's cheeks.

Father and daughter had packed their few belongings in two battered leather valises. They traveled second class, on wooden benches, north to Finland, then to Lithuania, and at last, in December of 1924, he and the seven-year-old Gemma landed in Bremen. They arrived destitute and lived on the street, begging for handouts, until Ugo's father could send him a money order. The humiliation of that experience led Ugo to decide to use his father's contacts and metamorphose from a revolutionary into a merchant of shoes. He rationalized the decision by telling himself that with the money he earned, he would fund European socialists and those left-wing groups opposing Hitler. Thus was born Ugo Rosselli, businessman and footwear distributor to the German high command.

His influence among the party faithful enabled him to acquire his villa, albeit illegally, after having lived in two rooms at the Schlüterstraße address. The Nazis had given the owners, a Jewish family, notice that the property was to be requisitioned. Ugo had conducted business with the man of the house, who agreed to transfer ownership to Ugo for exit visas and passports to allow his family to leave for the United States, where they had cousins. Instead of relying on forgeries, Ugo implored his friends on Friedrichstraße to issue the real thing in return for regular deliveries of soft leather Italian shoes. The Jewish family put the house deed in Ugo's name and left, with the hope that someday they would return to reclaim their property. Thinking he would live like a gentleman, puffing on his pipe in the library, he found that he missed the hubbub of the apartment house. As a result, the house had remained virtually empty, except for a trusted housekeeper and the clandestine activities taking place in the basement. Not long after Gemma's poisoning, when he felt she needed the quiet and greenery of the villa, he asked me to join Gemma and him to enliven the company.

Chapter Thirteen

Upon hearing the news of her father's stabbing, Gemma told no one, grabbed her passport, and hailed a cab for the train. She wished Baruch could have accompanied her to Amsterdam, but, as she told him later, she consoled herself with the knowledge that it was more important for him to continue working with Mendel Brand. From the station, she went directly to the hospital. On the way there, the talkative, multi-lingual cab driver spoke darkly about an attempted murder in the city, without his knowing that he was transporting in his taxi the intended victim's daughter.

"Rumors. Lots of them. They say a Bolshi tried to kill an Italian national. Those Reds are always causing trouble. Germany once had that problem, but not anymore, thanks to Hitler."

A perturbed Gemma gave the driver a smaller tip than she had first intended.

In the hospital, she was directed to the third floor. Exiting the elevator, she walked down a long hall, past several open doors, in which patients and family huddled at bedsides. A police guard was stationed outside her father's room. She identified herself and went to Ugo's bedside. Shocked to see her father's state, swathed, as he was, in bandages, she asked if any vital arteries had been severed. No, but the knife had just barely missed the aorta. His nurses said that underneath the bandages, the stitches ran from sternum to bellybutton, causing him to look as if he were wearing a zippered garment. His breath came in spurts, and his smile hardly registered owing to his sunken cheeks. After closing the door, Gemma told her father of the villa's successes, recounting all their skullduggery. Her enthusiasm was interrupted by a nurse entering and carrying a floral display, which she put on a table next to Ugo's bed. After the nurse left, Ugo read the card.

"We know where you are. You will never leave Amsterdam alive. Our agents are everywhere."

Ugo laughed, but his attempt to pass it off as a joke did not succeed. Gemma took his hand and said softly, "Given your condition, it's time you told me everything."

Sig. Rosselli, never having told his daughter about his work in the Trotskyist movement, was at a loss for words as she sat at his bedside. He assumed from her request that she was privy to medical information about his physical state that he lacked. "First, you tell me what you know."

Actually, she knew very little, just that her father's heart was holding up well under the stress, and that the hospital, which had a well-known cardiac unit, had taken immediate steps to prevent a coronary episode.

The facts were that Ugo, stabbed in the chest, had ironically escaped death because the knife, aimed for the heart, was deflected by a small hardcover book in his breast pocket, *The Communist Manifesto*. A sympathetic ambulance attendant had had the good sense to remove it, though Ugo was ignorant of that fact. He did, however, ask his daughter if his bloody shirt remained in the room. No. Would she be so kind as to inquire about it? She went to the nurses' station, where she was told that the shirt had been laundered and, judged to be unwearable, made into rags. The nurse, exhibiting a sly wit, said their hospital now had the only silk rags in Amsterdam. Guessing that her father might have had something in the breast pocket besides the book, she asked, but the nurse said that the shirt came to them, and here she punned, "bloody clean."

Back in the room, Gemma thought her father's mind was wandering when he said, "Lev Sedov was assassinated in February. How many others since? And now me."

"Papa, I don't understand. Please, explain."

Ugo stared at the ceiling and mechanically confessed to his membership in the Left Opposition. His work as a Trotskyist was to deliver messages from the movement to fellow travelers in Germany and nearby countries. "Stalin," he said, "is determined to wipe out all opposition. He'll go to any lengths. He's undoubtedly behind the death of Trotsky's son, Lev Sedov."

After Ugo explained the philosophical basis of the movement, he expected his daughter to inundate him with a flood of questions, but she said nothing. A minute or two later, she excused herself, saying she needed time to think.

On the sidewalk, she had the impression that she was being trailed. To be sure she wasn't imagining dangers, she wandered in and out of shops until she found herself at the Prinsengracht canal, the very location of her father's stabbing. A kiosk selling magazines, newspapers, tobacco, postcards, and stamps caught her attention. A sign read: German and English spoken here. Across the front of the kiosk, photographs of street scenes and stylish women hung from clothespins and strings. One of the photographs had been taken by Yva Simon: "Woman in Shadows." The picture, a copy, admittedly a good done, meant that someone was bootlegging Yva's pictures out of Berlin for sale in other countries. Reaching up and removing the photograph from the clothespin that held it to the string, she asked the tradesman where it came from.

"Turn it over," he said. "You'll see it's an original from Germany."

Looking at the back of the picture, Gemma said, "That's what it claims, but the picture is a copy of one hanging in Berlin. I even know the owner, my father."

Caught off guard this way, the tradesman could only stutter that he was just a poor vendor and that his artwork came from a Dutch art gallery, "The Palette." Gemma bought the picture and stood along the canal studying it. Glancing across the canal, she could see in the sunlit window of a barge parked along the opposite bank the reflection of a man coming up quickly behind her. His arms were raised as if he intended to push her into the water. But he was suddenly shoved into the canal by another man who seemingly materialized out of nowhere. Calmly walking to a post supporting a buoy, Gemma's savior threw the miscreant a life saver and helped him out of the canal. Her would-be assailant stood shivering in the cold, held firmly by her protector, who identified himself as special agent Geert Bos, assigned to her father's case. He spoke German fluently.

"While I keep an eye on this poor excuse for an assassin, alert the police. There's a call box just down the way. The telephone operators speak German."

"Who is he?" she asked.

"A Stalinist."

When the police arrived, Geert took a card from his wallet and took them aside. After a few private words, they put the scruffy man in a van and drove off.

Gemma tripped over her words as she excitedly inquired, "Where did you come from . . . how did you know . . . ?"

"I was at the hospital and saw you leave. I followed, and it's well I did. Come, let's have a hot chocolate. The wind has picked up, and you've had a frightening experience."

They walked a short distance along the canal to a café. Inside, floor heaters took the chill from the air. Geert suggested they sit at a table in the back, lest someone be tempted to take a shot at them through the front window. He removed his peaked hat and leaned back in his chair. She studied his face, feeling an understandable attraction to him. Besides having protected her, he looked the part. Except for acne-scarred cheeks, masked by a day-old beard, he had Aryan good looks: blonde and blue-eyed, with high cheek bones, and a square jaw. His smile revealed a perfect set of teeth, a rarity in these hard times. The one incongruity that she wondered about was his long locks, which fell carelessly over his forehead and ears. Most policemen, like the ones who drove off with her would-be assailant, had cropped haircuts. She'd have to ask him about it, but not until she got to know him better, a hoped-for eventuality.

"Who," she asked, "assigned you to my father's case?"

"Security."

Although she wished to dispel the vagueness of his answer, she chose to drop the subject. She could always return to it later. A rush of self-consciousness reddened her cheeks. Like a naïf, she wondered whether this was the man of her dreams. Then she told herself to act her age, and at the very least feign maturity. She cleared her throat and began again.

"You live in Amsterdam?"

"In the poorer part . . . for all of my thirty years."

"Married?"

"No, divorced."

She thought: How could such an attractive man not make his marriage work? What were the defects she couldn't see? Another subject for a later date.

"And you?" he asked.

She wondered what to tell him. In these troubled times, silence was safer than words. Lest she appear impolite she replied innocuously:

"I help my father and hope to attend university in the fall."

"A young woman as pretty as you must have innumerable suitors."

"No."

"Then I'll play that role."

She felt a charge of electricity run through her body, gulped, smiled, and thanked him. "For now, I'd just like to see some of the famous sights in Amsterdam."

"Finish your chocolate, and we'll brave the cold."

Stepping out of the café, they started down Prinsengracht, and then paused at a store selling pectin and spices. Through the front window, they could see a number of women seated in folding chairs and listening to a man presumably pitching his product. Out of curiosity, they entered the store and sat. Geert translated. The man's name was Otto Frank and he was selling Opekta, a gelling agent for making homemade jam. The women were housewives, who eagerly asked questions and just as eagerly bought the product. Gemma likewise purchased a jar, saying that with the coming of winter she could make jam from the fruits collected in her garden.

To Geert's surprise, she asked to see the red-light district. "I've heard the area is famous."

"It's called De Wallen," he said, "because many years ago it was walled off from the rest of the city. It also houses the Oude Kerk, the Old Church, as well as window brothels, cafés, restaurants, and normal living quarters. But I would stay clear of the quarter for the rest of the day. The fascists plan to rally outside the Old Church, and things could get nasty."

"It all sounds deliciously dangerous," she replied in girlish fashion, "take me." Actually, she felt the information might prove useful to Mendel Brand and the resistance group her father headed. "Know your enemy," her father often repeated.

As they entered the neighborhood, she wondered aloud why the women sat behind windows with the curtains almost closed.

Geert explained that the prostitutes, called street daisies, used to stand in doorways and lure clients into the house. The police forbade that practice but allowed the women to sit in windows.

"To shop their wares," she remarked.

"You might say that."

A gathering crowd made Geert obviously nervous. She put an arm through his. He tried to dissuade her from staying and tried to lead her away from the crowd.

"At least let me see the church," she said, as she pulled free and made her way to the Oude Kerk. Inside, she was awed by its vastness. Originally built as a Catholic cathedral, it had become a Calvinist church after the Reformation in the sixteenth century. She read from a plaque that the roof was the largest medieval wooden vault in Europe. A small group of singers, surrounding the altar, were singing a Bach motet. Gemma had never heard such fine acoustics. She stood frozen, listening.

Geert commented that the church was reputed to have the best acoustics in Europe.

"Perhaps," he said, "that explained why Rembrandt and family regularly visited the church. His wife is buried here."

Only then did she realize that the stone floor held the tombs of innumerable Dutch dignitaries. From outside the church came the sounds of a crowd. She started for the door.

"If you'll translate, I want to hear what nonsense the Dutch fascists are spouting." When Geert tried to object, she promised, "Just five minutes."

He looked at his watch. "Five minutes."

As they exited, a torchlight parade turned the corner heading for the Old Church. The marchers, mostly young men, were boisterous but small in number, which suggested to Gemma that the danger was slight. She and Geert scooted off the porch and took up a position to the side. Geert pulled his hat down, making it difficult to see his face. A pale, flabby, rotund man strode to the front of the church and identified himself as Rudolf Frumpel. He wore a black overcoat that reached to his shoes. Unprepossessing as he was, with cheeks roughened and reddened from the elements, he held the crowd's attention as he bellowed about the purity of women and race, decrying the brothels in the square and those who frequented them, especially Jews.

"Our view of racial purity and its genetic basis," he shouted, "comes not from science, but from our political convictions that National Socialism will cleanse the world of the whore and the hunchback." His minions roared their approval. "To build a healthy state, with fit people, we must make racial thinking the center of our National Socialist worldview and see the world as a process of constructing and renewing the Dutch nation by nurturing its Aryan roots."

The mob began chanting, "Aryan purity, Aryan purity!"

"My fellow countrymen, to save the beloved homeland, we must do three things: We must increase the birth rate, but not with the spawn of whores; we must deracinate the sick and get rid of unfit genes in our people; and we must cease the mixing of Dutch blood with that of lesser humans, namely, Jews."

A counter demonstrator held up a pole holding a picture of the Virgin Mary and the child Jesus. He yelled, "Do not yet again crucify Christ."

"To our Christian critics, we say: Continue to concern yourselves with the view that your kingdom is of another world, and leave us to build the kingdom of this one. To those who call our racial policy 'unchristian' and say that we are sinning against the will of God, we reply that we are doing the Creator's work when we prevent the propagation of unhealthy life and keep children from immeasurable misery."

Cries of "Yes! Yes!"

The protester started loudly singing Christian hymns, which inflamed the fascists all the more. Surrounding him and ripping from his hands the depiction of Mother and Child, they crushed the picture underfoot.

The speaker seemed not to notice. "Therefore, if we believe in Dutch purity, the whores and the hunchbacks must go. By ignoring the most valuable genetic elements in our people and spending millions on care for the inferior, we are squandering our wealth on the eugenically ill at the expense of the healthy and hardy."

The amen corner yelled its assent. "Root out the weak!" cried someone in the crowd, and others chanted in agreement.

"To the party faithful, I say: Only when our population swells with Aryan youth will we be able to look forward to a future of military strength, freedom, and honor, for all time."

A paroxysm of madness seemed suddenly to affect him as he pointed his puffy fingers toward the brothels. His face glowed a bright red as he expostulated, "Those vile cesspools of misbegotten genes deserve nothing less than the torch, and the whores immediate sterilization. Believe me, the Netherlands can be great again, populated with superior people, but only when the pimps and prostitutes have been driven from our midst. Exterminated!"

A voice in the crowd croaked, "You fat hypocrite, you are the worst whoremaster of all." A dangerous growl ran through the ranks of the fascist faithful. "We've seen you coming and going from the brothels numerous times," added the hoarse protester. But it was the last time he spoke, because several men jumped him and beat him to the ground.

Although police skirted the crowd, no one came to the man's aid. Then Mijnheer Frumpel left the speaker's stand and strode up to one of the brothels. He carried a baton that he produced from inside his overcoat. At the front window of the house he struck it with the stick and cracked the glass. Calling to the girls inside to come out, he stood with his legs astride and his arms folded across his chest. But no one exited the house. It was then that Gemma left Geert's side, pushed through the mob, and confronted the agent provocateur.

"By what right," she asked in German, "do you command these girls? By what moral right do you set yourself above them? You are nothing but a bully, an obese pest."

Mijnheer Frumpel must have understood, because whether offended by her defense of the girls or by the mention of his weight, or for some other reason, he struck her on the forehead with his baton, drawing blood. An incited Geert flung him to the ground. Before Mijnheer Frumpel's bodyguards could react, the police patrolling the rally arrived and led the fat fascist to a police van, which whisked him away, preventing the crowd from organizing themselves to keep the vehicle from leaving. Geert sat with Gemma in the front seat, holding a handkerchief to her forehead. Mijnheer Frumpel kneeled in the wire cage at the back, vociferating that when the National Socialists came to power, the injustice done him would be avenged.

******

After a nurse dressed Gemma's flesh wound, Geert accompanied her to the hospital to see her father. But for some reason, he stopped short of the room on seeing a policeman at Ugo's door. When she asked him why he didn't join her, he mysteriously said, "Later."

Gemma entered the room by herself and told her father the whole story. On learning the details of her misadventure, he expressed his disapproval of her wandering around Amsterdam alone, and his dismay at the treatment she received.

"No more political activities for you," he said.

She nodded in agreement.

"I fear that you have been targeted because of my political affiliations."

She tried to diminish the seriousness of the situation by remarking, "At least no one tried to poison me."

After sitting with her father for a few minutes, she said that someone was waiting for her.

"And who might that be?

"The man who saved me at the canal."

"Invite him in. I'd like to meet him—and thank him."

But when she went to the door, except for the policeman standing guard, the hospital corridor stood empty. "That's strange," she murmured, and returned to her father's bedside.

"Well?" asked her father.

"He must have gone downstairs." Not knowing what else to say, she lied. "He's shy."

"Some other time, then," said her father, and gave her leave to meet her friend.

Taking aside the policeman at the door, she asked if he knew a Geert Bos? "He was assigned to my father's case."

"Never heard of him," replied the policeman, and said that she could check with headquarters. "Here, let me give you a name and a number." He took a small pad from his breast pocket and jotted down the information. She thanked him and left.

In the main lobby, she found Geert sitting by himself and thumbing through a magazine. "I have to make a call," she said.

He looked uneasy and expressed surprise that she knew anyone in the city.

"It's for my father."

She entered a telephone booth just off the lobby. Dialing the number given to her, she asked for Police Detective Swart. A moment later, Geert appeared behind her, took the phone from her hand, and returned it to the cradle. A tongue-tied Gemma fumbled for an explanation.

"What . . . how rude . . . why . . . who are you?"

"A secret agent, assigned to undercover work."

She couldn't decide whether to laugh or to cry for help. "I don't believe you," she said. "Let's just go to police headquarters and inquire."

"I had better explain," he said earnestly. "You and your father have been targeted by the Stalinists for assassination. I've been assigned to protect you."

"By whom?"

"Can we save that information for another time?"

"No!"

"To prove that I'm here for your protection, I'll see you and your father safely back to Germany. Is that fair?"

A conflicted Gemma weighed his secretiveness against his preventing her from being shoved into the canal, and his attacking Mijnheer Frumpel in her defense. "Do you anticipate our having difficulty returning to Berlin?"

"We live in perilous times. Who knows?"

"But that's true for you as well."

"I have friends, and you do not."

Gemma found this response all the more perplexing. Perhaps the only way to dispel her skepticism was to let him guide them back to Germany. In the meantime, while waiting on her father's recovery, and bearing in mind his admonition, she would stay away from politics and have Geert chaperone her through the city. But she neglected to take into account the romantic effect that such proximity would purchase. With each passing day and each new attraction, she grew more attracted to Geert. A pretty young girl and a handsome man stopping at every alluring café, cruising the canals, strolling in Vondelpark, visiting the Rijksmuseum and Heritage museum, strolling hand in hand through the Royal Palace, touring the fishing villages of Volendam and Marken, admiring the Zaanse Schans Windmills, eating at a traditional cheese farm, and standing in the Rembrandt house when the sunlit windows cast a golden glow—how could it not result in Gemma being irresistibly drawn to her guide and telling herself that she was utterly and devotedly in love with Geert Bos?

Chapter Fourteen

After Ugo felt strong enough, Gemma took him home. With Geert smoothing the way, they had no trouble at the borders. Sig. Rosselli invited him to lodge at the villa, an offer that the latter asked to defer because he already had accommodations in Berlin, and prior commitments. Gemma wondered whom he would be seeing. After all, he had only recently decided to accompany them back to Berlin. She found the words "prior commitments" disquieting, though she wasn't sure why.

******

The reunion between Gemma and me led to hugs and confessions. I told her that my mother had suddenly disappeared and that Mr. Fertig wanted to adopt me; and she, after listening to me, related everything that had happened to her, including her fondness for Geert, whom I found quite likeable, notwithstanding my jealousy. Later, Mendel materialized and brought us up to date on pending antisemitic legislation.

"Under the new laws, Jews would have to register all their wealth and property, and Jewish doctors and lawyers would be forbidden to practice. They want to require Jews over age fifteen to apply for identity cards to be shown on demand to any police officer." Putting a hand to his mouth, he pensively stared into space. The others waited for him to speak, sensing that even more dire information would be forthcoming. "They want to close or torch the synagogues. They want all Jewish women to add "Sarah," and all men to add "Israel," to their names on legal documents, including passports, which also have to be stamped with a large red "J." They want all Jewish children secretly attending public schools expelled. And by year's end, they want all Jewish businesses to be owned by Aryans."

I always marveled at Mendel's sources of information, which enabled him to remain one step ahead of the official announcements. Having seen little of Mendel since Sig. Rosselli's departure for Amsterdam, I felt that the "old team" was again coalescing. The forgery operation had come to a virtual halt, waiting on Ugo's return. To dispel my loneliness, I had returned to Mr. Fertig's flat. As conditions daily worsened for Jews, Walter had repeated that he would like to adopt me. He said that if I changed my names, suggesting Hans Fertig, I would be less conspicuous. The name Baruch Rosner made me an easy target. But in deference to my father,

I resisted this generous offer. Mr. Fertig explained that his had been a sorrowful life, having lost a wife in the 1918 worldwide flu epidemic.

"At the time of her death, she was pregnant. After the tormenting fever and chills, I thought she'd survive. Oh, Baruch, how I prayed for her! When she died, I swore that I would never pray again and would do all I could to help needy children. I started my book collection for the neighborhood youngsters. They would come to me and ask whether I had certain books. I distributed them freely. If I didn't have the ones they wanted, they could browse through my collection and pick another."

Gemma suddenly asked, "Any news about Yva Simon?"

"I have told both Yva and Alfred that I can secure them exit visas. And though I would miss them terribly, I wake each day hoping that they will pack up and leave the country."

"What did they say?"

"Yva has, in fact, received several offers, from England and the United States. But Alfred thinks that life outside of the German cultural sphere would be ruinous, and that the best instincts of the German people will eventually prevail. So they remain. I can't understand why Yva listens to him. How can they fail to notice that their circle of friends and acquaintances continually shrinks, and that the staff members are seeking employment elsewhere?"

"The train has already left the station," said Mendel. "The gate is down."

Noting the consternation of Gemma and Ugo, as well as Geert's perplexity, I tried to change the subject, "You haven't told me about Amsterdam. I understand it's a beautiful city."

It was then that Mendel and I learned the details of Ugo's near-death experience, and of Gemma's rescue by Geert. Wishing to

Berlin Revisited

downplay the events, Sig. Rosselli suggested we continue our conversation in a nearby Greek restaurant, notable for its hospitality and good food, to say nothing of the soft musical background. Once seated, we all tried to ignore the ugly and dwell on the positive. But the moussaka, seared red mullet, Stamatis, and filo triangles, known as spanakopita, with spinach, feta cheese, and mushrooms, accompanied by Agiorgitiko wine could not dispel our concerns. Life intervenes. Facts matter. The Nazis were increasing border patrols, learning to detect bogus stamps and paper for passports and exit visas, offering rewards for the capture of forgers, and not least using Jewish collaborators to identify "enemies of the state." Throughout the dinner, as we shared our fears for the future, Geert remained strangely silent. Was he ill? No. He said he was thinking about his prior commitments, a statement that for some reason caused Gemma to flush. On the way back to the villa, she and Geert walked arm in arm, whispering, while I comforted myself with memories of Gabriella.

At the villa, after some schnapps, Geert departed.

******

I could feel the weight of Geert's absence on Gemma. His infrequent telephone calls merely intensified her wish to see him. Absence indeed makes the heart grow fonder. How well I knew the feeling. Not having once heard from my father, I had replaced letters with imagined discussions, which usually took place as I lay in bed. Tonight was no different.

Lieber Vater,

I cannot deny the fact that Gemma loves Geert Bos, but he seems not to care. Although he occasionally telephones, the calls are abbreviated. Hardly a day passes that Gemma doesn't confide in me and share her concerns. Where is he, she asks? The days become weeks, the weeks, months, and the months soon add up. But to what: a year, a furlough, an escape, an end of a young girl's fantasies? She shows admirable restraint, neither imploring him to see her nor seeking his place of residence. I have offered to help, but since she knows my own feelings about her, I think she tries her best to minimize my involvement. Being her confessor is one thing; riding out to find the dragon is another.

It pains me to love someone whose affections have a different person in mind. Is that how you felt about Mutter before you left? I am just beginning to understand what it's like to suffer from longing. Sometimes I think it would be better to leave than to stay and hope that Gemma's feelings for Geert will eventually fade. But he has become an unquiet ghost who haunts her, and when I consider how much pleasure I take in her friendship, I know that leaving will only intensify my longing and make her presence all the more needful.

Never having spoken to her father about her feelings for Geert, I wonder if now isn't the time to do so, although I suspect that he disapproves of an older man courting his beloved daughter. Surely, he can see that she is showing signs of depression.

Alles Liebe,
Baruch

******

As 1941 dawned, Geert's calls came to an end, and with Germany seizing Czechoslovakia and then invading Poland and the Netherlands, Gemma feared he might have died in the fighting. With each passing day, she grew more worried. Finally, she asked me to approach her father for help finding Geert, without mentioning her. As requested, I spoke to Sig. Rosselli and asked him to keep the undertaking just between us, so as not to upset Gemma. I said that the wish to find Geert Bos originated with me. Initially, Ugo hemmed and hawed, questioning my motives, and only after convincing himself of my sincerity did he agree to make inquiries among his Nazi contacts, whom Gemma rightly hazarded made it their business to know everyone else's.

"And those they don't know," she had said, "they are looking for now as we speak."

During this period, which witnessed the defection of so many of Yva's crew, Gemma and I had to assume most of the technical responsibilities. As the studio languished, Dr. Charlotte Weidler soldiered on the best that she could, and although models still showed up, mostly Jewish ones seeking work, the omens were not good. The Nazis wanted Jews to emigrate and relinquish all their valuables before leaving the country. To prevent penury, Jews tried to leave illegally with some of their wealth, including gold and silver items. Those who insisted on remaining in Berlin were forbidden rights as tenants and were relocated into Jewish houses. Henceforth, no German Jew could hold a government job. With the fall of Czechoslovakia and Poland, Great Britain and France had declared war on Germany and World War II had begun.

Given the confiscatory laws and the worsening international situation, the demand for forged passports and exit visas soared. For all his enterprise, Mendel, who had managed to imitate a die for Nazi stamps and to locate the paper he needed for passports and visas, found himself overwhelmed. I tried to help, using Yva's former studio for the work. I had just enough technical knowledge and familiarity with the equipment that I could prepare the documents on which Mendel would put the finishing touches. Fortunately, the studio was not far from the villa; but even so, Gemma and I had to take every precaution not to be stopped while transporting our contraband. To avoid detection, we used cellars, coming up for air only when the basements led to a dead end. Then we would walk to the next block of buildings and descend into the darkness to move the sacred papers closer to their destination. Once, while passing through Ludwigkirchplatz, a policeman stopped us. Gemma immediately elbowed me aside, suggested a rendezvous that evening with the officer, and continued on her way with me. She never kept the date.

One evening, with Gemma upstairs and out of hearing range, Ugo told me to meet him in the library.

"Sit, my boy, sit." I slid into a parlor chair. "You asked me to look into the matter of Geert Bos. I may have a useful lead for you. My police contacts tell me that two Romani, last name Bos, a mother and daughter, were sent to the Ravensbrück concentration camp."

I sat ramrod straight. "Tell me! What else did you learn?"

"The official, after looking through his files, said a Geert Bos, Dutch, was working for them—and here's the disquieting part—as an undercover agent. Relationship to the mother and daughter: unknown. When I pressed him to look further, the man produced a government note. 'What do we have here?' he said and read the note, which he copied for me. 'Geert Bos, without claiming any marital ties, requests that we release the two Romani.' At the bottom is the official response: 'Pending.'"

"Do you have an address for this Geert Bos?"

"Neukölln. The official wrote the information on a card and handed it to me. I thanked him and promised that a new pair of shoes would be shortly forthcoming."

When Ugo passed the letter and the card to me, I vowed not to reveal its source or its dangerous nature. The address was Allerstraße in Neukölln, in the southeastern part of Berlin, a shabby part of the city. I pondered how to proceed. If the Geert to whom I had been introduced was the same man living in Neukölln, a Nazi enclave, then he must be a Nazi, a fact that Gemma would find hard to accept. And if the same man also had a Romani wife and child, she would feel betrayed.

That night I mulled over the information given me and how to approach the situation. If I went to the address and indeed found Geert Bos, what could I say: Although Sig. Rosselli would not take kindly to your wooing his daughter, Gemma fancies you and would be delighted to receive your attentions? Or: If you're married with a child, stay away from the villa? Or: Is there anything I or anyone else can do to get your family released from Ravensbrück? The best I could hope for was that the Geert Bos who had accompanied the Rossellis from Amsterdam was another person.

Allerstraße, which had seen better times, had only the nearby parklands to recommend it. The house number I had been given led to a Lebensmittelmarkt that sold canned goods and day-old fruits and vegetables. When I asked about the Bos family, the woman behind the counter looked over my shoulder, as if to determine that I was alone, and replied with one word: "Upstairs." I left the store and rounded the corner to the door that led to the second-floor flat. The wooden steps sagged, and the hall smelled of lives sustained with greasy foods. I knocked on the door and waited. Nothing. I knocked again. And again nothing. Returning to the grocery store, I asked the woman if she knew the whereabouts of the Bos family. As before, she peered around me and then whispered that the mother and daughter had been taken away.

"They're gypsies," she said, as if that word explained everything.

"Geert Bos is Dutch," I replied.

"But not his girlfriend and daughter."

"Have you any idea when they'll return?"

"Good question. I've heard rumors that he has government connections and may be able to work something out." Again, she surveyed the surroundings. "The barber told me. His shop is just down the way. We call him Herr Friseur. But don't mention me."

I walked down Allerstraße to a small place with one padded barber chair, holding a sallow-looking fellow with sunken cheeks and a crooked nose. I sat next to a rickety table with dozens of old magazines, all of a fascist persuasion. As I thumbed through one, my eyes alighted on a picture of a fashionable woman standing next to an expensive automobile. It was one of Yva Simon's photographs. A red verboten line ran from the top right-hand of the page to the bottom left-hand corner. Splashed across the middle of the picture was the word "Degenerate." The Nazis had appropriated Yva Simon's work for their own propaganda purposes. The accompanying article inveighed against rich Jews and praised the Volk for their earthy, healthy values. I tossed the magazine aside. The man in the chair pointed to an unruly hair on his cheek, and the barber plucked it out. "If only," said the man, as he rose from the barber's chair, "we could rid Germany of all the undesirables as easily as you tweeze a hair."

"That would be an effort worth the Führer's undertaking," replied the barber, shaking out the covering sheet that had protected the man. After he left, I took the chair.

"Trim?" the man asked, seeing that my hair was not long.

I answered, "No, I want information, for which I'll gladly pay." If the hairdresser's stiffened posture was any indication, my reply had put the barber on alert. "I'm a friend of Geert Bos's from

Amsterdam. I dropped by to say hello. Do you have any idea when Geert might return?"

"Don't know the man," said the barber.

I acted as if I hadn't heard. "Geert wrote me about his girlfriend and daughter. Ravensbrück. He hoped to arrange their release. Do you know when that might be?"

"A trim?" the barber asked a second time.

I handed the barber a large bill. Herr Friseur tucked the sheet over my chest and started snipping. After a minute of snip, snip, which were the only sounds in the shop, the man murmured, "Next Friday." Snip, snip. Nothing else was said.

I returned to the villa and, at Sig. Rosselli's request, closeted myself with him. Having divined Gemma's motives and my reason for finding the missing Geert Bos, he crossly advised me that Gemma would soon forget Geert, and that I would only endanger their operations by contacting him.

"Given what we now know about the man, I can foresee only trouble. Inviting him back to the villa would be like putting the fox in the henhouse. We have too much to lose; and too many people depend on us."

After a sleepless night of tortured conscience, I decided to return to the grocery store on the Friday. For the rest of the week, I ran innocuous errands for Mendel. Ugo said that it was time for everyone to lie low, and that as much as we could, we should look as if we were living a normal life. I guessed that Ugo had some inside information, especially since Mendel moved all the equipment to a safe room behind a false wall in the basement.

Fortunately, I had not shared with Sig. Rosselli the return date for Geert and family. Friday morning, I nonchalantly ate breakfast and then sat down to read a book. Around ten, Ugo, with sample cases in hand, left to show some shoes to a department store. At the suggestion of her father, Gemma was reading Petrarch in Italian. Ugo didn't want her to lose her knowledge of the language. In fact, he often spoke to her in Italian; it was their private code, which no one else in the villa understood, though I did recognize a few words.

Shortly before noon, I left for the train station, saying I planned to meet Herr Fertig and would return un poco. Gemma smiled. She knew how limited my Italian was but admired my attempts to speak it. I exited the train and circled Allerstraße, just in case I was being shadowed. Poking my head in the grocery store, I nodded at the lady behind the counter, and she nodded back. I went around the building, ascended the steps, and knocked on the door lightly. A pretty, olive-skinned woman appeared. I asked for Geert; she asked me to wait and closed the door; a minute later Geert faced me. We stood looking at each other, neither really knowing what to say. For all my imagined scenarios, I had not really prepared myself for this moment. Tongue-tied, I made some unintelligible sounds. Geert saved me by saying that we should have a talk—at a nearby café.

"But first let me introduce you to Heidi, my companion, and Nina, my daughter."

The flat was furnished in good taste and clean, nothing conspicuous or kitschy. Off to a side, two traveling bags suggested a recent arrival; or did they indicate an impending departure? A child knelt on the sitting-room rug playing with a ball. Before Geert could introduce me to mother and daughter, I sank to the floor and told Nina my name, asking her if she had a boyfriend.

"I'm too young," she said smiling.

"Your papa told me you were married."

The child looked at him incredulously and then laughed. "He did not."

"I must have misunderstood."

It was only then that I rose and met Heidi. But the child, clearly quite taken with my silliness, invited me to join her in a game of knocking down some pins with the ball. I joined her immediately, and suggested we add a cup, lying on its side, as a specific target to aim for. Who could, from three or four feet away, roll the ball into the cup? This new wrinkle to the game delighted her, as we oohed and ahhed at our near misses.

"You're very good with children," observed Heidi.

"I like their openness and love of new adventures."

Twenty minutes later, Geert and I sat sipping coffee at one of the four tables in a shabby café. The others were unoccupied. A tired gray-haired woman served us. On one wall hung a large photograph of the fashionable Unter den Linden Boulevard and the Brandenburg Gate. On the opposite wall, Adolf Hitler's face peered out of a cheap print. I couldn't believe how much Geert had aged in just the last few months, since I had last seen him. Crows' feet trailed from under his eyes, and his former shining black hair was now streaked with gray.

"I work for the government."

"I know."

"Heidi has only two weeks before she has to go back. It's a kind of furlough, arranged through a friend at the camp."

"If you married her would it make any difference?"

"None. She and Nina have been racially typed as gypsies."

"What happens to you now?"

"I am being sent to Lublin, Poland. There is talk of building a Konzentrationslager there or very close by. As far as I can tell they are planning to make all of Poland one large concentration camp."

"Can't you smuggle Heidi and Nina into Switzerland?"

"They have no papers."

"Maybe I can help."

"Baruch, although we really hardly know one another, I feel I can trust you. I saw you with my daughter. You're a kind young man. I owe you and the Rossellis the truth. My days are numbered. I was originally assigned to Ugo Rosselli because the Gestapo suspected he was a Bolshevik. Of late, the authorities have been watching the villa. It's time for you and the others to save your own skins. As for me and my family, there's nothing to be done."

"I heard Sig. Rosselli say that some Romani are working as servants in the homes of German officials. Perhaps . . ."

As if he had not heard a word, Geert censoriously muttered, "And all because they said I polluted my Aryan blood by having a child with a gypsy."

Chapter Fifteen

At my request, Mendel prepared documents for Yva and Alfred Simon, in the hope that the worsening conditions for Jews would finally convince the Simons to leave. Gemma and I had ceased working for Yva earlier, when the Nazi invasions began. It was then that Albert Simon was forced to labor as a street sweeper, and Yva, owing to her expertise with a camera, was sent to the Jewish Hospital on 2 Iranische Straße in the Wedding district to work as an X-ray technician.

The Krankenhaus der Jüdischen Gemeinde, the Hospital of the Jewish Community, which survived the war, was a spacious compound of seven buildings in a large garden. The director of the hospital, Walter Lustig, whose name in English suited the man, given his lusty sexual appetite and numerous amours, arranged for a technician, expert in the taking of X-rays, to train Yva, who quickly became adept at running the machinery. At Gemma's suggestion, and with her father's approval, she volunteered to apprentice as a nurse's aide. Sig. Rosselli, now aware that the villa had become a location of Nazi interest, decided that it was safer for Gemma to work at the hospital than to continue acting as a courier for Mendel. He advised me to do the same, since the Nazis had already arrested me once before. Gemma liked the idea. Clearly, neither of us wanted to be apart from the other and from Yva, who recommended that I be trained to keep the X-ray equipment in working order.

A week later, both Gemma and I were employed at the hospital, returning to the villa each night. It slowly but undeniably became clear that the Nazis were using the hospital as a Sammellager, a collection point, a way station, to deport Jews to the East, particularly Poland. Inexplicably they brought seriously ill Jews to the hospital, and as soon as the patients were well enough to travel, they were put on trains for deportation. The Nazis said the camps were places of resettlement. Many Jews, encouraged by this news, thought it meant a new life away from the dangers of the city. But one day, a German soldier, suffering from a back injury, arrived at the hospital. He had been sent home from Poland. As Yva was X-raying him, he whispered to her that he could no longer remain silent. The camps, he said, were for forced labor and extermination. She was shocked, persuaded that the soldier's pain had disordered his mind. When she told Gemma and me what she had heard, we urged her to leave with Albert as soon as possible. But Albert dismissed the information as the stuff of old wives' tales.

It might have appeared to a casual observer that life in the hospital was proceeding the way it had before the war. Doctors and nurses in their starched uniforms circulated throughout the buildings, ministering to the sick. Patients were admitted and discharged, operations performed, medications administered. The cafeteria prepared and served meals. Clerks and typists kept registers, and the details of the institution's daily life were documented with Germanic efficiency, including a list of the evenings set aside for musical performances.

Nazis regularly visited the hospital to check on its running, on the patients, and on the Berlin Jews sent here for transport to other parts of the country. On the morning of Easter Sunday, 13 April 1941, the Gestapo brought to the hospital a Jewish man ostensibly suffering from an intestinal obstruction. The Nazis registered him under an Aryan name, Ernst Walter, but once Yva heard his Yiddish-accented German, she became suspicious. Who was this man, and why did he enjoy the protection of the Nazis? Gemma asked her father to inquire, but Sig. Rosselli could learn nothing. Based on Yva's impressions, Gemma concluded that the man couldn't be trusted; she therefore laid a trap. While sitting at his bedside, after the attending nurse had left the room, she alluded to the disillusionment of some German soldiers, and faintly suggested a German resistance movement existed in the hospital. The patient, rather unresponsive before, behaved as if he had just received a shot of adrenaline. He sat up, wide-eyed, and asked, "Who?"

From that moment on, he eagerly anticipated her every word and often substituted his own fancies for hers. He whispered that he could be trusted, and that his friends often commented on his discreetness. His keenness and gullibility grew equally. Like the other Jews collaborating with the Nazis, he thought that he and his family would be safe. The more credulous, like Ernst Walter, imagined they'd enjoy whipped cream and fresh fruit at the Adlon Hotel. Instead they were served sour grapes.

"Never mind who. They have stored arms in the garden, under the rose beds. They even have an anti-tank gun in the basement. And believe it or not, they hope to commandeer an airplane." She put a finger to her lips. "But that's just between you and me."

Herr Walter sat mesmerized, his jaw agape. He shook his head, and then a thin smile ran along his lips. "You're sure of what you say?" he asked.

"I work here, don't I?"

An hour later, he asked to have the portable telephone wheeled to his bed. He dialed, waited, and whispered.

That evening, a backhoe dug up the flower beds, and soldiers rummaged through the hospital basement. When nothing turned up, the officer in charge could be heard berating Ernst Walter for being so naïve and for blowing his "cover."

"Who is this nurse?"

"I forget her last name but the first is Gemma."

When confronted by the officer, Gemma said she had no idea what he was talking about. "You do know," she said, "the patient is subject to hallucinations?"

"We'll have him moved immediately," said the officer.

"Yes, perhaps a Catholic hospital would be more suitable. Although this hospital treats typhus, cholera, tuberculosis, whooping cough, scarlet fever, and myriad other diseases, it does not treat mental disorders. Yes, I think Herr Walter would find another hospital more to his liking."

Berlin Revisited

******

When the Nazis raided the villa, only Mendel escaped. He had luckily been visiting a woman friend. Sig. Rosselli, Gemma, and I were all interned, ironically, at the Jewish hospital, waiting to be transported elsewhere. The first to be processed, Sig. Rosselli, was sent three days later to the Mauthesen-Gusen complex in Austria, but not before he embraced his daughter and asked her to remember him and think only pleasant thoughts. As he departed, we wept and feared for his safety. Among those waiting for transfer was a young Jewish laborer, Zygmunt Poznanski, who had been forced to work on the new camp outside Lublin. He had escaped and joined the underground resistance, only to be caught in a dragnet of Jews hiding on the outskirts of Berlin.

"My guess," he said, "is that most of us will be headed for Majdanek."

"Majdanek?" I repeated, barely above a whisper. "Never heard of it."

"The official name of the camp is Prisoner of War Camp of the Waffen-*SS* Lublin, Kriegsgefangenenlager der Waffen-*SS* Lublin. The name 'Majdanek' comes from the nearby district of Majdan Tatarski, whose residents first nicknamed the camp in 1941. It is about three miles from the center of Lublin, in plain sight of the nearby highway. The Nazis made no attempt to hide the camp, which is built on a flat field covering more than six hundred acres, surrounded by an electrified barbed-wire fence and guarded by the *SS* in nineteen watchtowers. They're planning on housing forty-five thousand prisoners in the twenty-two barracks."

Imagining a Babel of prisoners, desperate to make themselves understood, I asked, "You're Polish but you speak German. Is that true of others?"

"Of many Poles, yes. But the Jews, who account for the largest group of prisoners, mostly speak Yiddish. You can also hear a lot of Russian. The Nazis shipped Russian POWs from the front. There are also Polish resistance fighters, and other nationalities."

Barely able to speak the words, I asked, "Does anyone ever leave alive?"

"The Nazis are turning Majdanek into a center for processing clothing from other camps. When I escaped, they had just opened a shoe repair shop, where the prisoners worked on the boots of the German soldiers, also shoes taken from Jews."

He then described the initial disarray of the camp, saying that before the Germans could define the different camp functions, there was little to do at Majdanek. "The prisoners mostly sat all day long, and sometimes the guards took you out to work. Half of the time, the people never came back. Work!" he scoffed. "They had me breaking up big stones into little ones, or digging ditches and holes, and covering the ditches up. That was the work. As for food, there was very little. Very little food."

With each passing day, Gemma and I wondered and worried whether we, like so many of the patients, would simply disappear in the rear of a truck headed for the train station. At the hospital, death became an absence. An empty bed meant the patient had been herded into a cattle car, destination unknown. Majdanek was just one more name we now heard whispered in the halls, like Auschwitz. To keep our sanity, Gemma and I made time for chess matches and card games. But we never stopped counting the disappeared ones. Ironically, the more frantic the hospital became, the better for the staff. They had less time to think of themselves. The hectic pace even drove incompatible men and women into relationships that they normally would never have entertained. Little wonder, then, that couples sought dark corners for a few minutes of affection. The women, though, knew to stay out of the clutches of the hospital director, Walter Lustig. His unsavory reputation led nurses to team up when they had to be in his presence. One evening, he made the mistake of cornering Yva Simon in a basement room. He came away from that encounter with a cut lip and a bloody cheek. She had hit him with a metal ferule. He retaliated by marking Eva and her husband for an early departure to Majdanek.

When Gemma and I heard the news, we embraced and wept. To keep from despairing we took turns reassuring one another that perhaps Yva and Alfred could survive in the camp or even escape, like Zygmunt. Grasping for straws, we put our hope in the fact that the departure date had not yet been set. In a moment of mordant humor, Gemma remarked:

"When we are sent to Majdanek, we'll have a grand reunion."

If the best way to palliate pain in oneself is to ease it in others that occasion presented itself when two new patients were admitted to the hospital, Geert's daughter, Nina, and his companion, Heidi, the first suffering from scarlet fever and the second from cholera. Geert was nowhere in sight but had somehow managed to have them transferred from Ravensbrück to the Jewish Hospital. The young woman and child were immediately quarantined, seen only by staff wearing masks and gloves. I recognized them at once and reluctantly revealed their identity to Gemma. Although shocked and hurt, she swore to herself that she would treat them like family. In the evening, I visited the pediatric ward and sat down next to Nina's bed. She was breathing heavily and coughed painfully. Her eyes were closed. On a stand at her bedside rested a pan of cold water and a washcloth, which I dipped in the water, rung out, and neatly spread across Nina's forehead. She opened her eyes but did not recognize me. When the other hospital staff members temporarily left the ward, I removed the mask, and Nina's smile, a semaphore of recognition, indicated that she felt safe.

The next day, I made it a point of visiting Heidi. She too smiled in the knowledge that she had fallen among friends. I whispered:

"Geert? Where is he?"

She found it difficult to talk but managed to say, "After he arranged our transfer, the Gestapo came for him. They said he was playing a double game . . . warning people."

I hoped that mother and daughter would take a long time recovering. With this thought in mind, I whispered:

"Even when you feel better, tell them you are still sick."

"And Nina?"

"I'll explain to her."

That evening I went to see Geert's daughter. As I let myself into the room, I heard a familiar voice. Gemma was speaking to the child.

"When I was a little girl, my parents told me fairy tales. After they went away, I lived in an orphanage, where I repeated their stories and even changed some of them. Here's one I think you will like."

A poor farmer and his wife had one child, a pretty daughter, eighteen years old. "It's time for her to marry," said the farmer's wife. "We are too old to care for her." The husband agreed. So, he went to the village and rang the church bell, summoning all the people. "Which of you," he asked, "has an eligible son or relative who will marry my lovely daughter?" Immediately the question arose: How much was the farmer willing to pay? "I am a poor man," he said, "and I have no money or goods for a dowry."

Gemma paused to ask Nina whether she had ever heard of a dowry. She shook her head no. "It's the property or money brought by a bride to a husband on their marriage." She then continued her story.

Not a single family in the village or the neighboring ones would let a son marry without a dowry. What were the parents to do? Their daughter, Ludmila, suggested they travel to see the king of the mountain, Chernomor, the sorcerer with magical powers. The parents agreed and set out. On their way to the mountain, they met a beggar on the road and told him of their destination. He asked them for a crust of bread. Although the old couple had just a bite of bread left, they gave it to the beggar, who said that in return for their kindness, he would give them one piece of advice. Since they were headed for the mountain, they should beware of Chernomor's net. Puzzled, they asked why, and the beggar said:

"Prince Igor's son, Ruslan, met me on this very road, and I gave him the same advice that I am giving you. But he failed to heed my warning. Chernomor ensnared him in his net. Now he is a goldfish in a silver pond."

With those mystifying words, the beggar slipped into the forest and fled. The old couple, too scared to continue, returned home and told their daughter everything that had taken place. Ludmila, however, had a brave heart. And since she was the one who had suggested that her parents speak to Chernomor, she set out herself. Once again, the beggar appeared on the road; and once again he asked for a crust of bread.

"I have no bread, but I will gladly give you my apple."

He thanked her and repeated his advice about the net.

"My parents told me what you said," replied Ludmila, "but how should I protect myself?"

"Chernomor is very proud of his magical net. Praise its fine silken threads and its emerald color. Ask to hold it yourself, and then throw it over Chernomor's head. More than that I cannot say."

"May I ask one further favor?"

"Ask," said the beggar.

"Dress me in fine clothes and shoes so that I may appear before the king of the mountain as a suitable caller."

The beggar snapped his fingers and vanished into the woods. Ludmila, looking down, found herself arrayed in velvet and lace, with shoes made of the softest leather and buckled in brass.

Arriving at the mountain, she climbed the winding stairs to the top, where stood a marble castle and a silver pond that held a single goldfish. Chernomor came from the castle to greet her, much impressed by her fine clothes. He decided immediately that she was a woman of high degree, perhaps a princess. On his belt hung a beauteous net that sparkled in its emerald radiance.

"What a beautiful net," she said, admiring its richness and shape.

"It has magical powers," said Chernomor. "It can turn a person into a fish or a toad. It all depends."

Snatching the net from his belt, she threw it over his head, and a second later he turned into an ugly toad. Even more marvelous, the goldfish sprang out of the pond and landed by her side, now in human form and dressed in the robes of a prince.

"My name is Ruslan," he said, "and I have been living under the curse of Chernomor, who swore that my becoming a prince was as unlikely as his becoming a toad. But having said those words, he provided a cure for the curse. So, for your boldness and beauty, I will make you my wife."

And for the rest of her life, her parents lived in splendor and she in a palatial palace.

"Did she have children?" asked Nina.

"Two, a girl and a boy."

"And the girl's name was Nina!"

"How did you guess?"

"I just knew."

Quietly slipping away, I headed for the X-ray machines in the basement, passing the door to Lustig's office, which stood slightly ajar. Lustig was conferring with a Gestapo officer wearing polished boots, a shining jacket, and jodhpurs. I wondered if the man administered some sort of horse brigade; but then Nazi costumes were often nothing more than the expression of what these misfits imagined themselves. I heard the word "Majdanek" repeated, as well as "plat." I kneeled, pretending to tie my shoe, and listened.

"We want you to be fully informed," said the stranger.

Lustig replied, "I would rather not know."

"Ah," said the other, "but your knowing guarantees your loyalty. You are then one of us."

"Please," said Lustig, "just pack up the map and papers, and take them with you."

The man laughed. "We want you to have them." On his way out the door, the man nearly tripped over me, still kneeling. "Idiot!" he swore, kicked me, and briskly proceeded down the corridor. I rose, brushed myself off, knocked on Lustig's door, and, without being given permission, entered. On a long table against the wall lay a map. Lustig, who still bore a red mark on his cheek from Yva's blow, asked me what I wanted. I replied:

"The child, Nina Bos, needs thicker soup, if she is to gain weight."

"For this you interrupt me. Out!"

Convinced that the papers and map answered the question most often asked by the Jews at the hospital, "What's to become of us?" I knew that I had to enter Lustig's office that evening, before the papers and map disappeared. And I knew how to obtain a pass key. Gemma had been wooed by one of the janitorial custodians, Max Teufel, a dim-witted fellow. By using her considerable guiles, she could get it. When I broached the subject with her, she asked what I hoped to discover.

"A map of the Majdanek camp and who is to be sent there."

She paused, studied a fingernail, and said, "I'll get it."

Her account of her dealings with Max still linger, so humorous were they. Finding Max in the furnace room, she watched as he oversaw a coal delivery. With the anthracite roaring down the chute into the holding bin, a black cloud enveloped the room. Her coughing attracted Max's attention.

"You, here?"

"Looking for you."

"Why?"

She waved the dust from her line of vision and said, "Can we step outside?"

They left the coal dust for an airy room. As they brushed their clothes, he said, "Well?"

"Ah, you've trimmed your mustache."

"Not for a long time."

"Good, I think a scraggly mustache is manly."

He wiped a coal-stained hand on his overalls and grunted, "Messy."

"It takes a man of experience to oversee the furnace room."

"Jürgen's the boss."

"But you wisely keep an eye on things."

He parted his lips in a half-hearted smile, revealing broken teeth. "You never know."

"Ah, but you do."

"Know what?" he asked.

"The people and possessions of every room."

"My job."

"An important one—with keys."

He proudly produced a large key ring from a trouser pocket, rattled the keys, and returned the ring to his pants.

"I suppose there is a master key for each building at the hospital."

"Also, for the cabinets and closets."

"May I see them again?"

He removed the ring.

"Let me guess which of them is the master key for this building." She thumbed through the collection. "This one."

He guffawed. "Nope!" Then he singled out another key.

"May I borrow it?"

"What for?"

"So I can let myself into your room tonight."

His eyes glazed as he thought about her proposition. "In the attic? I'll leave the door unlocked."

"Don't! It's safer not to."

"Tonight?"

"Yes."

He breathed deeply and weighed his good fortune. Removing the key from the ring, he handed it to her. "What time?"

"Whatever's good for you."

"After nine."

"See you then."

PAUL M. LEVITT

******

That evening, with pass key in hand, I made my way to Walter Lustig's office, hoping that the director was not working late. Through the window in the door I could see only darkness. Good. But what, I thought, if Lustig's office has its own key, a special one? I slid the master into the lock, paused, and then turned the bow. The key glided past the tumblers, and the door quietly opened. I entered. The flashlight I'd purloined from one of the storerooms glowed dimly. I had taped a piece of cloth over the lamp. Tiptoeing to the long table, I found the map and its accompanying documents, which included plans for the development of the Majdanek camp and this disquieting statement:

"From *SS* Headquarters. Commandment Karl Koch initially hoped that the camp would hold between 25,000 and 50,000 prisoners. But we now see that this number will not suffice. Instead, we would like to expand the camp to 150,000 or even 250,000 prisoners, although it currently holds approximately 50,000 prisoners."

A map of the camp lay in full view. I stared at the map until its image became indelible. I would never forget it.

Absorbed by the plans for the camp, I continued reading, deaf to the approaching steps. Not until someone said, "I saw it . . . a light in the director's office," did I realize that I had been discovered. Two men entered, one a Jew in the employ of the Nazis, and the other a security guard at the hospital, Friedl Schmidt.

"By what right are you here?" hissed Friedl.

At that moment the snitch seemed to disappear.

I told myself not to apologize, but to speak clearly and forcefully. "I heard a rumor that there would be an attempt to steal important documents from the director's office. So, I came to check."

"On whose authority?" asked Friedl.

"Herr Teufel's."

"That underling! Well, we'll just see about that."

Friedl shoved me from the office and marched me upstairs to the custodial dormitory; but no one there seemed to know Max's whereabouts. Although Gemma had told me how she secured the key and what she had promised, she assured me that she would shove the key under the attic door and fail to meet Max. Given the circumstances and possible consequences for both me and Gemma, I rolled the dice and bet on brazenness.

"Try the attic," I told Friedl, who seemed utterly confused by my suggestion.

"Why there?"

"Just try it."

Using his own pass key, Friedl opened the door to the attic and discovered a speechless Max Teufel, seated on a cot in his underwear. Before Friedl could speak, I rapidly discoursed on the matter.

"Here's your key, Max, and thanks for spreading the word about an attempted break-in of the director's office. You saved the day. Who knows what might have happened if you hadn't sensed trouble. I didn't want to see a woman given the responsibility of protecting secret documents, so I took the key you gave her and went myself. How you learned of a possible security breach is anyone's guess. I won't ask for your sources, but they were certainly useful. When I entered the director's office, two men brushed past me. How they gained entry is beyond me, but I could see that they were up to no good. They wore scarves over their faces, making it impossible to recognize them. And rather than chase after them, I chose to see what they wanted to steal."

I paused and shook my head, exhibiting disbelief. "You won't believe it." By now both Max and the guard gaped in shock. I continued my concocted explanation, saying that on a long table in the director's office lay a map and plans for the expansion of Majdanek. And from what I saw, I concluded that the high command hoped to double or triple the number of prisoners, some of whom—the strong ones, the healthy—would come from this very hospital. Reason enough, I said, for the authorities to protect the hospital patients. They want to heal the sick and wounded to work at Majdanek.

"Now you can understand why some of our patients don't want to get better. They know that the minute we declare them fit, the authorities will ship them out to the camp. Even the staff, people like me, won't live many more months." With that statement, I gambled on the sympathy of Teufel and the guard. Their rapt attention had misled me into thinking that they would protect me. "So, I urge you," I concluded, "to watch for spies, like the ones who tried to steal documents from the director's office, and to protect your good and faithful staff—I admit, I count myself among them—from removal and shipment to the camps."

The guard, the first to speak, wondered aloud, "If what you say is true—"

I interrupted. "Then Max deserves a medal."

"But," continued Friedl, turning to Max, "why did you give such an important assignment to a woman? Why did you not go yourself?"

To protect Max, who seemed to believe that he had actually behaved heroically, I said, "Max intended to use the woman as a decoy. Then I came along. Before they could act, I did. Right, Max?"

A bewildered Max replied, "Ya, ya."

Friedl, now more confused than ever, and more skeptical, asked Max, "Why didn't you take your concerns to the director?"

I answered for him. "And miss the chance to catch the traitors?"

"But you did miss them. By your own admission you bungled the job."

"True, sadly true," I sighed. "But the next time—"

Friedl, now utterly convinced that neither Max nor I could be trusted, declared, "Let me assure you, young man, there will be no next time. Max will be confined to his dormitory quarters and you shall be sent . . . to a camp . . . just as soon as I can make the arrangements." With this pronouncement, he abruptly turned and left the attic.

Forcing a smile and trying to encourage Max and myself, I remarked, "Friedl doesn't mean it. He'll soon forget."

Max, looking forlornly at the pass key in his hand, asked, "Will he want this back?"

Chapter Sixteen

Watching from a second-story window as Heidi and Nina Bos waited for the truck that would take them to the train station, I played my wild card. I left the building, caught up with the soldier in charge, and loudly declared, "My god, man, they're infectious. Tuberculosis! Just listen to them cough." Heidi, taking her cue, whispered to her daughter, and the two of them started hacking. The soldier paled and ordered them back inside the hospital. The truck left without them.

Deportations took place unannounced. One day a patient occupied a bed, and the next day it stood vacant, waiting for a replacement. In the absence of lists or announcements, rumor became the principal source of information. I made it a point to rise early and stand at a window that looked down on the front entrance of the hospital, where the transports parked and loaded.

When I saw Yva and Alfred Simon clutching their modest possessions waiting for transportation to the train station, I could think of no way to save them. As tears ran down my face, I ran out the front door to say goodbye. After hugging and kissing them both, I asked who would replace her in the radiography department, eliciting the last words she ever spoke to me.

"For sure it won't be a fashion photographer."

Only later did I learn that the train the Simons boarded bore instructions to head for the Sobibór extermination camp. But owing to a mishap, the train moved to a sidetrack at Lublin, where the authorities selected 1030 prisoners to continue to Sobibór, and the remaining ones, among them the Simons, to go to the Majdanek concentration camp.

When the Nazi official in charge of the Jewish hospital heard that two of the patients had avoided deportation because of tuberculosis, he instructed the attending doctor to confirm the diagnosis. Once the report came back negative, I found myself standing with Heidi and Nina outside the hospital waiting for the Opel Blitz multi-purpose utility truck to transfer us and our few belongings to the railroad station. That same morning, Friedl had gladly informed me that my immediate deportation was owing to my "key" scheme.

"Now or later, it's all the same," I had recklessly said. But I did not plan to enter the train unprepared. Strapped to my leg, as

Zygmunt, the Pole, had advised, was a chisel that I had lifted from the lock shop.

In the back of the truck, the few able-bodied men immediately started planning an escape. But, as one warned, it would all depend on our traveling in the same cattle car. "So," he said, "we have to make every effort to stay together."

At the station, hundreds of "non-Aryans" crowded the platform, waiting for what the authorities called relocation. Divided into groups, some headed for one train, some for another. A medical orderly, who had ridden with me in the same truck, was directed to a distant platform. Five minutes later, he had somehow made his way back to the original group. A line of cattle cars stood waiting, with open doors, to carry their human cargo to some unknown destination. Soldiers, with barking dogs straining at their leashes, stood guard at the cars, strewn with straw and smelling of disinfectant. At the end of each car, welded on the outside, a booth housed a soldier with a machine gun. People desperately sought information from him and from others. Rumors swirled, and the word "camp" kept surfacing. A Nazi officer grinned and mendaciously assured the skeptics that the train would deposit them in a pleasant part of the country, with hills and dales and charming villages.

The cars at the front of the train started filling first. As people shuffled into a car, the guard would count to eighty, sometimes even more, and then point the succeeding group to the next car. Penned in and cramped, without any room to sit or lie, prisoners often stood with their hands above their heads. Before shutting and bolting the door, the guard would toss a water bucket into the car for use to hold human waste. I had positioned myself on the station platform at the back of the group. When my time came to board, I felt someone from behind tug at my sleeve. It was Gemma, holding a pass that allowed her entry to and from the platform. She held a satchel of food, and a garlic bag hung from her neck. Worried that she might be swept into the car, I reached for the satchel and begged her to leave. She whispered:

"Wither thou goest, I will go."

"But why? You are free to leave."

"Father is gone, you are next, and Geert has disappeared."

Ignoring my pleas to return to the station, she joined me in the cattle car. The guard shut the door and closed the vents to prevent escape, leaving Gemma and me and the others in darkness. Air entered through only the cracks. In this condition, the train pulled out of the station, with Gemma and me standing by the bolted door.

Someone cried "Who's here?" and the prisoners each called out a name. At hearing Heidi and Nina identify themselves, Gemma passed word to them to try to reach us. After a great deal of pushing and shoving and apologizing, Heidi and Nina appeared. I yelled for Peter and David and Daniel to find their way to the door. Again, pushing and shoving took place until the men reached me. They were the ones who had talked in the truck of escape. The cracks in the wall boards allowed us to see landmarks we recognized. Taking turns using my chisel to dislodge the bolt and a board, we inched open the door. Then we waited. To jump into an open field would invite suicide. The guard in the booth would pick us off like fish in a barrel. Hours passed. Finally, on reaching the border area with Poland, the train entered a forest. I took Gemma's hand. Her other hand held fast to Nina, whom Heidi had implored her to take, feeling that her daughter's chances of survival were greater with Gemma than with herself.

As the train chugged through the wooded area, the group debated whether they should wait for night or take their chances in the fading light. They decided that rather than wait and run the risk of the train coming onto an open plain, they would use the forest to their advantage. Forcing the door open, we prepared to jump. But Nina reached out to her mother, crying for her to join us. At the last moment, Gemma, fearing to yank the child and increase the chances of injury, released my hand and stayed behind as I and the others leaped, amid a hail of gunfire. Never swift of foot, I made a good target. Bullets sliced the air and ricocheted off the trees around me. When my right side throbbed as if I'd been stabbed, I knew I'd been shot, though I couldn't see or feel any blood. The train slowed to a halt so that the guards could fix the broken door and apprehend the escapees, who had separated in the forest. To outrun the guards would be impossible, so I hobbled across a creek, which I hoped would mislead the dogs, painfully climbed a tree, and hid in the foliage. From a short distance away I could hear shouts, barking, and then shots, which came from three different directions. I waited. Two guards broke through the foliage and stopped at the creek. Their dogs sniffed the bank and whined but didn't cross. They had apparently lost the scent. One of the guards unbuttoned his pants and urinated in the water. Then the men took their animals and left. Minutes passed. Other than the forest sounds, I heard only a whistle and the clickety-clack of a departing train. After waiting several hours, I climbed down and stumbled through the woods until I saw in the distance a small village and a church spire.

In the darkness, I crept to the church and found a crawl space underneath the building. I removed a single rotten piece of wood and wriggled into the dank place. To the delight of my stomach, I discovered that the crawlway served as a storage area for dried fruits and vegetables, handfuls of which I stuffed in my mouth and pockets. In the morning, I heard footsteps overhead and people conversing in Polish. Never a gifted language student, I wished now that I had applied myself to learning more than a smattering of English in school and some Italian from Mrs. Levy. That night, listening for the last parishioner to leave, I thought constantly of Gemma. Before the priest could secure the front door, I emerged, bedraggled, and begged entry. The priest, Father Nowak, seeing that I was hurt, led me to a couch in the vestry and telephoned the village doctor, a Polish physician who had served in the Great War.

Dr. Gajos had heard rumors of an attempted escape from a "Jew train," and although he suspected that I was the prisoner being sought in the neighborhood, he disliked the Germans even more than the Jews. A short man with an S-shaped arthritic back, rheumy blue eyes, and a bald head, he spoke to me in German, which he claimed was the only profit he had taken away from the First World War. Cleaning my wound, he announced that the bullet had passed through my body and exited above my right kidney.

"The bullet probably just missed a lung. Only an X-ray can confirm the degree of the injury. If you piss blood, then you'll know it nicked your kidney," said the doctor. "But I see no infection." He bathed the wound with iodine and covered it with gauze and tape. "My advice to you is to get the hell out of here as quickly as you can."

"I have no money," I said.

"The doctor removed his wallet, counted some zlotys, and gave them to me. "Just remember me in your prayers."

I stayed on the vestry couch for several days, fed by the priest, who advised me in sign language and broken German which roads to take and which to avoid.

"My bike," said Father Nowak. "You keep. No need it."

When I felt strong enough to leave, I left the church at night and scanned the neighborhood. My eyes lit on the bicycle, leaning against a tree, just where the priest had told me to look. I felt the tires to check the air pressure, gingerly climbed onto the seat, and started slowly pedaling. With Father Nowak's directions in mind, and my side painfully throbbing, I took to the road.

In the countryside, cycling proved treacherous. The uneven roads and potholes made me fearful of falling and gave me cause to worry about my bicycle tires. After several hours, I slipped into the bushes and immediately fell into a deep, exhausted sleep. When I awoke in mid-morning, the route looked clear, so I decided to risk moving during the day, reasoning that I could slip off the road at the first sight of a vehicle. Approaching a town, I passed a farmer with a horse-drawn wagon. He took little notice. His lack of interest emboldened me to carry on past other farmers, who also ignored my presence, and led me into making a grave mistake.

As I entered the town, people suddenly seemed interested in my presence. I tried to calm myself. Many of the peasants who had come into town that morning wore bedraggled dirty clothing like mine and rode bicycles. But they clearly recognized the cut of my city clothes and therefore marked me as an outsider.

Coming around a corner into the town square, I saw to my horror a number of German soldiers milling about a fountain, or sitting on tanks, or smoking cigarettes and flirting with unresponsive young ladies. Stopping would have aroused suspicion, so I rode on as nonchalantly as I could. At the end of the square, an *SS* officer, leaning against an official-looking sedan and smoking, was wearing the black uniform and black boots that evinced such terror. I could feel my hands trembling but behaved as if I came through this square every day. He seemed uninterested in me, eyeing lasciviously a young Polish woman in a print dress walking briskly down the opposite side of the street.

About twenty yards past the square, the buildings gave way to fields. I began to feel a sense of relief, a sense that somehow, I had come through unscathed. Suddenly I heard, from a distance, the *SS* officer shout, his distrust aroused for some reason.

I could feel my heart fibrillate, but somehow my legs continued pedaling mechanically at the same pace. To speed up would draw suspicion. I therefore continued as if I hadn't heard the man's order. He shouted again, louder, with minatory authority, "Halt! Halten Sie sofort!" Stop immediately! Continuing to pedal at the same casual pace, I dared not look back, though I felt it imperative to see whether I was being pursued. My fear of capture and execution became a reality when a shot rang out and hit what I immediately recognized as a railroad sign a few yards distant. Almost simultaneously, I heard a train approaching. Another two shots from the *SS* officer's pistol pinged the sign. If I pedaled faster, I just might clear the tracks before the train blocked the way. Otherwise, I saw no chance of escaping certain arrest.

The road inclined down to the tracks, and even though it didn't seem steep, I covered the descent like an arrow shot by an archer. The train, unfortunately, was also rapidly moving, and above the din of the engine's coal furnace, I heard two more pistol shots. The engineer sounded the warning whistle several times, but he had no time to engage the brakes. The two of us seemed destined to simultaneously reach a point on the tracks that would result in my death. Resolved to such a fate, I knew that an instant death would be the most merciful.

The bicycle flew across the tracks with the train so close behind that the buffer of air pushed in front of the engine almost knocked me over. Joyful that a long freight train stood between me and the *SS* officer, I found the energy to flee into the countryside and dart off into the woods through a myriad of trails that made my capture unlikely.

For the next few days, I proceeded with extreme caution, avoiding all contact with other people, slipping into barns and henhouses to steal a bite to eat, and having learned my lesson, disappearing quickly into the bushes along the side of the road whenever I heard the distant sound of an approaching vehicle.

But most stop and go progress led me to conclude that to bicycle all the way to the Polish border would be impractical if not impossible. I would have to risk enlisting help or to die from fatigue and starvation.

Although unable to speak Polish, I did know the word for Sweden, Szwecja, a name that I had heard repeated on the train, a name associated with freedom. I hadn't gone more than a few miles, when I saw in the distance a lorry driver stopped along the road, tightening the ropes around the canvas covering his cargo: cases of beer. I bicycled to the spot, said "Szwecja," held up my shirt to reveal my bandaged side, waited, and prayed for a miracle. The driver, built like a barrel and in need of a shave, pointed to himself and repeated the name "Jakub." He easily lifted the bike with two fingers, put it in the back of the truck, and then motioned for me to join him in the cab. I guessed from his sad blue eyes, exuding resignation, that the man wanted someone to dispel his loneliness.

When it became apparent that neither of us could understand the other's language, we communicated with our hands and in the few German words the driver knew. Without trying to explain my desperate situation, I could see from his expression that he understood. As if to confirm our companionship, he opened his wallet and showed me photographs of his two children, a boy and a girl. I nodded and smiled appreciatively. Removing another picture, this one of his wife, he indicated with his arms and shoulders that she exuded strength. I chuckled and Jakub shook his head approvingly. He registered that he'd like to see photographs of my family, but all I had managed to salvage during my escape was a small snapshot of Gemma and her father. Jakub said *dziewczyna*, girlfriend, but when I held up the palms of my hand to show incomprehension, he took a pad from his shirt pocket and drew a heart. After several false starts, I finally comprehended. Shaking my head yes, he extended a hand to me, and I shook his large and calloused paw.

After an extended period of silence, Jakub began to sing what sounded like folk songs. His pleasing baritone lulled me to sleep. I dreamed of Gemma. But in my happy memory, just as she reached a hand to me, I felt the truck slowing down. Snapping into wakefulness, I viewed in the distance a roadblock manned by two German soldiers. Jakub, who had sensed my vulnerability, saw the danger at once. He opened the glove compartment of the vehicle and removed papers. Pointing to them, he gesturally asked me if I had any. No. He leaped from the cab. At that moment, I momentarily feared arrest and deportation. The soldiers met Jakub in the middle of the road. He handed them his papers, which they read and returned, and then pointed toward the truck. More discussion followed. One of the soldiers accompanied Jakub to the rear of the lorry. Jakub pulled back the tarp, revealing cases of beer. The soldier muttered and returned to his post at the roadblock. Jakub lifted a crate of beer from the flatbed and put it at the feet of the two Germans. After further words among them, Jakub returned to fetch a second crate, also left with the soldiers.

As we drove past them on the road, the Germans looked the other way.

On reaching Szczecin, Jakub pointed to a forest road and with his hands imitated the motion of waves to tell me that it led to the Baltic Sea. Three days later, after sleeping in the woods and living on berries and nuts, a skeletal me reached the coast and passed from one fishing boat to the next asking, Szwecja? An old man, whose leathery skin would have taken an awl to pierce, wiped his dripping nose with his sleeve, pointed to his small craft, and allowed that I could board. Besides the old man, two others bunked on the boat, his son and son-in-law. Sitting down to a meal of herring and black bread, I kept repeating the words I had bestowed on Jakub, the beautiful words Dziękuję Ci that in Polish mean thank you.

Docking in Stockholm, the old man gave me a hug and a hunk of black bread. I found someone who knew German and asked directions to the Jewish Relief Agency, where I remained for several weeks, undergoing further medical treatment, waiting for a boat to Lisbon that would bear me and other Jews to this gateway city that pointed West, away from the terrors of Europe.

******

My return to Berlin, and the Bogota Hotel, having inspired me to recall the memories of times past, I left Yva's former studio and took the elevator to the lobby, where Viktor Bobel, the caretaker, leaped to his feet and warmly invited me to chat, lass uns reden. Let's talk. Herr Bobel used the desk phone to call someone, presumably his wife. "Bring a pot of coffee and some cakes." The two of us retired to a couch in the lobby, and Viktor pulled up a low table for the refreshments.

"I want you to know," said Viktor, "that although I briefly served in the Wehrmacht, I am not one of them. By training, I am a carpenter, and still am. Anything goes wrong in the building, I fix it." He let out a good belly laugh. "Why, I was the one who turned Skaller's former apartment into a projection room to evaluate the weekly propaganda newsreels. I also converted the first-floor salon into an office for *SS* Brigadier Führer Hans Hinkel, the Minister of Culture." He quickly added, "At the direction of the Nazis, of course. You see," he said defensively, "they had to find a building to house the Ministry of Public Enlightenment and Propaganda. The old one had been bombed. So, they confiscated this property from Oskar Skaller, a Jew. Would you believe that Benny Goodman played his clarinet here, in this very building, in the 1920s?"

"I don't suppose," I said wryly, "Herr Hinkel's guest list included Benny Goodman. In fact, if I'm not mistaken, Charlie Chaplin in *The Great Dictator* based his character Adenoid Hinkel, the dictator of Tomainia, on Hans Hinkel."

Looking deflated, Viktor rallied with the observation that Herr Hinkel entertained important visitors, like King Boris III of Bulgaria.

I ironically commented, "And everyone remembers good old King Boris."

Impervious to the sarcasm, Viktor proudly talked about the Nazi film industry and Hans Hinkel's role in popularizing Third Reich movie stars. "Would you believe I saw Joseph Goebbels, Minister of Propaganda, usher into Hinkel's office the beautiful Kristina Soderbaum!"

"Soderbaum, a household name not only in Germany but also in America."

"Really?" Viktor exclaimed credulously.

"Every antisemite knows the story of *Jud Süß*, the pure Aryan girl who drowns herself after being raped by a Jew."

Viktor started to say something, but a hefty woman with a pretty, freckled face entered from a side door pushing a cart with a coffee urn, cups, saucers, spoons, sugar, and biscuits.

"My wife," said Viktor, "Geraldine Bobel."

The woman shifted her shoulders to adjust her considerable bosom and extended me her hand. "I hope Victor isn't boring you with his stories about 45 Schlüterstraße. He takes great pride in the history of this building."

"As do I," I said.

"He once lived here," added Bobel.

"Ah," said a surprised Geraldine, "were you here when the Germans occupied the building and stored their stolen goods in the basement?" She paused. "I don't remember seeing you."

"Geraldine! Watch what you say," Victor admonished.

"Sorry!" She winked at me. "I had better return to the kitchen before my husband divorces me."

The two of us sat silently sipping our coffee. Viktor broke the quiet with the comment that all the "so-called stolen goods" had been removed at war's end. "The only things that remain," he said, "are discarded valises and junk the previous tenants left behind."

"May I see the basement? I hardly remember it."

Viktor, looking uncomfortable, agreed that after we finished our coffee, he would lead me into the cellar.

"As far as you know, Herr Bobel, which Jewish family left the building last?

"That's easy. The Levys. His wife made such a fuss—"

"Magda."

"I had been recently hired to work on the building. She kicked the police and struck them with her fists, saying that as a non-Aryan she had every right to stay right where she was."

"And their belongings?"

Viktor looked puzzled. "They took them when they left, of course." He thought a moment. "Except for a moldy valise with a wooden frame. That's still downstairs."

"Perhaps, just perhaps," I murmured to myself, hoping to find in the detritus of death, a memory of life.

Viktor continued with his history, explaining that the same year the Simons left the premises, the Nazis seized the building, which, he said, partially in wonder, had escaped the bombings. Others on the block had not been so lucky. "There's something special about 45 Schlüterstraße. You can feel it."

After declining another cup of coffee, I followed Viktor down the cellar stairs. The two of us brushed aside cobwebs and sidestepped old newspapers and broken furniture.

"As I recall, I once hid a book down here." Proceeding to the rear of the cellar, I reached above my head, and removed a brick from the wall. "It's still here." I took the book and thumbed through the pages."

"What is it?" asked Viktor?

"*Lady Chatterley's Lover*."

"Never heard of it."

I put the pirated copy in my pocket and replaced the brick. Continuing through the rubble-strewn basement, I saw the valise that Viktor mentioned. Ribbed with rounded blonde wood, and covered with heavy leatherette, it had a brassed back and catches. Inside, the fully cloth-lined space held a few moldy socks and an old pair of slippers. The pockets held only dust. Gripping the lining of the lid, I pulled it loose from the cover. A small folder fell out. Inside were some negatives. Viktor stood awe-struck, his expression begging for an explanation.

"I saw a slight bulge and acted on a hunch."

"What are they?" asked Viktor.

"I won't know until I can hold them up to the light, but if I had to guess, I'd say fashion photographs." Viktor looked confused. "The Levys and Simons were friends. You said the Levys were the last to leave. That means the Simons left before them. When they went to say goodbye, I suppose they left these negatives with the Levys."

"Are they valuable?"

"No idea."

Suddenly proprietary, Viktor said, "I think you ought to leave those films with me, and I'll turn them over to the authorities." He held out a hand.

I ignored him and pointed to another old suitcase.

"Herr Fertig's," said Bobel.

"I thought it looked familiar."

"After he died, I cleared away the books in his flat, sold the furniture, and moved his papers down here."

"In the suitcase?"

"Yes."

I blew the dust off the top and gently opened the valise, as if opening a door to a secret garden. Although the volume of paper stored here gave me pause, I quickly realized that most of the contents were organized in labeled folders. Without taking the moment to read any of the contents, I did note the names on some of the folders: Ruth Rosner, Last Will and Testament, Books Read and Unread, Correspondence. I shut the lid, secured the clasps, grasped the handle, causing its leather covering to flake away, and said, "Walter was like a father to me. I owe him the gratitude of reading his last thoughts. We can leave now."

Viktor mumbled something about "stealing," as I lugged the luggage upstairs to the main floor.

To satisfy the disappointed caretaker, I suggested he would do well to go through all the discards downstairs, even to the point of removing the linings of old travel bags. Viktor gulped and looked gulled.

Chapter Seventeen

As I exited 45 Schlüterstraße, anxiety seized me. My hands shook, and my temples throbbed. My longed-for reunion with Gemma awaited me, but would the reality satisfy my expectations? I had dreamed of this day so intensely that the dream had taken on a life of its own. With the weight of Mr. Fertig's valise and my own reminding me that I had several blocks to go to reach the villa, I weighed the advantages of taking a cab or walking and savoring the sounds and smells of my former neighborhood. Even though the old Charlottenburg lay widely in ruins, I decided to walk a block or two, hoping to find a few familiar landmarks. After all, 45 Schlüterstraße and the villa had survived, what else had escaped allied bombs?

Berlin Revisited

Most of the rubble had been removed or stacked in piles. An urchin, with patched pants and a streaked face, picked his way through a demolished site and offered to carry my bags. The boy asked for a pittance, and I puckishly replied:

"Yes, so long as you agree to double the price."

The boy gawked, his open mouth revealing broken and missing teeth. "What a deal," he exclaimed, and immediately turned entrepreneur, yelling for a friend, who materialized out of the rubble, and offered him one-third of the take if he would help. I now had two porters. I asked the boys which buildings remained intact. The enterprising lad who had first approached me readily answered:

"The chocolate maker on the next block. Let me show you."

Memories reeled off pictures in my head. The little corner shop, like the one in Firenze, had exhibited in its store window chocolates molded into every shape and design. I remembered one scene in particular: a desert landscape of pyramids and palm trees, pharaohs and a meandering river, presumably the Nile. Countless times I had stopped to buy a single chocolate or a bag of bonbons. Gemma and I had frequently come to the shop, sitting at one of the three tables or standing when the tables were occupied. Her favorite was chocolate caramel. I would buy a box of them now, if available. A bell tinkled over the door as we entered the shop. The man who greeted us was not the stooped man whom I remembered. This one, younger and robust, answered my question about the old man by introducing himself as the master chocolatier's son, Paul Fredericks.

"No one can match father's artistry. He should have been a sculptor." He thought a moment and continued. "In fact, he was: a sculptor of chocolate."

"And oh, the taste!" I added.

By this time, the two young lads were virtually salivating. So, I told them each to pick a chocolate, and I would pay. As often happens, too much choice can paralyze. The boys couldn't make up their minds. While they pointed and assayed each piece on display, I asked whether Herr Fredericks could prepare a box of chocolate caramels as a gift. Paul flew to the task. By the time he had finished, the two lads had finally settled on their choices. I paid the bill and the three of us continued our neighborhood stroll.

The park seemed unchanged, although a bit ragged. The church stood undestroyed. What struck me, though, was how poorly dressed and shabby the people looked. A once prosperous area of Berlin had been reduced to penury. On street corners, men and women hawked their wares, like the Eastside in New York City. From pushcarts and folding tables, they sold household items, used clothing, a lamp, a chair, a bicycle, a pair of ice skates, a violin, a set of books, a lawn mower, a tea set.

The sight of people selling their belongings was just too painful. I told the lads that I had had enough sightseeing and would like to go directly to the villa. When we reached Schloßstraße, I was out of breath and sat on the curb. Paying and thanking the boys, I dismissed them. In truth, I felt overcome by the sight of the mostly intact old road, with its familiar houses and the wonderful villa in which I had briefly lodged. I knew that I had to take the last steps of my journey alone.

Shouldering the valises, I crossed to the villa, opened the metal gate, closed it behind me, and paced the familiar distance to the front door, where I paused. The old door knocker, in the form of a key, had been replaced by one shaped like a bulldog. I knocked. And waited. In the background, I could hear children's voices. A young boy opened the door. I asked for Fraulein Gemma Rosselli.

Berlin Revisited

The boy, in accented German, asked me to wait while he summoned his "mother." Each second that passed felt like an hour. A girl about nine or ten peered around a door. I stared. She looked hauntingly familiar, but I could not put a name to the face, perhaps because my mind was elsewhere.

At first, I heard a voice, then footsteps. The voice became more distinct. I recognized it. And suddenly Gemma stood before me in all her youthful beauty, but no longer an adolescent, a woman now. We stared fondly at one other. Gemma held out her arms, and I, leaving my luggage at the door stepped into her life. We hugged and clung, knelt and wept. The children watched, both awed and frightened. Gemma turned to them and said:

"This is the man I told you about. I said he'd return, and he has."

Once Gemma introduced the children, I remembered Nina, the train, and my escape, with Gemma clinging to the child at the door of the cattle car, afraid to jump. Lucas proudly declared that he was learning German, and Nina said she now had two mothers, one in Lublin and one in Berlin.

I replied, "I've come to find mine."

******

That evening at dinner, I heard all about the children and their family stories. After she put the children to bed, I finally had a chance to speak frankly with Gemma. But before doing so, I presented her with my gifts, the chocolates, which brought a wide smile of remembrance, and the Yva Simon picture that I had bought in Prague. She held it up, studied it, pressed it to her breast, and broke into tears.

"I was there when they carted her off to the ovens. Albert died first and later Yva. I will never forget what I saw."

"How did you survive?"

"I worked sorting clothing. Frequently I found some valuable items in a pocket or a seam or in a lining. By giving them to prison guards, I traded for time, staying alive long enough until the Russians liberated the camp."

"And Nina and Lucas?"

She explained.

"But after all that had happened, why did you return to Berlin? I happily fled."

"My father . . ."

"Even though you knew that when they took him away, he'd never come back."

"I had to know precisely."

"And?"

"Shot." The word caught in her throat. "Once the Nazis discovered his communist sympathies, they wasted no time lining him up." She paused a moment. "The Germans keep good records, even regarding the manner of death."

I hugged her and told her how much I admired her father. "And Geert?" I asked.

"Tried and hanged for treason. They cited his warnings to people facing impending arrest and used his pleas for his wife and daughter against him, accusing him of impurity."

"I suppose one shouldn't look too closely, unless you're prepared to live with what you find."

She nodded and then disclosed her good luck. "In the city files, I learned that the villa was still registered in my father's name. With help from the Americans, I reclaimed it, as well as a trust fund my father had established in my name. Most of the furniture had been stored in the basement. The empty rooms were ghostly but hardly mute. They rang with memories."

"My reason for returning," I said, "was to see you. So, please fill in all that I missed. Bring me up to date. Tell me everything you remember. I want to share that part of your life that lives only in remembrance. Speak your memory."

PART FOUR

Chapter Eighteen

As Gemma related the missing years, I held a hand to my face to cover my tears.

******

She and Heidi had found just enough room in the boxcar to squat. They took turns holding Nina. The modest amount of food Gemma had brought with her had been dispersed among the neediest. By the second day, the car smelled of excrement and the small portion of drinking water exhausted. When the train made its first stop at a station for refueling, the prisoners begged for water. A voice from outside the train replied that the cost would be five golden watches, which were immediately collected and handed out through a small vent in the ceiling of the car. A few minutes later, a pail of water was spilled through the vent and a soldier sarcastically hollered, "Here's your water. Don't drink it all at once."

The best one could do was lick a drop or two that might have fallen nearby.

Slowly, the train moved eastward. At each stop, the dead and dying were slid out of the car and carted away by the local authorities. Those engaged in this activity could hardly say, as so many did later, they didn't know that these were death trains, especially since the prisoners would beg for a morsel of food, a bite of a cold potato or turnip. The unsanitary conditions and the absence of food and water provoked in Heidi and Nina a recurrence of their ills, cholera and scarlet fever. Gemma could see the sickness in their faces and feel it on their skin. That she escaped the infection, she attributed to nibbling on the garlic that she carried around her neck. Urging Heidi and Nina to try it, she swore by its medicinal qualities; but they had passed beyond appetite.

The swaying of the train induced drowsiness. Gemma faded from one dream to another, most of them touching on Geert. Had he really been married before? Why hadn't he married Heidi? Or was she merely a temporary girlfriend who had accidentally become pregnant? And yet he had stayed with her and even tried to protect her. Clackety-clack sounded the train wheels. Gemma wondered why he had flattered her, told her she was pretty, praised her maturity, defended her, sought to save her family, and, not least, hinted at a future. He had, in fact, promised to resume their friendship, a word she took to mean courtship. Clackety-clack. Perhaps he had hoped to use her to spy on Sig. Rosselli and discover the secrets of the villa. But she saw no evidence of such behavior. Maybe her father had scared him off; or maybe he thought that Baruch was a suitor in waiting and didn't wish to interfere.

Why were there only questions and no answers; and why did one question always invite another? If that was the nature of learning, then perhaps she didn't want to attend college. The only people who felt the satisfaction of permanence, she decided, were those who treated their ideas or faith with religious certitude, which put them beyond questioning.

Her father never seemed to doubt the rightness of his ideas, nor did his adversaries. Others were full of unease, like the Jews, who understandably feared from one minute to the next. And she? To dispel her disquieting reflections, she told herself to think pleasant thoughts, as her father often advised. Leaning back against the splintered boxcar boards, she happily recalled his reading Benjamin of Tudela's exotic descriptions of Sicily and Palermo, where her father had visited in his youth. So great was her pleasure at hearing these word pictures that she had often asked him to repeat them.

Palermo, he had recited, lies in a part of the country rife with springs and brooks of water, a land of wheat and barley and plantations and parks. You will not find its equal in the whole world. Here, he said, is the king's domain and garden, Al Harbina, which contains fruit trees of every variety, and a large fountain. The garden is encompassed by a wall and has a great lake, called Al Buheira, with many sorts of fish. In the lake are ships inlaid with silver and gold, and friends go out in them for pleasure trips. In the park stands a great palace whose walls are brightly painted and decorated with precious stones. The floors are paved in marble, with gold and silver mosaics. You will see no other building like this one in all the world from Spain to China, and no other island that contains all the pleasant things of this world in such measure as the island of Sicily. Clickety-clack.

The old quarter of Palermo, the Sari-al-Qadi, with its crescent-shaped streets, is walled and built on a peninsula between two inlets of the sea. Here you'll find a water clock made by a Maltese Arab, said to be as famous as the one once belonging to Charlemagne. You'll also find a great sundial, which is inscribed in Palermo's three tongues—Latin, Greek, and Arabic. In the evening's freshness, you can ride on horseback to Favara, which is the place of paradise, with its lilac sprigs and summer roses, where the waters run like liquid pearls and great fish swim in brooks, and birds chant songs in lemon trees.

Before I die, she told herself, if time and means allow, I want to see Palermo. There I shall plant a tree in father's memory.

******

The day Gemma arrived at Majdanek, a Polish Red Cross team, sent to inspect the camp, paused to watch the prisoners as they left the cattle cars. Those who had died in transit remained lying in the fetid straw until later that evening, when POWs disposed of their bodies, out of sight of the Red Cross. Among the corpses lay a woman dead of cholera, Heidi Bos. Gemma, clutching Nina's hand, led her into the camp. Before they had proceeded much past the front gate, a nurse from the Red Cross stopped them. She recognized in Nina's red cheeks and paleness around the mouth the markers of scarlet fever. Fearing the disease could easily spread, the nurse, a devout Catholic, whispered to Gemma, who found her words magnanimous and told Nina to go with the woman and receive medical care. The woman had said that she would take Nina to her own home and treat her. Gemma stared into the nurse's face so that if she survived the war, she would have etched in her memory the appearance of this guardian angel. The nurse had said that she lived in Lublin, which constituted the total of Gemma's information. Nina, too sick to protest, left with the nurse, looking back once at Gemma and wanly smiling.

Berlin Revisited

It took Gemma, assigned to process clothing, only a day to find Yva Simon, who had been appointed to the medical ward. Alfred was digging ditches. With some photographic equipment at her disposal, Yva suggested that she and Gemma clandestinely make a record of the camp, Yva with pictures and Gemma with written descriptions. If they failed to survive, perhaps their records would provide evidence for others to see and know what had occurred in this place. Yva buried her pictures, to this day still unfound, under the boards of her barrack. Excerpts from Gemma's diary read:

Far from arriving in a pleasant valley with quaint villages, we detrained on a flat plain at a concentration camp surrounded by electrified wire and numerous watchtowers. In the distance we can see Lublin, also a highway. The people who live in the vicinity must know about the presence of this camp and the forced labor occurring here. Do they notice? At least Nina is safe.

Initially built to house Soviet prisoners, the camp opened in September 1941 and now, I am told, holds inmates from fifty-four nationalities and twenty-eight different countries. Besides Soviet prisoners of war, the camp includes Jews from Poland, Germany, Czechoslovakia, the Netherlands, France, Hungary, Belgium, and Greece. Non-Jewish political prisoners, used as slave laborers, come mostly from Belorussia, Ukraine, and Poland.

Every day prisoners die simply from being here. Yva tells me that the most common deaths result from disease, starvation, exposure to extreme temperatures, overwork and exhaustion, or from beatings by camp guards. Others die from mass killings.

Yva has become a cultural anthropologist, photographing the prisoners in every stage of camp life: digging trenches, suffering illness and pain, standing naked in the cold and enduring frostbite, and coffined in their barrack beds. Nothing escapes her expert eye:

prisoners fed rancid bread and watery soup, prisoners starved, whipped, hanged, and shot. On a single day, 3 November 1943, the Germans shot 18,000 Jews. The victims stood on the edge of large pits, which they fell into, while in the background loud music muffled the noise of the killings. Alfred Simon, part of the shovel detail, had to help cover the bodies with lime and dirt.

Only later did the dead escape burial in the trenches; the Kapos burned them in newly built ovens. By then, Majdanek had become a death camp, as the Germans shot many thousands of victims. They seemed especially pleased to "eliminate" sick Soviet war prisoners and Soviet Army officers. But Jews also ranked high on their list. The smell of burning flesh shall never be absent from my nostrils, that dreadful coppery, metallic smell, mixed with the ghastly odor of burnt liver. And who can forget the skies blackened by the ashes of the innocent?

Many of the Jewish prisoners went right from the trains to the gas chambers. Alfred looked like a skeleton and, sick from malnutrition, requested death by shooting. Yva, like Heidi Bos, succumbed to cholera. I saw her body, but not Alfred's, carried to the ovens. May her memory live on in her art.

As we lie in our beds too weak to stand, we can hear the *SS* evacuating the camp. The day escapes me; the month, July, the year, 1944. Those strong enough to stand in the doorway describe the *SS* demolishing the crematoria chimney and much of the evidence. But the speed of the Soviet advance prevents the *SS* from destroying the gas chambers and prisoners' barracks. On 24 July, a date I do remember, the Soviet Army liberates the camp but finds just a few hundred prisoners alive. I am removed to a field hospital and fed intravenously, but I continue to record what I recall.

Berlin Revisited

When I regain my strength, I will go to find Nina, residing in some unknown house, cared for by some unnamed woman, whose unnoted life remains a mystery, but not her face, which survives in memory.

******

According to Gemma's account, when she left the hospital, she moved to a Russian encampment, where she received a daily ration of hot soup and black bread, boiled meat and cabbage. Assigned a cot, she remained for ten days until she felt strong enough to start her search. But for what? If she found Nina alive, the child might think her a stranger. Or an unwanted interruption. And even if the child did recognize her and looked upon her kindly was Gemma prepared to become a surrogate mother at age twenty-eight, looking after a little girl who, like herself once, had known abandonment and foster parents who spoke a strange language? Did she enjoy good health? Had she been medically cared for with inoculations and regular examinations? Surely not. Could she read and write? What kind of school had she attended: parochial or state or none? And not least, what if she didn't like the child? She could hardly walk away.

Not until this moment had she considered these questions. Nor had she considered the cost. To raise a child is expensive. Was she prepared to clothe and feed and house Nina? Or to spend time with her: taking a walk in the park, buying her an ice cream, putting her on the carousel, reading to her, answering her questions, treating the child as her own bone and blood? As much as she wished she could answer affirmatively, she knew that until you actually live in the experience there is no way of knowing it. And since we change from one day to the next, she might change her mind. Foster parents were known to return children to orphanages. She did not wish to join their ranks. But to guess what tomorrow will bring is to engage in sorcery.

Without money, she depended on the Russian soldiers for the little she had. But she knew that to find Nina, she would need zlotys. The few items of value she had managed to hide from her jailers came from the processing center, where she had occasionally found jewelry sewn into the confiscated clothing she was assigned to sort. One piece she thought especially valuable, a sapphire ring, which she had found wrapped in a note: "For your sixteenth birthday. May you have wonderful days and long life." Catching a ride to Lublin in a Russian truck, she replied, when asked which area she wanted: the office of the Polish Red Cross. But as no one in the truck knew the location, or if it still existed, she accompanied the soldiers to the center of the city and exited there.

She reasoned that those made destitute by the war would be selling or exchanging their possessions for food or money or both. And the few people with money would be acting as pawnbrokers in a thriving black market. Among all those people, surely someone would know the location of the Red Cross. With her few words of Polish, she found the square where the money changers had set up shop. They made no effort to hide their activities, and the police, perhaps for a price, turned a blind eye. She needed Zlotys. Without money she'd never find Nina. She spotted a table with jeweler's tools: pliers, loupe, magnifying glass, hammer, mallet, scales, and even a sizing machine. Despite the warm weather, an elderly man wore a black woolen overcoat and threadbare muffler. He kept rubbing his hands, either to warm them or to express his willingness to deal. He was haggling over a necklace with a woman wearing a frayed sealskin coat that had once been grand. Gemma could not understand the verbal exchange, but she could see that the woman had rejected the man's assessment or offer. She couldn't tell which, but she could see from the woman's gestures and her frequently holding up the necklace for the man's admiration that she highly regarded it. With feigned disgust, the woman took her necklace and started to leave. She had gone only a few feet when the old man called to her. A minute or two later, they quickly settled.

This play acting provided a useful lesson for Gemma, who decided that if she didn't like the price, she would take her sapphire and pretend to leave in a huff. She put the stone on the purple velvet cloth that lay on the table. The old man smiled and said "jak się masz?" How are you? She replied "Jestem głodna," hungry, a word that every camp prisoner knew by heart. Studying the stone under a magnifying glass, the old man shook his head, sighed, and uttered a price. Gemma gestured that he should write down the figure. He scribbled a number on a piece of note paper that he tore from a small pocketbook. She looked at it and imitated the old man, shaking her head and sighing. He shrugged, as if to say there's nothing more I can do. "Schade," she muttered. He asked was she German? She answered yes. Then he summoned a jug-shaped (big bottom, slim neck), pasty-faced merchant who spoke Deutsch. After the two men conferred, the second one told Gemma that the jeweler fully appreciated the value of her stone but lacked the funds to buy it. She thanked both men, wrapped the sapphire in a handkerchief, turned, and stepped away from the table. Expecting a summons to return, she heard nothing. What was she to do now?

Bravely, she started across the square. Before she reached the other side, a young boy pulled at her sleeve and pointed toward the jeweler's table. She looked and saw him motioning for her to come back. He held up a handful of zlotys. How had he come by them and did he intend to haggle? If the latter, she would remain firm. Only then did it occur to her that she had not made a counteroffer. What would she ask for the sapphire? Double the price! He would offer less. If she came down would he go up? She returned to the table, which exhibited the pile of cash that the man had been waving and that he hoped would prove an inducement. Gemma wrote down a number on the same piece of paper. As before, the jeweler sadly shook his head to indicate that he couldn't meet her demand. He wrote another figure, higher than his original but lower than hers. Should she press her luck? The jeweler was offering a sizable sum. She gestured that they ought to split the difference. He rubbed his stubby chin and mumbled "Jezus." She waited. They locked eyes. Her only fear now was that the old man would withdraw his new offer. She waited. He repeated "Jezus." At that moment, for some inexplicable reason, she crossed herself. The old man did likewise, and, without further ado, opened a drawer, removed additional zlotys, and added them to the pile stacked on the table. As if to prove his honesty, he insisted she count them. Once she did, she opened the handkerchief and handed him the sapphire.

Only later did she give a thought to the sixteen-year-old girl who had been given the ring, and by whom. She had kept the note that had come with the ring. She would keep it always.

The young boy who had drawn her back to the table stood just a few feet away. She spoke to him in German, which prompted him to point to the same fellow with jaundiced skin who had translated for the jeweler. She asked him the location of the Polish Red Cross and explained the nature of her quest. The sallow-faced man gave directions to the young boy, whom he called Lucas, and then rubbed his thumb and forefinger as a sign to Gemma to tip the lad. Gemma did. Looking like mother and son, the two of them, hand in hand, left the square in search of the Red Cross office, which was situated some distance away. After an exhausting walk, they arrived at their destination. Lucas related to the desk lady what he had been told. She retreated to the back of the office and returned with the director, a burly woman who reminded Gemma of some of the camp guards. But the woman's personality belied her looks. She spoke kindly, inviting Gemma, in German, to tell her every detail she could remember about the events and the lady in the Red Cross who took the child.

Poring over a ledger, the director studied dates and days and assigned duties. After nearly thirty minutes, she said that she felt sure of the woman's identity, Hanna Kowalski. Gemma asked if she could see a photograph of the person to validate her memory. Sadly, the office had no pictures. She gave Gemma an address and told Lucas how to find it. It was a distance; a hired car would be best. A few telephone calls later, the director secured a car, told Gemma the cost, and departed for an emergency. Gemma indicated to Lucas that she'd like him to join her to communicate with the driver and answer any questions that might arise. She assumed, correctly, that the driver spoke no German.

They pulled up at a row of tenements, half of them unlivable owing to bombing and strafing. Lucas led her to the door and knocked. A man in overalls answered and acknowledged his name, Kowalski. He and Lucas then engaged in a brief exchange, which led to the man inviting them into the flat and offering to share a tea bag: "I have only one." His wife and daughter, he said, had gone looking for food. He guessed that they would be returning shortly, because they had nothing of worth to barter. The man went into the kitchen and, a few minutes later, returned with a tea kettle, some chipped cups, and a single tea bag, which each of them took turns dipping into the hot water. While Lucas and the man chatted in Polish, Gemma scanned the room. A sagging sideboard held a silver crucifix and some cheaply framed photographs. Gemma put down her teacup and went to look at them. Yes, she had come to the right address. To keep from gasping as she stared at a picture of Nina, she held her breath, causing her to feel light-headed and to seek the security of her chair.

"My daughter," the man said, pointing at the photograph, "spricht Deutsch," speaks German.

From the looks of this sitting room, Gemma concluded that the family was painfully poor. The one tea bag spoke a thousand words, as did the seedy couch, the rickety chairs, the worn rug, the tattered window drapes, and the absence of heat in the flat. The war had not only destroyed lives and homes, but also left survivors hungry, cold, and jobless. When Mrs. Kowalski returned with Nina, they both took a minute to recognize Gemma. After their initial shock, they embraced, and Nina, now much taller, translated. Mrs. Kowalski held three potatoes, her embarrassment palpable.

"It's all I could exchange for my bread knife."

Unable to endure Hanna's obvious discomfort, Gemma asked if the local market had any food supplies. Nina told her that they had just come from the corner black market, where today's prices were beyond their means. The local farmers had been unable to make a delivery. Gemma asked if the market had chickens. Only one, but for an outrageous price. Removing some zlotys from her pocket, Gemma handed them to Nina and suggested she return to the corner and purchase the chicken. Nina looked at Mrs. Kowalski, who at first seemed dumbfounded, and then nodded. With the money in hand, Nina shot out the door.

Berlin Revisited

That evening, over boiled chicken and potatoes, Gemma made the Kowalskis an offer. Just as they had cared for Nina while she was interned, she would care for Nina in Berlin until the husband and wife could financially get back on their feet. The offer brought a stunning silence to the table. To sweeten the offer, Gemma added:

"I have enough cash to tide you over temporarily, and once in Berlin, I'll have access to more. Nina will have the best education money can buy. Her knowing both Polish and German will virtually guarantee her future."

When Hanna Kowalski found her voice, she forced a smile and asked Nina her preference. The child couldn't answer. Instead she buried her head in Hanna's lap. Lucas, who had followed those parts of the discussion that had taken place in Polish, blurted:

"Take me! I have no parents and live on the street."

Gemma seemed unable to speak.

Lucas continued. "I'll learn the language and be a good student. I earned top marks before bombs destroyed our school."

While stroking Nina's hair, Hanna said, "I have an idea. Keep Nina with you for six months. She can then decide whether she wants to remain longer or return."

Gemma, finding the compromise reasonable, said, "If Nina agrees, I'll be happy to sign legal papers to that effect."

Lucas asked lugubriously, "And me?"

Perché no? thought Gemma, and immediately fell into self-introspection.

I've already reviewed all the reasons for not adopting a child, and even so went ahead. If I continue down this path, I will simply compound my problems. At least Nina knows German. Lucas does not, though he seems a quick study. Weigh both their cases and you'll see. See what? Nina will probably be lonely, at least at first. He can keep her company. She'll be disinclined to misbehave if he's looking on . . . unless they team up against me. Hmm. She can help in the house and garden, and he can help with repairs and heavy lifting. Perhaps they can share the shopping and cooking. I'd see to it that they're both introduced to the culinary arts. Gemma! You know nothing about him. At least you knew Nina's parents. He may even be lying, and his parents living just around the corner. I must learn something about him. And the downside, apart from everything else, is the effect on your own future. Who would want to marry a woman with two children, adopted ones at that? Waifs, so to speak. Nina is swarthy, Lucas is not. People might think you've had affairs with two different men. And even if they don't, are the German people open to this kind of arrangement? Well, "Tutta la vita è un lancio di dadi." All life is a throw of the dice.

Lucas soundlessly pleaded with Gemma, his eyes tearfully signaling for help.

Gemma nodded and said, "Anche tu." You too.

******

The villa had grown dark. We embraced and remained, silently, in that posture until the poisonous past exhausted itself in the telling and set us momentarily free. The hour was late. Gemma turned on a light and showed me to my old bedroom. In the morning after the children had departed for school, we sat in the kitchen drinking coffee. I refrained from telling her that the coffee she had made could not hold a candle to Gabriella's. Mostly, I just wanted to sit and stare at Gemma, incredulous that this dreamed for moment had actually arrived.

"A penny for your thoughts," she said.
"I can't help thinking about my mother."
"More coffee?"
"No thanks."

She removed the coffee pot from the burner and rested a hand on my shoulder. "There are transcripts . . . you can read them yourself . . . of your mother explaining herself. Knowing how much you admired your father, I don't think you'll find much pleasure learning how she really felt about him."

"Is there a file on him?"

"Yes, but it's brief."

After clearing the dishes, Gemma and I took the train to the former *SS* Gestapo and police headquarters on Friedrichstraße. The archivist greeted Gemma warmly and made me feel welcome. Having hosted her on several occasions before, the archivist knowledgeably led her past the thousands of uncatalogued files to the ones that she sought. I wished to see the same files and, particularly, the ones bearing on my parents. The archivist removed the relevant ones and led me to a leather-topped desk. Gemma sat facing me. Through a window at my elbow, I glanced at the sidewalk below and wondered how many of the people had a past that they wished to hide. Are we not all, I thought, the sum of our memories, looking to an unknowable future and living through a momentary present?

As Gemma had indicated, the file, compiled at Dachau and marked "Professor Meyer Rosner," held very little. Physical details: height, weight, hair and eye color, identifying marks, and a few notes bearing on the prisoner's conduct. Apparently, my father had not protested when assigned, with other intellectuals, to clean latrines. However, one note captured the life and death of my father. "Prisoner has formed a group that meets in the barracks at night to study history. When Professor Rosner was asked by Camp Commandant Weider to include in his lessons the heroic rise of Hitler and the grandeur of Nazi Germany, he refused. Whipped for insubordination, he took ill from his festering wounds and crawled to the electrified fence, where he was warned to stay back. Ignoring orders, he was shot by Emile Franks, a guard in watchtower seventeen."

The file made no mention of whether my father had left behind his pocket watch or books or fountain pen or anything else. He had disappeared with no mention. The files said nothing of the body or the ashes or a grave. I lowered my head and studied my empty hands. I had been left with not a material thing to remember my father, except for the mug shot, clipped to the file, taken of father on entering the camp. In some ways I found this state fitting. Meyer Rosner had always said that death constituted an absence. The person standing there a minute before was now gone, and the resulting void was filled with either good or bad memories, or maybe both, or even nothing. That was to be my endowment.

I waited several minutes before opening the next file, my mother's. I knew from Gemma that it contained interviews with a psychiatrist assigned to her case after her arrest and sentencing, and briefly during her incarceration. The psychiatrist, Rudolph Eckstein, given the unsavory work of trying to determine why Jews would collaborate, had conducted several interviews with Ruth Rosner, all of them taped and then typed. The thorough Germans knew that over time the tapes would disintegrate and therefore committed them as well to the written record.

While I thumbed through the interviews between my mother and Eckstein, Gemma asked the archivist whether he knew of any files bearing on 45 Schlüterstraße. His eyes lit up.

"Ah, the office of *SS* Brigadier Führer Hans Hinkel, the Minister of Culture. Believe it or not, I once ran an errand for him. I brought a movie actress to that building. At the time, I was driving a taxi, having lost my job in a school library for allowing the children to read a favorite playwright of mine, Bertolt Brecht."

He turned on his toes and disappeared into the stacks to retrieve the file for an address that had attracted considerable attention, given the fame of those who had resided there. When he returned with a full trolley, Gemma invited me to share in the reading, but my absorption in the Eckstein-Rosner papers would not brook any interruptions.

Chapter Nineteen

I quickly read through the initial interview, in which my mother and the doctor introduced themselves and merely exchanged niceties until they felt comfortable with one another. When I reached den Kern der Sache, the heart of the matter, I read each page slowly and repeatedly, as if I had come upon a sacred text. My mother was talking about my father. I could hear her voice and recognized the repetitions.

"Meyer tried to convince my parents and me to leave the country. He said it was becoming unsafe. But unsafe for whom? He was the outspoken one, the critical one. My parents and I pleaded with him to give the new government a chance. Yes, they discriminated against Jews, but that was from envy."

"And he said?"

"You're blind! Blind?" I said. "Are you not making a good living? And my parents . . . no one has touched their bakery."

"It's just a matter of time," he said. "Read their racist literature. They make no bones about who's to blame for all of Germany's troubles."

"You must admit, Meyer, the Jews can be arrogant—and pushy. A little humility and it will all blow over. Admit it."

[Eckstein added] "I gather his desire to leave led to discussions that took place over several weeks."

"Months! Months before I had told him to leave if that's what he wanted. My parents were too old to learn a new language and new ways. Then he said that leaving would be good for my son, a chance to thrive in another country. I said, 'He stays with me.' He suggested we ask Baruch what he wanted. I told him Baruch was too young to know. Know what? How much he would miss his own country."

"Did he speak to your son?" asked the doctor. "I see nothing unreasonable in it."

"Yes, and I told both my husband and son that the only way Baruch could leave would be over my dead body."

"But you sent him away . . . to live with someone else."

"You must understand, Doctor Eckstein, Walter Fertig was a good friend, a very good friend. I knew he would be a father to Baruch, the father who was no longer there for my boy."

"Do you feel any guilt about causing your husband to wait, while he tried to persuade you, thus leading to his arrest? If he had fled the country when he wanted, he would probably be living safely in Switzerland now."

"Conjecture. Pure guess work. More likely if he had kept his opinions to himself, he'd still be . . ."

"Not teaching. Jewish professors were all expelled."

At this point in the interview, bracketed material indicated that Dr. Eckstein reminded my mother of specific events. [The universities and schools made Judenrein. No Jews. Intellectuals and artists of every stripe considered subversive because they represented a possible source of discontent and criticism. Jewish businesses confiscated. Internment camps built. Racial laws passed. Gypsies and the mentally and physically disabled liquidated. Thousands told to leave the country, dispossessed of property and personal possessions, and made to pay exorbitant exit fees. Many Jews went into hiding. Some Jews collaborated.]

"Ruth, why did you collaborate?"

[Tearfully]

"I was always the invisible child in the classroom. Insecure, scared, unnoticed. I knew that to be seen, I would have to be perfect."

"You seem to be mixing up two different things: insecurity and perfection."

"Don't you see. When you're the best, you're noticed."

[The prisoner is remarkably attractive and has probably exploited her looks since her youth.]

"What were you best at?"

"Nothing."

"But you just said—"

"I quickly learned that to excel at anything, you have to practice, over and over again."

"And you lacked the self-discipline."

"Yes. I also learned that if I never finished a project, I could never fail. If you're a beginner, you're excused for making mistakes. No one expects you to be perfect. You're excused. I tried violin, art, pottery, guitar, piano, French, voice. I never finished projects because I didn't want to fail. My excuse was always the same: I'll get back to it."

Dr. Eckstein added, "Being pretty didn't take any work. It was your natural state. Was that how you made friends and got noticed?"

"Meaning?"

"A smile, a flirtatious manner, genial, accommodating," Dr. Eckstein said.

"Who wouldn't want to be the class favorite and queen of the dance?"

"People who want to be loved have a hard time saying no."

"I always said yes and no."

"Decisions have consequences."

"Precisely."

"I can't imagine that your husband or son found your ambivalence easy to live with."

"They found it exasperating."

"And you?"

"For me, the ambivalence was genuine. I never knew what to say or do, so I would go and do what I wanted."

"That sounds like a contradiction to me. You didn't know what to do, but you went off to do what you wanted. Which was?"

[Eckstein: She looked baffled. After several attempts to explain, she resorted to her wish to be noticed.]

"I wanted to do things or go to places where I would be admired."

"Faculty events?"

"I always felt insignificant at those." [She started to pick at her fingernail polish.] "To attract attention and to compete with my husband, I would find some point he was making and disagree."

"Did your disagreements succeed?"

"They led to one of his colleagues sarcastically remarking, 'I see you wholeheartedly support your husband.'"

"Then where did you find the praise you sought?"

"With people less educated or much younger than me. They found me interesting."

"And pretty?"

"Of course."

"What did they find interesting about you?"

"My ideas."

"But you admitted to not having many of them."

"I had a ready source: my husband and his colleagues."

"Was Gunter the first man you had an affair with?"

"No."

"From what you have said, I imagine you picked men who would find you 'interesting.'"

"I picked weak men who were needy, so I could affect their lives, just as my husband affected his students. All the men I fancied were full of faults. Full of them. That's why I liked them. Meyer seemed perfect. He was always on top of things. I was jealous of that because I too wanted to be at the head of the class. With these men I was."

"So instead of addressing your deficiencies, you slummed, if you'll pardon the word."

"I hated my inadequacies. But it's hard to admit certain things to yourself. In the past, I've been unwilling to educate myself and face problems."

"Like what?"

"Like admitting that I didn't know how to handle my son. Meyer did. I didn't."

"Certainly, your husband would have been willing to help if you had asked for it."

"It was easier to have an affair than to talk to him about those things that troubled me. Besides, I wasn't prepared to admit that I was mentally lazy and immature and selfish."

"What other problems did your ambivalence create?"

"Although I couldn't make decisions, my husband could."

"And you resented him for it."

"That's what he'd insinuate, saying, 'Ruth, be glad that I'm here. If you can't decide, I will.'"

"Which infuriated you."

"It made me feel worthless. Utterly worthless. That's why I contradicted him in company and tried to compete with him. But to compete, I found myself parroting his words. Then his colleagues would tease him, saying that when they spoke to me, they thought they were speaking to him. It was true. I plagiarized—and hated myself for doing it."

"Then why did you?"

"I just said: I had no ideas of my own. But using his made me feel as if he inhabited me."

"And having an affair was a way to prove to yourself that he didn't own you."

"I came from a home with traditional values. Women were not expected to shine intellectually nor say anything critical about people. I was really never taught to speak up or develop my mind. So rather than depend on intelligence, I developed social graces, dressing well and having perfect manners, all of which people noticed."

"At the time, were you aware of not developing intellectually?"

"I ignored what Meyer used to call 'the life of the mind,' and focused on being physically attractive. You'll laugh. But I wanted to look like the women in an Yva Simon photograph. You do know the name?"

"Yes."

"She died in a camp, I think."

"What did you like about her photographs?"

"The women always looked so self-assured—and chic."

"In a way your marriage gave you those things: a well-appointed flat, nice clothes, and a highly regarded professor for a husband."

"Ironically, he was in large part why I lacked self-worth. He eclipsed me. I lived in his shadow."

"I should think you'd find a life of ideas stimulating."

"Always his ideas. Where did I fit in?"

"When you slummed, weren't you bored? I can't imagine the conversations were very scintillating."

"I impressed them."

"Voicing his ideas . . . because you had none of your own."

"I've already admitted that I plagiarized."

[It's important that she understand the source of her behavior and her motives.]

"Which made you all the unhappier."

"He seemed so perfect, so self-controlled. I envied him his life."

"Would you agree that to have self-control and power you collaborated?"

"I could determine whether a person lived or died."

"Even your husband."

"A student denounced him."

"One that you knew."

"He came to our flat on a few occasions."

"When your husband was absent."

"Meyer's colleagues may have thought me simple, but his students didn't."

"Tell me about Gunter."

"He played the piano. He serenaded me. I'd sing along. He was much younger than me. We both worked for the secret police. His grandmother had a nice home, with a carriage house. That's where'd we rendezvous. I always circled the block first to make sure I was alone. The serenading and singing led to my thinking about him obsessively. Meyer found out about the affair and said I should live with Gunter. But I couldn't decide whether I loved him or not. Then I asked myself: How could I be feeling this obsession when I hardly know him?"

"He made you feel carefree, youthful."

"That's exactly how I felt."

"So, you sent your son to live with a friend, a decision that would allow you to be . . ."

"Free."

"Are you now prepared to understand yourself and take responsibility for what you've done and how it turned out? [She looked perplexed.] Your freedom proved costly."

"You seem to be saying that I am guilty of more than just collaboration."

"Just? Isn't that enough?"

"Enough to have sent me to prison, yes."

"But there's more."

"What?"

"When Meyer applied for an exit visa, his request was denied. In the files, I see that you objected."

"He had a family to support . . . and I thought he'd change his mind."

"Meyer's denunciation—"

"Yes?"

"It occurred when you and Gunter had become, shall we say, familiar."

"What of it? Meyer and I were no longer intimate."

"Convenient timing."

"Since you are familiar with my records, you can see for yourself that I was not the one who exposed him."

"No, you used feminine wiles to persuade Meyer's student to betray him."

[She could not hide her guilty expression, but she did what she had always done. She lied.]

"I have forgotten."

"Or do you refuse to remember?"

The interview ended with a note at the bottom. [Ruth Rosner's jail sentence of eighteen months includes medical attention. She has been diagnosed with a weak heart, and has difficulty clearing liquid from her lungs. I.e., She's in the early stages of congestive heart failure. After she completes her prison sentence, she will be sent to the St. Gertrude home for medical rest. She knows that her husband, Meyer Rosner, died at Dachau.]

******

Gemma and I debated whether to visit my ailing mother. We finally decided to see her because she could tell me what plans, if any, she had made for herself. But first we would visit the cemetery where Gemma had paid for a memorial plaque honoring her father.

The Friedhof Heerstraße cemetery, located at Trakehner Allee 1, in the district of Charlottenburg-Wilmersdorf beneath the Olympiastadion, covered an area of 149,650 square meters. Gemma had selected it for its proximity to the villa and for its wooded hills. The brass plaque had been costly. It read: "Here lies Ugo Rosselli, whose memory shall not be erased by time. He resisted when others lent themselves to evil." Tempted to ask her how she had found the perfect inscription for the plaque, embedded in a tree-shaded hillside, I silently laid flowers on the spot, and said the kaddish, "Yisgadal v'yiskadash sh'mei rabbaw b'allmaw dee v'raw chir-usei . . ."

As we left the cemetery, Gemma took my arm. "You are probably wondering where the money came from?"

"Not at all," I fibbed.

"Father left me money in a trust managed by the Deutsche Bank, the very one he assailed for collaborating with the Nazis. He felt it unlikely that my account would come under scrutiny in the fascists' own backyard."

I had my answer.

After we stopped for tea, we hailed a cab and directed the driver to take us to the St. Gertrude rest home, a former Catholic school surrounded by lawns and flowers and entered through a grand front door. At the desk, I checked in with the matron, showing my passport to prove my identity. When she cast a suspicious eye at Gemma, I said, to Gemma's surprise:

"My fiancée."

We took the steps to the second floor, while the matron explained that the home was trying to raise money for a new elevator. At the nurses' station, we met the principal attendant and were guided to room 207. My mother lay in a room with two beds that faced a small pond attracting larks, swallows, wrens, and other singing birds. The second bed was ominously empty, and, as we subsequently learned, the woman who had slept there had died of a cerebral hemorrhage.

Mutter, as thin as a twig, lay staring at the ceiling. Gemma hung back so that I could greet her first. She looked comatose. I stood at the side of her bed until she moved her head. She gazed and blinked, as if trying to bring into focus something elusive. I smiled. Her cloud of unknowing dissipated. Tears appeared in her eyes. Then she feebly held out a hand.

"You survived," she said, sniffling.

"In Cuba and now the United States."

She looked past me at Gemma. "Is she your wife?"

"Not yet," I replied, as Gemma blushed.

"A pretty woman."

"Her name is Gemma."

"I like that." She paused, owing to a lack of breath, with her words coming in pauses and bursts of air. "In school, I once had a friend called Gemma."

"Are you uncomfortable?" I asked. "What do the doctors say?"

"They talk in a language I don't understand."

"Then I'll speak to them."

"Even if I recover, I have no place to go."

I weighed whether to invite her to live with me and decided against it.

"Your father would have known what to do, but he's gone, isn't he?"

Only then did I realize that my mother was failing not only in heart but also in head. Propping up a pillow for her, I said, "Tell me about yourself."

Gemma moved to my side and whispered, "Be gentle."

"As I recall, the horror began on Kristallnacht."

"9 and 10 November 1938."

"Then came the yellow star."

"Nineteen forty-one."

"They promised to feed me and my parents. To house us, to clothe us, if I worked for them. Otherwise they would ship my mother and father to a camp. What choice did I have?"

"Vater wanted you to leave long before, but you wanted to stay. Was it because of some friendship?"

"The idea of leaving Germany scared me to death."

"Even though death stalked the streets."

"I never believed it would touch my family."

"You sent me to live with Walter Fertig. Why?"

She turned her head to the window. "Is it spring? Most people think spring the loveliest time of year. I prefer fall."

In her breathless fashion, she then related that as a little girl, she thought the gold in the trees was real. One day, she climbed a tree and reached for a golden leaf. She fell and broke her arm. When her parents asked her how she hurt herself, she lied. She told them some mean man had thrown her to the ground. They believed her. That experience, she said, taught her that it was easier to make up stories than to tell the truth. She even convinced herself that lying was an innocent form of storytelling.

She pointed to a framed photograph resting on the night table at her bedside. It showed a youthful—and stunning—Ruth Rosner. "Before you go, tell me I'm still beautiful."

"Mutter, you are still beautiful."

Silent tears wetted her face. Then she enigmatically said to no one in particular, "Who hears the faithless cry?"

******

A month later, she died, not from congestive heart failure, I thought, but from a broken heart. I had visited her regularly, holding her hand and watching painfully as she descended into her own world or, as she would have said, her own stories.

Instead of following Jewish custom and burying her in a plain wooden coffin, I had her cremated, spreading her ashes in the villa garden, in a tree well that held a sycamore sapling that I, with Nina's and Lucas's help, had planted in her unrecorded memory.

Lieber Vater,

If words outlast the ruin of time, and if great spirits, like yours, never die, this letter will, I'm sure, find you wherever you may be. My innumerable prayers have at last been answered. Gemma and I have reunited, living together in her former villa with her two adopted children, Nina and Lucas. The first is Geert's daughter, saved from Majdanek, the second is a war orphan. She brought them from Poland. Yes, she survived the camp, one of the few. Her protracted stay in Poland—and the reason my letters never reached her—was owing to the children and the complex paperwork involved in removing them from the country as adoptees.

Berlin Revisited

With Gemma's help, I located Nazi files detailing a series of interviews Mutter had with a court psychiatrist. They should probably remain buried in the archives. Were they made public, the Rosner name would suffer. After her eighteen-month jail sentence, she was moved to a rest home, where they could care for her congestive heart failure. Oh Vater, until her death, she lived a solitary and rueful life, where she had nothing but time to consider her selfish decisions. I arranged for her cremation and the burial of her ashes, in the villa garden, at the foot of a Sycamore sapling. Nothing more. No burial words. Not even a plaque bearing her name. Nothing.

Now I invoke your generous and imaginative mind to lead me to a decision. Gemma wishes to remain in Germany; I wish to bring the family to the United States. Berlin lies in ruins. If I stayed, I would be lending myself, at least spiritually, to rebuilding a city that wished to liquidate me. Gemma reminds me that she and the children know no English, the same excuse that Mutter used when she refused to leave. I have been wracking my brain for a compromise. What do you think of this idea: We move to Italy! Gemma has been talking to the children in Italian, which they mostly comprehend, though their speaking skills are limited. I briefly studied the language with Magda Levy, and can make myself understood. Sig. Rosselli's cousins live in Stresa, on Lake Maggiore, and just across the border in Switzerland I could find work in the gem trade. Advise me, if only in a sleeping dream.

Alles Liebe,
Baruch

******

With the blessing of the owner of 45 Schlüterstraße, Gemma and I married in Yva Simon's former studio. As a wedding gift, I had the two negatives (deemed originals) that I found in the Levy's valise printed and framed in the same style as Ugo's villa collection, which had not only survived the war but also formed the nucleus of a valuable private trove. A notary from the registry office conducted the ceremony. For a moment I could hear the echoing voices of the successful artists and free spirits and political pariahs who had lived in the building, and I could hear Yva Simon say, Hallo! Bitte Fühlen Sie sich . . . fühl dich wie zu Hause. (Hello! Please feel at home here.)

In 1976, when 45 Schlüterstraße became The Hotel Bogota, Gemma and I were among the first to book a room.

Respice Finem: Consider the End

After honeymooning in Venezia, we returned to Berlin, the villa, and the children. The one responsibility that I had failed to discharge, a task that I had deliberately avoided, now lay before me. I had yet to peruse Walter Fertig's papers. For the sake of privacy, I removed the valise to the basement and to Mendel Brand's former workbench, where I sorted the folders and, repairing to Mendel's old club chair, started reading the most innocuous: bills, budgets, receipts, purchases, sales, rents, taxes, letters, medical expenses, a marriage certificate, as well as one certifying Frau Fertig's death, and his will, in which he left his books to an orphanage, his money to charities, and a sum for his eventual burial costs and the maintenance of the gravesite that he and his wife now shared. His testament, the one document I intuitively feared would upend my world, remained unread.

PAUL M. LEVITT

It would take several days before I could summon the courage to begin.

******

I, Walter Fertig, being of sound mind, must sadly confess my behavior regarding Ruth Rosner. At war's end, she asked me to hide her. Desperate and disheveled, she appeared at my shop seeking to escape the occupying authorities. I had no idea why she feared the U.S. Occupying forces. Collaboration? Since her husband's imprisonment, she had worked in the government to make ends meet, but so too had numerous others. She called it clerical work, and we all know the passion for paper in every German office. Records and rules: the soul of German life.

Lodging her in the basement of my shop, among the books and second-hand furniture, I cleared a space for a sofa bed and a chest of drawers. Here she lived for several months, fearing to step outside. I brought her food from the local restaurants. She grew pallid from the lack of fresh air and sunshine, but adamantly refused to leave the safety of the basement. I don't know how long she would have remained there had not an unforeseen event occurred.

A camp survivor and his son appeared at my shop, looking for a desk and hoping to find a copy of Thomas Mann's Der Zauberberg, The Magic Mountain. They had heard about my collection of previously banned books. While I showed the father some desks, his son, who heard me mention the location of the books, ran down the stairs to the basement. Before I could stop him, he came face to face with Ruth Rosner. Although surprised by his arrival, Ruth greeted him warmly and showed him where among the shelved books he could find Thomas Mann's works. She even struck up a conversation with the boy about literature and his literary tastes.

The father, hearing conversation from below, joined his son. A moment or two later, the man cried, "You, the Greiferin who betrayed me!" Standing at the top of the steps, I listened as the man continued. "My wife and I begged you, for the sake of my other son, the one with the limp, not to turn us over to the Nazis. She pleaded with you not to send us into eternity. You said callously it was our destiny. She and my older son died. Aaron here and I lived, barely. And now you, I see, hide from justice. Before long, the authorities will post your picture on every lamppost in Germany. It is just a matter of time. Then what will you do . . . and the shop owner upstairs? Come, Aaron, let us leave this Gomorrah."

Having no idea what had possessed the man, I asked Ruth. She identified the man as a former suitor who wouldn't leave her alone, so she had reported him to the police. But matters took a turn when I saw a flier affixed to a lamppost. Then I knew. Taking the circular, I brought it back to my shop and showed it to Ruth. She cried and said it had all been a mistake, and she could explain everything. I listened. What I heard sounded like a story out of "The Thousand and One Nights." According to her, she had to choose between becoming the mistress of Gunter Beltz or becoming his Jew catcher; she chose the latter to preserve her virtue and to warn other Jews, whenever she could, of the danger bearing down on them. I suggested she go to the authorities and explain the situation. She refused.

PAUL M. LEVITT

So, I went myself to the U.S. Occupation Authority. And what I heard led me to reveal Ruth Rosner's place of hiding. Allowing the military police enough time to remove her from the premises of my shop, I then returned to pen this testament as an addendum to my will. At bedtime, I shall drink a schnapps and take a fatal overdose of sleeping pills.

Ende

ABOUT THE AUTHOR

Paul Levitt grew up in an iconoclastic family that revered education and thought that the measure of a great society was not how often it pandered to special interests, but how well it treated the poor. Newark, New Jersey, once a pleasant garden suburb of New York City, was his place of birth. Here the author received from learned women a public education in reading and writing that aimed at accomplishment, not self-esteem. He moved to Los Angeles as a teenager and fell under the spell of basketball, which taught him aesthetics and self-discipline. At the University of Colorado, he took a B.A. in philosophy and an M.A. in history. After a year in Florence, Italy, he attended Washington University in St. Louis and then matriculated at UCLA for an M.A. and a Ph.D. in English. He taught at the University of Colorado from 1964 to 2014, with a stint as a visiting professor at the University of Massachusetts, Amherst. His interests include travel, tennis, and swimming, but most of all the reading and writing of historical fiction, which has enabled him to visit the Jazz Age (*Chin Music*), McCarthyism (*Dark Matters*), immigrants to America (*Come with Me to Babylon*), 12th-century England (*The Saint-Makers*), and Soviet Russia (*Stalin's Barber*).

Berlin Revisited